Don't Shoot the Borloks

FROM THE SAME AUTHORS

By Richard Bessière:
The Gardens of the Apocalypse + *The Seven Rings of Rhea* (translated by Brian Stableford)
The Masters of Silence + *They Came from the Dark* (translated by Michael Shreve)

By Jean-Marc Lofficier & Jean-Michel Archaimbault :
Chevalier Coqdor vs. The Zodiac (translated by Michael Shreve)

Don't Shoot the Borloks

Don't Shoot the Borloks
by
Richard Bessière

No Mercy for the Borloks
by
Jean-Marc Lofficier
& Jean-Michel Archaimbault

translated by
Michael Shreve

A Black Coat Press Book

Visit our website at www.blackcoatpress.com

To Henri Gineste, the genial director of Vision sur les Arts, *painter of the imaginary and of reality... Science of man and Fiction of the canvas... A friend... fantastic!*

Richard BESSIERE

To Madame Mick Bessiere, this sincere tribute to her deceased husband, great dreamer and the first amongst the writers of Anticipation, *who has marked us for life since our childhood readings... without us ever imagining that we would one day be continuing his work. And to Roland C. Wagner, the last of those, who would have had a lot of fun reading this book.*

J.-M. LOFFICIER & J.-M. ARCHAIMBAULT

To Richard and Roland, as a personal recollection of an extraordinary debate at the second Rencontres de l'Imaginaire *at Sèvres, a real baptism of fire for a budding moderator...*

J.-M. ARCHAIMBAULT

ISBN 978-1-64932-370-5. First Printing: April 2025. Published by Black Coat Press, an imprint of Hollywood Comics.com, 18321 Ventura Blvd. Suite 915, Tarzana, CA 91356. All rights reserved. Except for review purposes, no part of this book may be reproduced or transmitted in any form or by any means, electronic or mechanical, including photocopying, recording, or by any information storage and retrieval system, without permission in writing from the publisher. The stories and characters depicted in this novel are entirely fictional. Printed in the United States of America.

TABLE OF CONTENTS

Introduction 7
Bibliography of the Sydney Gordon series 9
DON'T SHOOT THE BORLOKS 11
   PART ONE 13
   PART TWO...61
   EPILOGUE 119
NO MERCY FOR THE BORLOKS 121

Henri Richard Bessière

Introduction

French science fiction scholar Rémy Le Chevalier wrote an out-standing and very complete introduction to our edition of *The Gardens of the Apocalypse* [1] released in December 2010 detailing the life of Richard Bessière (b. 1923). Since then, Bessière passed away in December 2011. We refer our readers to this introduction for the purpose of discovering this great author and his works. You might also enjoy Stephen R. Bissette's introduction to our edition of *The Masters of Silence* [2] published in 2014.

Bessière's works were published primarily by Fleuve Noir, whose imprints *Anticipation* (1951-97) and *Angoisse* (1954-74) came to embody the French silver age of science fiction. Black Coat Press has translated and published a fair sample of these and we invite readers who wish to know more about this period to search our catalog for works by G.-J. Arnaud, André Caroff, Jimmy Guieu, Gérard Klein, Maurice Limat, Pierre Pelot and Kurt Steiner.

This work owes its genesis to my friend and collaborator Jean-Michel Archaimbault. We are both fans of the *Anticipation* imprint and, after I founded our sister company *Rivière Blanche* in France, we tracked down some of our favorite authors, either to print their unpublished works, or, in some cases, new works (both fiction and non-fiction) based on their classic novels.

Our most notable effort was the publication of three novels based on Maurice Limat's *Chevalier Coqdor* series, the first of which was recently translated and published by Black Coat Press as *Chevalier Coqdor vs. The Zodiac*.[3]

Our next challenge was to write a novel set in one of the many universes of Richard Bessière. We quickly settle on a Sydney Gordon novel, first because it was without a doubt the most iconic character associated with the author, and second, because I had already written a Sydney

---

[1] ISBN 978-1-935558-68-2.
[2] ISBN 978-1-61227-297-9.
[3] ISBN 978-1-64932-340-8.

Gordon short story (not included in this volume) for an earlier Bessière book, and found its tongue-in-cheek style easy to master. And of all the S.G. novels that could lend itself to a sequel, Jean-Michel and I agreed that the 1968 *Ne Touchez Pas aux Borloks* was the best candidate.

Jean-Michel and my collaboration on these novels was simple: after an initial conversation, I wrote a very detailed plot, chapter by chapter, which was then handed to Jean-Michel, who wrote the full prose version.

Our book, *Pas de Pitié pour les Borloks*, came out in 2012 and we were both saddened that Bessière, who had passed away the previous year, had not had a chance to read it; but his widow, the indomitable Mick, told us she had enjoyed it very much.

(In 2014, Jean-Michel wrote another posthumous Bessière collaboration, *Katorga*, but I had little or no involvement with that one.)

Jean-Marc Lofficier

Bibliography of the Sydney Gordon *series*

1. *S.O.S. Terre* [S.O.S. Earth] (Fleuve Noir *Anticipation* 55, 1955)
2. *Altitude moins X* [Altitude Minus X] (*Anticipation* 75, 1956)
3. *Route du Néant* [Road to Nothingness] (*Anticipation* 81, 1956)
4. *Cité de l'Esprit* [City of the Mind] (*Anticipation* 85, 1957)
5. *Création Cosmique* [Cosmic Creation] (*Anticipation* 89, 1957)
6. *La Deuxième Terre* [The Second Earth] (*Anticipation* 97, 1957)
7. *Via Dimension 5* (*Anticipation* 101, 1957)
8. *Carrefour du Temps* [Time Crossroad] (*Anticipation* 111, 1958)
9. *Bang !* (*Anticipation* 121, 1958)
10. *Panique dans le Vide* [Panic in the Void] (*Anticipation* 129, 1959)
11. *Plus égale Moins* [Plus Equals Minus] (*Anticipation* 179, 1961)
12. *Les Poumons de Ganymède* [The Lungs of Ganymede] (*Anticipation* 198, 1962)
13. *Micro-Invasion* (*Anticipation* 210, 1962)
14. *Planète à Vendre* [Planet for sale] (*Anticipation* 232, 1963)
15. *La Planète Géante* [The Giant Planet] (*Anticipation* 255, 1964)
16. *Les Mages de Dereb* [The Wizards of Dereb] (*Anticipation* 289, 1966)
17. *Ne touchez pas aux Borloks* [Don't Shoot the Borloks] (*Anticipation* 342, 1968)
18. *La Machine Venue d'Ailleurs* [The Machine From Beyond] (*Anticipation* 372, 1969)
19. *Quatre « Diables » au Paradis* [Four Devils in Paradise] (*Anticipation* 438, 1970)
20. *Variations sur une Machine* [Variations on a Machine] (*Anticipation* 482, 1971)
21. *Quand la Machine s'emmêle* [When the Machine meddles] (*Anticipation* 646, 1974)
22. *Cette Machine est folle* [The Machine Goes Mad] (*Anticipation* 809, 1977)
23. *Tout va très bien, Madame la Machine* [All is well, Mrs Machine] (*Anticipation* 903, 1970)
24. *Quand la Machine fait boum* [When the Machine Goes Boom] (*Anticipation* 1032, 1980)

25. *Faut Pas Pousser Mamie dans les Schlingniarfs* [Dont Push Granma into the Schlingniarfs] (short story in *Le Carnaval des Enclonés*, Rivière Blanche 2029, 2007) by Jean-Marc Lofficier

26. *Pas de Pitié pour les Borloks* [No Mercy for the Borloks] (Rivière Blanche 2100, 2012) by Jean-Marc Lofficier & Jean-Michel Archaimbault

DON'T SHOOT THE BORLOKS

FROM YOU TO ME

First, a question:

"Do you believe in Santa Claus?"

No, of course not and I'm not blaming you. In fact, my illustrious boss, James Funnigan, did a quick job of dispelling any personal illusions of mine on this subject when, on the morning of December 24, I walked into his office to ask for a raise.

The big boss of the *New Sun* looked at me while chewing his awful Italian cigar.

"Come on, Syd, you believe it, don't you?"

I didn't need him to name it. I immediately understood WHO he was talking about. You'll tell me it's a catchphrase, a completely banal expression that says exactly what it means, but, as French singer Sacha Guitry said: "Whether you believe it or not, the main thing is to get presents."

Jolly good! For that, there's only one date in the year when you can try your luck.

You know it: it's December 24th.

So, go on, wait patiently for that day and when the time comes, leave your shoes beside the fireplace.

After that... you will see what will happen to you.

Sydney Gordon

Interior illustration
by Gaston de Sainte-Croix

PART ONE

CHAPTER I

It often snows in New York City around Christmas time, but this time it's more of a "freak storm".

It's falling from the leaden sky like in Siberia, so much so that, behind the windows of my office, the skyscrapers have completely disappeared from view.

But it's Bud I'm thinking of instead.

One thing is certain. The kid will not spend Christmas with us. And all because of Margaret's grandmother who absolutely insisted on taking him with her on her pilgrimage to Lourdes.

Of course, I disagreed, especially about Bud. That damn kid doesn't miss anything and this time he got a nasty bout of flu.

But go and make a crazy old woman and an impossible kid, both as stubborn as each other, listen to reason!

Result: the return canceled, kisses and all the rest...

I'm thinking about this when the phone rings. Miss Grant, my delightful secretary, picks up and hands me the receiver.

"For you, Syd. Your better half on the other end of the line."

I do indeed recognize the voice of my tender and sweet Margaret.

"Hello, Syd darling... I got lucky, I was afraid you had already left the *New Sun*."

"Where are you?"

"At the hairdresser."

"Well, he must be getting to know you pretty well!"

"Oh, Syd, stop grumbling. I'm calling about Bud."

"Yes... What now?"

"I got a second message from Grandma. Bud is over the worst of it."

"I'm sure he is. A flu is a flu, that's all."

"But, Syd, it's a French flu that Bud caught."

"So what? Whether it's French or Chinese, it's still a flu, right?"

"I'm not so sure."

"Anyway, we'll see..."

"What scared Grandma is that a French flu in the Pyrenees is almost a Spanish flu. I hope you've heard of that, at least, Mr. Know-it-all?"

I roll my eyes.

"It's all right. Just tell grandmother that as long as the kid doesn't play castanets in his delirium, he's in no danger."

"Silly!"

"Is that all?"

"No. When you get home, watch where you step. We've got so many toys for Bud that the living room is a mess. Adios!"

A sharp click batters my eardrum and I hang up with a sigh.

Behind her IBM, Miss Grant gives me a smile that I prefer not to encourage.

As I put on my leather coat, she stands up and walks towards me, swishing her hips.

"If you're wishy-washy about your evening, come celebrate New Year's Eve with us. We're organizing a Martian evening at the Waldorf."

"Mmmm! And what role do you play in it?"

"Venus!" my voluptuous secretary shoots back at me.

Since I really want my peace and quiet, I prefer to leave it at that.

"Very original for a girl who's always in the clouds!"

She doesn't take offense but bursts out laughing, which finally cheers me up.

"Merry Christmas!" she says to me good-humoredly.

"Merry Christmas!"

And here I am, driving my Buick through the streets of New York.

It's still snowing and I feel like I'm driving on an ice rink. And what a hustle and bustle, cripes!

Mind you, it's always like this on the eve of the holidays and this Christmas snow doesn't change the traffic problem at all. On the contrary, it's worse!

Even the sidewalks are taken over by a thick and rowdy crowd loaded with parcels, bottles, all kinds of provisions.

And just look at the long lines coming and going between the lighted fir trees whose endless rows of replicas are dizzying. But it's especially in front of the toy stores that the traffic jams are the most intense.

Personally, I've never seen such a crowd in front of the lavishly decorated and illuminated shop windows. A real record!

Of course, this all brings me back to Bud. Poor kid, a flu on Christmas Day, that's definitely bad luck...

But, whatever Margaret says, the flu in Lourdes, under Bernadette's protection, can't be so very bad.

It is with this rather comforting thought that I park my car right in front of my building. The main elevator drops me off a few seconds later on the 24th floor and when I slip the key into the lock my next-door neighbor comes at me with a big smile.

"Merry Christmas, Mr. Gordon, and thank you!"

He pats me on the shoulder in a friendly manner and winks at me.

"It's great that you thought of my little one. The electric train, my wife immediately said it was you. The signaling is amazing. We haven't stopped since this morning... Thanks again, and Merry Christmas!"

"Merry Christmas!"

He disappears into the elevator and I shrug. Margaret, I guess. It's possible, although we don't socialize much with our neighbors. But, if he says so...

I have to admit that Margaret was not lying when she talked about the "mess" that awaited me in the apartment.

A real clutter! Toys on all the tables, on the armchairs, on the carpets. And then boxes, packaging, bits of string... And come on... Is it or isn't it Christmas...

I find rugby balls, a remote-controlled lunar exploration tank, a fire engine, an astronaut's costume, a big cybernetic "ladybug" that obeys whistles and a bunch of other clever toys, not to mention all kinds of play sets, toy soldiers, electric trains, a menagerie of stuffed animals and painted clowns.

A normal kid, playing 24 hours a day would take ten years to play with them all. But with Bud, I'm sure that everything will be done and gone within ten days. And that reassures me.

Somehow I manage to wind through the toys, pushing aside a few boxes, which Margaret certainly didn't have time to open, and I stumble into the kitchen, tripping over a roller skate.

I nibble on an apple, a ham sandwich and return to the living room to pour myself a Cutty Sark. To find the bottle is another expedition, but I find it on the bar behind a pile of carefully tied comics.

"Good morning!"

I swing around, almost spilling my drink. Instinctively, my eyes go to the front door. But no, it's still closed.

"Hello. Hello and Merry Christmas!"

And there it goes again. Again the same small, soft, monotone voice. Well now, since when do people just let themselves into the homes of...

I step forward through the clutter, scanning the room.

"Hey! Where are you? Come out of your hidey-hole so I can see you!"

"But you see me very well. I'm right here..."

I swivel forty-five degrees in the direction of the voice.

No, it's not true, it's not possible... It's not coming from that doll sitting comfortably on an Empire armchair!

I walk around the chair but there's no one behind it. Then I look at the doll, a lovely doll the size of a two-year-old child, all blonde with green ribbons tying her braids. The dress is white silk decorated with gold braid.

I look at it and it looks at me too. Two big blue eyes of celestial clarity, which stare at me with an almost angelic sweetness.

A little pout curls her lips and makes her cute dimpled cheeks swell.

"You are not polite. I said Hello and Merry Christmas! You must return my greeting and wishes. It is in the instructions."

This time it's gone too far. A toy that says "Hello and Merry Christmas" is great, but a toy that has the gall to remind you to be polite is a bit excessive.

There are indeed instructions in the long cardboard box lying at the foot of the chair. Without really knowing why, I pick it up still watching the incredible doll that's giving me a bad feeling.

"My name is Pat," she says, her big blue eyes still fixed on me. "And you?"

I stammer, "Um... Sydney... Sydney Gordon..."

"That's a nice name."

I take the opportunity to swallow the rest of my drink in one gulp while she goes on:

"I am very happy to be in your home. It is very nice and very comfortable."

"Uh... Thanks a lot for the compliment, Pat, but..."

"You do not have the right to talk to me informally. Only children have that privilege and you are not a child."

She points me the instructions with her chubby little arm.

"It is written, you can check."

A sweat begins to bead on my forehead. I take time to go back to the bottle of Cutty Sark and pour myself another dose.

I point to the box.

"I suppose... you were in that box?"

"Yes."

"Where are you from? Who sent you?"

"Who?"

"Yes. Which store made you? There's nothing in the manual about that."

"I don't know."

"Listen... since you seem to understand everything. You should know that I am a reporter... a journalist... Do you see what I mean? I haven't written anything good for several weeks, you can probably help me. Where are you from? Answer! It's really very important."

"Yes, I see. You want to know my creator?"

"Exactly."

"Well, he's called M."

"M?"

"Yes, M. A capital M."

"And where is this... this capital M?"

"I don't know. The borloks have no right to know."

"*Borloks?* Where does this word come from?"

"I don't know."

"In short, you don't know much."

"Oh yes. I know how to entertain children, laugh and sing with them. But you can also take me with you to the theater, the cinema, to bars and cabarets. I am well brought up, a model doll..."

Third scotch, which is not extravagant in a situation like this, believe me!

"Are you married?"

My word, but this is an interrogation As I nod, she continues:

"Children?"

"Just one, but I don't think you'll do the trick."

"For what?"

"Well, first of all my son doesn't play with dolls. We're very strict in the family about this kind of... amusement..."

"At least wait for your wife's opinion. By the way, where is she?"

"At the hairdresser."

"Is she pretty?"

"Yes... yes... but..."

"You are also very nice. You are even very handsome. How old are you?"

"Thirty-five years-old."

"When your temples turn gray, I'm sure you'll look even better."

Then the door swings wide open and a Margaret disguised as a fury bursts into the middle of the living room.

At the time, I don't even notice that she's had her hair cut. I only see her flushed face and her glaring green eyes.

"No, but seriously... Now the guy is having his tryst at home?"

"Margaret…"

She cuts me off abruptly.

"No need, what I heard is enough for me. Where's the girl?"

She races across the living room like a Polaris rocket as I force myself to smile.

"Come on, calm down, I'll explain."

She glances towards the bedroom, then retraces her steps.

"Well, I'll give you some graying temples. Are you going to answer? Where is she?"

With my glass, I point to the doll.

"Here's who you're looking for."

"Stop, you want to make fun of me?"

"Not at all. She answers all questions and even asks a lot more."

"Like what?"

I turn to wink at Pat.

"Come on, Pat, show her."

But in the chair, the doll no longer moves. Her blue eyes have lost their sparkle and her face remains stone. She now looks like a regular dime-store doll, motionless and frozen.

I mutter, "I really don't understand. She was talking until you got here."

"Maybe I upset her, poor little thing."

I snatch up Pat, lift her dress in search of some mechanism, but find nothing. Nothing but synthetic skin, velvety, and extraordinarily supple.

"Something must have gone wrong inside."

I take the opportunity to take a look at Margaret's hairstyle.

"It wasn't a good idea for you to get your hair cut. I hate it."

"Don't try to change the subject. I want you to tell me the truth."

She grabs the doll from my hands and puts it back on the chair. She's about to start in again when, suddenly:

"Hello! Merry Christmas!"

Right away, Margaret smiles. She looks at the doll in awe.

"Oh... Syd... Syd darling."

But I pounce on Pat.

"What happened? Why didn't you answer me?"

"If you had read the instructions carefully, you would know that I have periods of disconnection. From time to time, my energy cells need to recharge."

Triumphant, I turn to Margaret, but my wife shrugs.

"Well, what, it's a talking doll."

"And that's all you can say? But don't you get it?"

"Oh come on, you know, with technology..."

"But she talks like a human being."

"Don't worry, I'm not deaf."

"And it's a borlok."

"A what?"

"Well, apparently that's the name of this toy."

I think and whisper, "Who could have sent us this thing?"

Under Pat's watchful eye, Margaret examines the box.

"Yes, I remember this package. It was in the pile the doorman brought up this morning. But there was no card."

"Someone had to send it to us, right?"

Margaret scratches her forehead,

"Wait a minute, maybe it's Aunt Emma. She's so forgetful..."

"Aunt Emma? Are you completely crazy?"

"And why, pray tell?"

"She's been dead for a year."

"Oh my, that's true." She frowns and decides "So, it was Funnigan."

"What, the boss? He's way too cheap.It must've cost a fortune, a toy like this. No, it's probably Archie and Gloria."

"Impossible! Look, you know very well that they take great joy every Christmas in giving their godson his present themselves. By the way, do you at least remember that we're celebrating Christmas Eve at their house tonight?"

I slapped my forehead. By Jove, I'd completely forgotten.

A burst of laughter from Pat, "You two are really funny."

"Funny or not, I intend to find out."

"What are you going to do?" Margaret asks me.

"I want to know where she comes from."

"And you intend to search all the shops in the city?"

And then suddenly, inspiration strikes.

"M! Capital M! Damn, I think I've got it!"

I pick up some cardboard boxes and show them to Margaret.

"Macy's! Almost all of these toys come from Macy's. That's where this doll was bought. No doubt about it. With any luck, I'll find out who played this prank on us."

Without waiting for Margaret's answer, and even less for Pat's opinion, I grab the doll and place it delicately in the long cardboard box.

Two seconds later, with the package under my arm, I rush into the elevator.

CHAPTER II

Anyway, my mind is made up. I will not keep this doll. This android, as fantastic as she is, does not inspire confidence in me.

I have always felt a kind of repulsion for robots built in the image of man and a mechanism capable of reasoning with such poise and confidence poses a very serious problem.

Because, in short, one has the right to wonder where the line is drawn between a fun toy and a serious model! And I'm wary of intelligent toys that have their own initiative.

Still, one question bothers me. Who could have made this terrible toy? Macy's is certainly only the distributor... but for what purpose? How many androids of this kind could have been launched on the market for the Christmas holidays?

It's not possible that this doll exists in only one copy... Or else I don't understand anything.

In any case, I'm determined to find out what brilliant mind is behind this extraordinary discovery.

I'm thinking this when I suddenly realize that I'm about to take a wrong turn.

Angry horns honk around me and finally a shrill whistle announces the arrival of a policeman with a frost-covered face.

I roll down the window and his big round head pops through the opening.

"Now what's gotten into you? Don't you see the sign? Pull over!"

I obey and he comes over to me grumbling while I try to apologize as best I can.

"You know, with this snow..."

"Yeah, yeah, it's always something. Come on, license and registration."

I hand them to him. He steps back and examines them carefully. Then suddenly I'm aware of Pat beside me. She must have jumped out of her box during the ride and now she has slipped into the front seat. I feel her little hand tugging at my jacket.

"I do not like that man," she says. "He looks funny, don't you think?"

I cough to cover my voice and manage to sputter, "Pat, for heaven's sake, shut up... This isn't the time."

"It's in the instructions. I have the right to express my opinions freely. This cop looks nasty, it's the truth and I stand by it."

"Be quiet, damn it, be quiet!"

All of a sudden, the policeman's head reappears at the window. His bulging eyes search the interior of the Buick then rest on me with a strange expression.

"Hey, tell me, who are you talking to?"

Then he looks at the doll and hands me the papers back with a suspicious look.

"I see, you're a ventriloquist, I guess. In that case, a word of advice. Go do your thing somewhere else, before I get mad. It's okay this time, get out of here!"

With a sigh of relief I set off, leaving the policeman behind, while Pat, at my side, seems to be having the time of her life.

"He took you for a ventriloquist. That's funny, really very funny."

"Pat, if you keep trying to cause me trouble. I warn you this could end badly."

"If you threaten me, M will get revenge. It's in the instructions."

"To hell with you and your instructions. Enough of this now, go back to your box and shut up."

I have a hard time getting her to return to her box, but she finally makes up her mind when I park the car not far from Macy's department store.

It's a veritable human tide flooding the sidewalk and the entrance to the store.

I slip through the crowd, the box under my arm, elbowing my way through, and once inside the store, I barrel towards the elevators.

A series of floors, aisles, moving walkways, then more aisles and I finally arrive at the administrative offices.

Hundreds of typists, accountants, an army of secretaries amidst a din of humming IBMs and the whirring of calculating machines.

Messengers are running around all over the place. One of them hesitates at my request but finally agrees to take me to the main corporate office. There, a charming girl looks me over from head to toe as if I were the devil himself.

Really, what audacity to just show up here like this, Sir! She thinks so loudly I believe I can hear her.

"Mr. Marshall, the chairman and CEO, sees people by appointment only. Make your request, explain the reasons for your visit and we will get back to you."

The same old story. Without flinching, I slide my card to the elegant secretary whose false eyelashes keep fluttering behind big round glasses.

"I know Mr. Marshall personally. Insist, please, he will see me."

"That's impossible. Mr. Marshall has been very busy all morning. He has given strict orders that he is not to be disturbed under any circumstances."

I see the door to the his office, on the right.

"Very well, I'll deal with it myself."

Without waiting for the girl's reaction, I cross the room and push open the large, leather-padded door. Suddenly, I feel like I'm entering a concert hall rather than an executive's office.

An avalanche of sound greets me with a great crash of cymbals and thunderous brass, so loud that I hesitate to take another step.

But I spot William Marshall in the middle of the vast room, comfortably seated in a leather armchair. His head thrown back, he isn't moving. Only his twitchy little fingers beat time on the armrest, signaling the "fortissimo" and the "pianissimo" with the fervent assurance of a music lover.

On a stereophonic device, a record spins round and round, reeling off musique concète with accents that are sometimes raging, sometimes smooth and modulated. In an asymmetrical commotion, the clichés and onomatopoeias follow one another from major to minor, highlighting the dramatic tension of this unknown, hallucinatory work.

Personally, I've never heard anything like it. Even at Carnegie Hall. It gnaws your guts as if the flesh itself was taking part in the suggestive power emanating from the dizzying symphony.

These violins howling in unison on the high harmonics, the tremolo harps, the massive assault of the trumpets and the wordless, aggressive chorus that formed the counter-melody... all of it has something haunting, something harrowing. Something both dreadful and sublime that gives me the impression of traveling to the limits of harmony and human music.

And the record spins... spins... spins...

I don't know by what effort of will I manage to uproot myself from the ground and move towards the stereophonic device.

Marshall still hasn't moved. Unaffected by my presence, he remains immersed in his musical reveries.

The record spins... spins... spins... but on the surface the needle is still traveling over the first grooves. It looks stuck. The arm doesn't even move.

Then, abruptly, I shut it off and the music stops. Relieved, I walked over to William Marshall, who has just been roused from his stupor by the brutal silence.

He shudders, wipes a hand over his forehead, then looks at me with a mixture of surprise and incomprehension.

"Good God, it's Sydney Gordon! How the hell did you get in?"

I point to the door with my thumb, while in the midst of his embarrassment he holds out his hand and tries to smile.

"Really, it's nice to see you again."

With his face transformed, he turns towards the stereo device.

"I guess you were the one who stopped the record? Great, isn't it? You must have heard it. What do you think? Personally, I think this symphony is brilliant. And you know I know a thing or two. By Jove, if only there was something written on the label! How am I supposed to know who composed this masterpiece?"

He shrugs his shoulders and jumps from one subject to another without even giving me time to answer him.

"By the way, we sent you a gift for your Bud. I hope you got it?"

I put the box on a table and grab Pat.

"This doll, right?"

Marshall grimaces like he's constipated.

"Where did that come from?"

"What, it's not from you?"

"No, I sent you a cybernetic ladybug. It's something else. As for your doll, I've never seen anything so pathetic."

"But she talks... she talks..."

"So what? Ours talk too. They say, 'Daddy... Mommy-pee...' What more do you want?"

"Well, I've got you. This one can hold a conversation. You'll be the judge. This is a borlok."

"A borlok? Hey, hey, that's funny."

I turn to Pat, but there she goes again. Complete disconnection. She doesn't react to anything I do to loosen her tongue.

A mocking smile stretches the CEO's thin lips.

"Your doll's a real cold fish. Just good for the deaf. Come on, forget it, someone played a trick on you."

I don't push it. In any case, I was barking up the wrong tree so there's be no point in pushing it, especially since Marshall, after glancing at his watch, suddenly swears out loud.

"Damn it! Already five o'clock! It can't be..."

I point to the stereo.

"How long were you listening to that record?"

"I found it on my desk this morning at nine o'clock and..."

"How many times have you listened to it?"

He thinks about it.

"Well, I... I put the record on right away... I wanted to know what it..."

"Since nine o'clock this morning?"

"Yes."

"Who sent it to you?"

"I don't know. There was no card, no address. But what do you care?"

"A word of advice, if I were you, I'd smash it."

"Smash it? You're crazy!"

I don't have the courage to tell him why. Deep down, I don't know myself. It just came to me like that... spontaneously. A kind of aversion to the music. Pretty much the same as I feel towards Pat.

But am I taking things too far with these strange ideas I'm stuffing into my head? After all, it's his record, not mine, and Marshall has every right to like what I don't like.

I leave the office without another word, but as I step through the doorway, a harsh chord erupts behind me, shaking me from head to toe. Marshall has turned the stereo back on, at full volume.

Brass, tam-tam, cymbals! Clarinets whining... in pursuit again of an inaccessible coda!

CHAPTER III

When I stop in front of my house, Pat is still silent, so much so that I begin to wonder if the automaton's internal circuits have not finally exhausted all of their energy potential.

In any case, I'm determined to have this mysterious doll examined by my excellent friend, Professor Archibald Brent, at whose house Margaret and I are supposed to spend Christmas Eve tonight.

I leave Pat in the car and rush into the building, but no sooner have I entered the elevator than I'm greeted with a "Merry Christmas, Mr. Gordon" in a small, raspy voice.

It's Gino, a young boy I often run into between the ground floor and the 15th floor where his father runs a small Milanese pastry laboratory. A nice kid whose face is starting to blister with unsightly little pimples as he approaches puberty.

He has a tennis racket and a ball that he bounces on the elevator floor.

"This thing is really cool," he says to me. "I wowed all my friends. Oh, if you could've seen them!"

"Your Christmas present?"

"No. It's for Pietro, my brother. But, since we won't give it to him until tomorrow, I'm playing with it today."

"Well, you'll both have plenty of time to play with it together."

"Oh, no need for two of us. This thing can be played alone."

As the elevator stops at the 15th he waves me an invitation.

"Come and see."

We go out into the long central hallway and immediately Gino launches the ball with a swing of his racket. What happens then takes my breath away. The ball flies down the hallway and as it starts to peter out, it stops in the air and returns straightaway to the young boy who hits it with another swing of his racket.

It bounces off, flies off again, comes back changing its angle, ricochets off a wall and hits Gino square in the nose, who missed his shot this time.

In other circumstances, I would probably have burst out laughing, but what I have just seen gives me no desire to do so.

"That happens sometimes," the kid says, rubbing his nose. "You got to be really fast for this game."

I pick up the ball and examine it, but it looks like any other ball. I mean, how the hell is this possible?

What mysterious force could possibly be acting on this foam ball, able to change direction as if another player had tried to "block" Gino? It's unbelievable.

"Gino, who gave you this toy?"

"I don't know. The instructions say it's a borlok. We found it this morning with the other presents. Dad says it must have come from Italy. We have a lot of family there and…"

I don't listen to the rest. This is the straw that broke the camel's back. I rush to my apartment and shoot across the living room like an arrow.

Here, it's still the same mess and I find Margaret in front of a game table with a series of multi-colored squares. In front of her are game pieces, bundles of fake dollars, a die, fake stocks...

"Margaret, please hurry up. We have to go to Archie's immediately."

She doesn't even look up, frozen in an almost ecstatic attitude.

"Margaret, what's happening is very serious. We absolutely must..."

A yellow light comes on on one of the squares. Pieces are spewed out of a slot and Margaret lets out a little cry of joy.

"I won the castle, Syd! I won it. Look!"

"What is this game?"

"A kind of Monopoly but way more fun."

"Where did it come from?"

I hesitate before asking the question again. Margaret shrugs. I understand. Another one of those anonymous, mysterious gifts of unknown origin.

"I've already won a hotel chain," Margaret announces proudly, pointing to the squares, "plus three copper mines, a castle in Scotland and a monopoly on a shoe factory. If I manage to ruin the Independent Fund, I win."

She points to the small steel block at the very end of the squares. Something hums inside. A die pops out of a slot and Margaret rolls hers. But this time she loses all three of her lead mines.

She places her shares in front of the block and the block swallows them up with a sucking sound.

The next blow is the shoe factory, which suffers the same fate.

"Margaret, Margaret, listen to me!"

"If I succeed in ruining the Independent Fund," she continues feverishly, "it will blow up. Which means that it will destroy itself... fictitiously of course. And the game will start over. Otherwise, if I lose, I'll have to kill myself. That's the rule."

She bursts out laughing.

"Unless I cheat, which would be equivalent to fraud. In that case, the borlok does not accept compromises. I will be exterminated on the spot."

She shivers.

"Brrr..."

Suddenly, I feel myself turning pale. It's like an alarm bell has gone off in my head. Unconsciously, I have a presentiment of danger awaiting Margaret as she tries to discreetly cheat with her die after another failure.

With a nervous finger, I press the "stop" button. The squares go dark and the buzzing of the device fades. Margaret straightens up with the dazed expression of a sleeper pulled out of a nightmare.

"Syd, but why? What's gotten into you?"

Horrified I look at the Monopoly with the instructions also bearing the name borlok.

"Margaret, get dressed. We have to leave immediately."

For once, she obeys without question. Ten minutes later, the Buick starts up and we drive into the big, bright city, heading towards Blue Cottage.

It's almost nine o'clock when we pull up in front of the brightly lit luxurious bungalow.

The snow has stopped falling, but a bitter cold shakes us to the core as we climb the steps to ring the front doorbell.

Of course, I haven't forgot Pat.

The doll "woke up" during the trip and despite Margaret's protests, who still doesn't seem to realize the seriousness of our situation, I had to tape the lid of the box shut so that I didn't have to hear the awful little voice that has become unbearable to me.

But the android is still moving around in her box and her nervous little fists keep drumming against the cardboard. Unmoved by her anger, I press the doorbell a second time, but still no answer.

What the hell are they doing? By chance, I turn the door knob and it opens without any difficulty.

"A broken door bell, surely," Margaret whispers to me as she enters first.

The hall is empty. We enter the living room, visit the office, the library, the three other rooms and the kitchen. But it's all the same. No Archie or Gloria.

We call out but in vain. Nobody answers us.

I whisper, rather intrigued, "It's not like them to do this kind of thing. The door's open, everything's lit up, it's very weird."

Margaret suggests, "Take a look in the lab, I'll check upstairs."

I quickly dash down to the basement, but the lab is as empty as the ground floor. Just as I'm getting back into the hall Margaret's voice booms over my head.

"Syd, hurry up, hurry up!"

It hits me like a lash. I throw the box onto an armchair and rush up the marble stairs, taking them four at a time.

Margaret is at the end of the hallway, in front of our friends' bedroom, the door of which is wide open. With a trembling hand, she points inside the room.

"Oh... Syd... look..."

And I see. I see Gloria, from behind, in the middle of the room, motionless in a charming pink silk negligee. She looks like she's admiring herself in a mirror. A tall, oval mirror on legs. A mirror whose beveling, in the ambient lighting, seems to reflect all the colors of the rainbow. But what's astonishing is the image that the mirror reflects back to us.

It's a different Gloria. A Gloria whose pink negligee has been replaced by a long black dress that is somewhat reminiscent of the feminine extravagance of the 17th century. Long, all gathered, and puckered, with a low, black, round neckline embroidered with a line of pearls.

And then, a coat suddenly appears, with a big green velvet hood framed in black fox.

Just for a second or two.

Then the image disappears, as if through a veil of moving water. Undulating shapes appear in the mirror, surrounded by ghostly lights, while from the misty surface another Gloria emerges. This time, in a salmon-colored crinoline dress, decorated with little green and white bows. A Pompadour dress!

At this moment, Gloria (the real one) turns slowly three-quarters and her bent right arm begins to wave lazily. In the mirror appears a lace fan, which the pseudo-Gloria begins to wave in the same slow and regular movement. Then comes the powdered wig out of the blue, inexplicably. A beauty spot on the right cheekbone and another between the breasts.

"Syd, the dress of my dreams!" Margaret whispers, as I feel her slipping under the spell of these extraordinary visions.

I must admit that it takes a serious dose of willpower to escape the grip of this magical mirror and it is at the moment when the other Gloria reappears in a long wedding dress, Directoire style, that I rush forward.

I pounce on the mirror and turn the whole thing around. The image blurs, fades and vanishes completely. It's nothing more than an ordinary mirror reflecting my own image.

Meanwhile, Margaret has come into the room and Gloria has turned around. Her face is cadaverously pale. She looks at us with astonished eyes.

"Syd! Margaret!"

Her long brown hair is messy. She brushes a strand away from her forehead, turns her head toward the mirror and tries to smile.

"Oh! Lord, what happened?"

"Gloria! Where's Archie?"

"What's wrong? What's going on?"

I grabbed her firmly by the shoulders.

"Please answer, it's very serious."

She seems to be snapping out of it.

"Well, I... I think he was in the little sitting room next door when... I..."

Heart pounding and fearing the worst, I dash into the next room. Archie is there, indeed, and I find him comfortably seated in a Louis XV armchair.

He's wearing a bathrobe, his legs bare and his feet crossed. He's got a magazine in his hands but he seems so absorbed in his reading that he shows no reaction to my presence.

"Archie! Archie!"

He doesn't even hear me... turns a page and continues reading.

I walk around the chair and glance at it. The magazine is full of multi-colored drawings, text circled in red and black... with mathematical formulas that look like real puzzles.

Archie turns another page. I think that it's the last one. But no! Another one follows and then another and another, every time Archie's hand turns one. As if the magazine was gradually creating its own pages!

And it goes on forever...

Yet the thickness of the magazine remains the same. It's incomprehensible! In a flash, William Marshall's non-stop record comes back to me. There was no coda to that supernatural music, just as there is no end to this diabolical magazine.

With a shudder of horror, my eyes catch the title at the top of a page: "The Infinite and I!"

This time it's too much. Hastily, I snatch the magazine from my illustrious friend's hands and he jumps when he recognizes me.

His eyes are red, his eyelids swollen. He looks like he's exhausted, like the Wandering Jew who has traveled for thousands of light years on foot.

CHAPTER IV

Of course, it's not easy to explain the inexplicable, but what first of all gets me to seriously arouse Archie and Gloria's concerns is time!

In fact, this kind of enthrallment that they've both just experienced, one with the mirror and the other with the magazine, lasted for several hours.

It began around noon, when, back at the bungalow, Archibald and Gloria Brent decided to deal with the many presents that had been sent to them, mostly for their godson, who is none other, as you know, than our fine little Bud.

Of course, neither the mirror nor the magazine appeared to be intended for him and they were both astonished as they opened the packages, especially since there was no card indicating the name and address of the sender.

They had figured that it was an oversight and, with their curiosity piqued, Archie and Gloria had let themselves be caught in the trap.

Of course, we're hesitating to repeat the experience of the "Magic Mirror", but Gloria's account now lets me guess the incredible power of this object. Everything is in the imagination and Gloria only had to let her mind wander from one idea to another for all her dream outfits to immediately come true. Who, really, could resist such an enchantment?

As for Archie, he too had let himself be dragged down the dangerous slope, strewn this time not with frills and lace, but with numbers and mathematical formulas and more or less esoteric drawings that had obsessed his mind to such an extent that all contact between him and the outside world had been broken.

To convince him completely, I grab the magazine and open it to the last page. With a trembling hand, I turn the page, but another one pops up spontaneously, as if the sheet had suddenly split in two. And the phenomenon is repeated again, twice, three times, four times... as the pages turn... turn... turn...

Archie has turned pale. He in turn grabs the magazine, the thickness of which seems to remain unchanging. The first pages have disappeared, giving way to those that have just been spawned, thus keeping the object the same weight and thickness.

"A mass-energy relationship," he mutters under his breath. "But, damn it, I don't..."

Here his scientific mind is taking control, but... where's the energy? He guesses my question but I don't give him time to answer.

"The surprises aren't over yet, pal. Come and see."

I drag everyone downstairs and hurry to free Pat from her cardboard prison.

The doll is smiling again and starts in on her little spiel, gratifying my friends with "Merry Christmas" and all the goodwill of creation.

Gloria opens her eyes in astonishment and whispers, "Lord, how is this possible?"

Archie asks sharply, "Where did she come from?"

I calm them down with a wave of my hand and in one breath I spill everything about Macy's, the unending William Marshall record, Gino's ball and that horrible Monopoly game which, for a moment, made me fear for Margaret's life.

"And all these borloks are distributed anonymously. Nobody knows where they come from. That's the most serious issue."

Archie slumps into an armchair. His forehead is furrowed with deep wrinkles.

"If I understand correctly, every family has received one of these mysterious gifts?"

"I haven't had time to visit all of New York, but I am afraid that everyone is getting sent something."

"Do you realize the capital invested in the manufacture of these objects? It's all so unbelievable... scientifically incomprehensible... at least at our level of knowledge."

I nod.

"Let's leave that aside. The question I want to ask is this: For what purpose were these objects made?"

An uneasy shiver runs through us but the heavy silence that falls is broken by Gloria's voice.

"I... I think there's another borlok... but this one's definitely meant for Bud. Yes, now I remember... it's a kind of merry-go-round with..."

Gloria rushes to the fireplace and brings us the "gift".

"It looks like a miniature slide," Margaret exclaims.

Indeed, it does look like one. It's a long circular track, the right side clearly higher than the left. The track, set on an intricate metal scaffolding attached to the rectangular base serving as a stand, has two parallel rails with no cross ties. A small wagon mounted on four weird skates sits on a square with red hatching, obviously marking the start and finish of the course.

Archie steps forward and examines the toy minutely. After a moment, he says to us, "That's curious."

"What is?"

"Look! The two sloping sections are not the parallel. The one closest to us is normal but the one on the opposite side has a twist. Well, that's right... Yes... This track is made like a Möbius strip!"

We look at each other hesitantly, but Gloria has already grabbed the instructions that come with the toy. It's controlled by a small power unit with two buttons. One for "start", the other for "stop". Still the real nature of the toy completely escapes us.

Only one sentence at the bottom of the instructions catches our attention: "Learn to get rid of your possessions and do it as naturally as possible. Give an object to the wagon and press the button."

I deliberately throw a box of matches into the small vehicle.

"Go ahead, Archie, we have to get to the bottom of this."

After more hesitation, my learned friend places his finger on the button and presses it hard.

A faint hum comes out of the generator and straps of a sort unfold to hold in place the matches as tightly as could be, it seems. Immediately the wagon sets off down the twisting track, carrying its load.

The vehicle picks up speed, climbs the slope, goes around the semicircle of the raised track, continuing to pickup speed, then shoots down and into the twist. Now it's *upside down*.

This explains the harness that straps down the cargo and the complete separation of the two rails! In reality, they are rails between which the wagon slides and moves thanks to its four skates probably equipped with ultra-miniaturized inner friction bearings...

Upside-down, then, it glides over the lower section of the track and returns to its starting point – more precisely, under its starting point! – and starts a second loop at an ever-increasing speed.

Flying at a dizzying pace, it rights itself again when it goes through the twist, comes back towards us and starts another course with even greater speed. The wagon doesn't take long to hit the descent and turn upside-down for a shorter lap than the previous one.

At the precise moment when it turns itself upright, I could swear that a strange luminescent aura envelops it and hides it from us for a fraction of a second...

We see it speeding along at a dizzying pace and, after a fourth lap, it finally slows down and then stops abruptly at the starting point.

Margaret is the first to express her amazement.

"Oh, my word, the box of matches has disappeared!"

As incredible as it may seem, the wagon is indeed empty. The matchbox appears to have vanished... without a trace!

"Great, isn't it?" Pat's voice calls out to us.

Her tone sounds ironic and the intervention of this machine in the midst of our bewilderment is rather irritating. Maybe even appalling. I only regret that the wagon is too small to hold her. Ah, I swear, with what joy I would send her off to join the matchbox! Except that, really... Where could the box have gone? Where?

For, it has completely disappeared from our world and the same phenomenon is happening again with a tube of Nivea cream that Gloria tosses into the wagon. This one comes back empty and as if waiting for another package to be shipped off... God knows where!

"Well, as a city dumpster, you couldn't do any better. But come on, what's going on? What happened to all these things?"

No time for nitpicking... Now Archie grabs the track and feverishly drags us into the laboratory.

He opens a cage, grabs one of his guinea pigs, in fact an adorable little white mouse, and he places it in the wagon. This time again, the experiment is successfully repeated. If one can call it that. The mouse disappears but just when the wagon flips over on the twisted section. And in the same glow as the other vanishings.

Archie scratches his forehead thoughtfully.

"That's what I figured," he says. "Living beings are not immune to this strange phenomenon."

He furrows his brow.

"First the speed, then a twist in the continuum, that's what would perhaps explain..."

"Yes... but the landing point?"

He shrugs.

"In time... or in another dimension... How would I know? This is all scary... really scary!"

He looks at us for a long time and, after a sigh, continues:

"These toys threaten to ruin our entire civilization. We're in the presence of the most formidable psychological weapon that has ever been created."

"Explain what you mean?"

"There's nothing to explain. I observe, I try to be objective. First of all, these toys are not intended only for children. Put into all homes, they will become psychological traps that will spare neither young nor old. We've had the sad experience of this, Gloria and I, and if you hadn't come in God knows what would have become of us. Of course, the methods are different but all these toys, made with diabolical skill, all have the same goal: to excite the tendencies that we all feel to escape the present and daily reality. Man, whatever his age, is always only a child who can create toys to suit him thanks to the development of his knowledge. Look at a man at the wheel of his car. He knows that he's driving a dangerous toy, but he likes it. And what does he think about outside of work? To spend his free time exactly like a schoolboy during his breaks. He'll go to a fair to break clay pipes with a rifle or to ride roller-coasters, or maybe he'll go to play cards at the local bar. If he has the means, he'll try flying, canoeing or underwater fishing, archery or fencing. The braver ones will set out to conquer an inaccessible peak while others, more timid, will be happy playing with their children's electric train. When Carnival arrives, three-quarters of them will go and dress up, throw confetti and blow into kazoos. Yes, man has always felt the latent desire to take refuge in this period of childhood which marks his entry into the world."

He looks down at the track and shakes his head gravely.

"This is why these toys are dangerous. They were designed with a psychological ploy to tear man away from reality and plunge him into total passivity."

It's my turn to nod.

"Yes, I see where you're going with this. They want to grab our attention, to amuse us with all these baubles. In short, a kind of diversion when in reality all this ingenuity is only a purely militant means of subversion. But who's behind it all? Who?"

Archie stares at the track. He grabs a screwdriver and starts unhooking the energy cell from its metal shell.

The inside is just a mass of wires, coils and batteries. But the energy used by the device remains a deep mystery and Archie, after a quick study of the different parts, lets out a sigh.

"All this is beyond imagination," he admits. "If only we could understand the nature of the energy which seems to me to be at the heart of quite a few of these toys..."

"Maybe we could do a test with our electronic analyzer?" Gloria suggests thoughtfully.

Archie doesn't dawdle. With the help of Gloria, he pulls the analyzer off its stand and quickly hooks it up to the mysterious box.

"No danger of blowing up the house?" Margaret asks, who seems more suspicious than ever.

A spark flies in the connection but Archie reassures us immediately. Not the slightest sign of radioactivity or saturation in the toys batteries. No, there's no danger... at least I hope not.

Needles start oscillating on the analyzer's dials. Gloria fiddles with a few buttons as the hum in the track starts growing alarmingly louder.

"Archie, be careful... I don't like that noise at all."

Another spark flies from the connections and shakes the laboratory with unexpected force. The air around us starts vibrating strangely, as if the atmosphere were suddenly being sucked in by a powerful pump.

The whirlwind is concentrated in the middle of the lab and in the next second something comes to life before our astonished eyes, takes shape, materializes.

A massive silhouette... of a human being... A kind of old patriarch wrapped in a long red robe cinched at the waist by a silk cord.

From his hooded head emerges a thick white beard sprinkled with tiny stars shining like pearls.

He's an old man, a noble old man with a stunned expression. He looks like he's walking on clouds, expressing gentleness, shyness, fear and respect all at the same time.

His aged body is bent under the weight of a heavily laden sack. Snowflakes fly and dance around him in wispy sarabands.

He looks at us wide-eyed, like an angel lost outside his celestial empire and thrown into the midst of demons.

I can't resist. Despite the vice that's squeezing my throat, I still manage to whisper, "Who are you?"

He blows in his beard and shakes the snow off his shoulders. "But... I'm Santa Claus!"

CHAPTER V

I've never liked jokes of this kind, but I must admit that the mysterious appearance of this being who seems to have come straight out of a Christmas story leaves me perplexed.

"Santa Claus," Margaret cries out, stepping towards the old man. "Really, who are you trying to kid?"

The noble creature suddenly looks panicked, his swollen eyes still staring at Margaret.

"Lord God... But how am I here?... And you, madam, who are you?... Who are you?"

"Mrs. Claus," Margaret spits out through clenched teeth. "And my whole family is behind me."

"Oh mercy, do not blaspheme... Help me to clear up this mystery... My sleigh... Where is my sleigh?"

He turns his head to the right and left, then runs towards the stairs down to the ground floor. Instinctively, we set off after him, determined to get him back by hook or by crook.

We meet up with him in the living room, in front of the large bay window overlooking the park. His gaunt hand has pushed aside the curtains and a sigh of relief ruffles the hairs of his beard. In turn, we, too, see what has eased his mind.

A sleigh full of toys, harnessed to six reindeer with glittering antlers! The steel runners had dug straight furrows in the soft snow... only for around ten feet... as if... as if... Oh, come on! It looks like the sleigh had suddenly appeared in front of the bungalow... as if it had fallen from the sky... or simply at the wave of a magic wand.

"Where are you from?"

This time, it's Archie who is asking the question with his usual firmness.

The old man turns around, struggling against a fatigue that we imagine is eternal.

"Well, from... from Center."

"Which Center?"

"The Experimental Center, yes, where we study all the borloks that are destined for you... um... I still have some stuff on me that maybe..."

He slides a hand behind his back, rummages in his sack, but Gloria stops him.

"Please, let's try to reach an understanding. Where is this center you just mentioned?

"But I... I do not know... It is impossible for me to explain to you."

"Who do you work for?"

"M is the creator. He is also my creator."

I step forward feeling my top starting to blow.

"M... with a capital M, right?"

A smile from Santa Claus.

"Yes, that is right, how did you know?"

"Are you playing a joke on us?"

"Oh no, I would not dare... You are humans. We love humans. M says we should respect and honor them. Personally, I have never seen humans. You are the first. This all happened so strangely..."

He rifles through his long beard, then scratches the tip of his big red nose.

"I was in Center, busy examining the borloks, when suddenly... pfft, there was a kind of whirlwind. It was like an uncontrollable force that yanked me off the ground... and then, I found myself next to you, on this world... Please, what is going on?"

I catch Archie's eye. The short-circuit in the contacts... the spark... something incomprehensible must have happened at that moment.

The old man coughs slightly, then his beady eyes fall on Pat who seems to be following the scene with visible interest. Suddenly, a smile appears on Santa's lips.

"Pat," he exclaims, rushing toward the doll... "Pat, what a surprise! How are you, my young friend?"

His wrinkled hand caresses the doll's cheeks in a fatherly gesture.

"I am doing very well, Santa, and I am having a lot of fun... If you knew how funny these people are..."

"Adorable, isn't she?" the old man says to us. "She is the most complete borlok that has ever been made."

"Oh, you think so!"

"You seem to underestimate the psychology of toys. A toy must amuse for a long time and develop in the child's brain a taste for marvelous and surprising effects."

"That's what you say," Margaret retorts.

"No, that is Baudelaire," the old man shoots back with a little smile. "But Baudelaire's time has passed. Although today's toy allows the child to face life by ridding him of all his complexes, it is also a precious help for the adult. It allows the adult to kill time, boredom, bad ideas and daily worries. Myself included since I have never lived except among toys and I can guarantee you…"

He doesn't say anymore about the matter because at that moment footsteps echo in the hall and a creature that is not at all supernatural bursts into the living room.

It's James Funnigan, my beloved boss, all wrapped up in a big fur coat and dragging behind him a big cardboard box wrapped in silver string.

What now! This was all that was missing!

He puts his package on a table and crosses the room, all smiles on the outside.

"Hi guys, I hope I'm not too late for Christmas Eve? My wife has a terrible toothache so I thought I might as well make the most of it and go and spend Christmas Eve with my friends. What do you think of my idea?"

I shake his big hand with a strained smile.

"You have such inspirations…"

"Yes, that's how it comes to me… Besides, I always know how to find the good places to have fun and to eat even better."

He bursts out in loud laughter and then finally realizes the other creature's presence.

"Well, I think we're in for a laugh here. Very good disguise! Who is it?"

"Santa Claus," Margaret tells him impassively.

JF winks at me, "A friend of yours?"

"We'll tell you again it's Santa Claus. The real one!"

"Always your little jokes, huh? And to think that I planned to play the same prank on you. I wanted to come here in the same costume."

"That would've taken the cake."

"Bah, you have to have a little fun from time to time. And I'm in a good mood tonight. Okay, what's on the menu? Turkey with chestnuts, I guess? Mmm, I love that. But first, we're going to have a friendly whiskey, right?"

As he heads over to the bar, the low hum coming from the lab reminds us that we forgot to unplug the analyzer.

We rush to the basement, leaving JF to his bottle of Cutty Sark, and we turn everything off. An unpleasant smell of ozone floats in the lab where it's become abnormally hot. Heavens, I think we were just in time.

Archie wipes his brow looking overwhelmed by events.

"Syd," he says to me, "we must urgently alert the government, otherwise..."

A scream from Funnigan cuts him off. Fearing the worst, we go back up to the living room, a mighty fear hot on our heels.

JF is on all fours in the middle of the room, his head tilted under an armchair.

He mumbles, "Wow, where did he go?"

"Who?"

"Your two-bit Santa Claus!"

He straightens up, huffing like a seal.

"Say, weird things are happening here! Your friend was right here in front of me. I was going to pour him a drink when suddenly, nothing. He disappeared just like that."

He looks at the large bay window. The sled has disappeared too. Only the tracks in the snow remain.

"And that doll that won't stop talking? Where did you get it from, huh? Where did it come from? What nonsense it spews!"

"She's my sister," Margaret tells him, "but she's very touchy, I warn you."

Funnigan looks at us with the baleful glare of a stillborn calf.

"None of this is human... Listen, I know that with you I have to expect anything, but don't do things like that to me. It drives me crazy!"

"Well, the doctors gave up on you a long time ago, you're safe now, come on!"

A burst of laughter from Pat punctuates Margaret's retort, while poor Funnigan collapses into an armchair, his teeth chattering.

Just then the phone rings and Archie rushes over to it. A short conversation, then the young scientist turns to us with a frown.

"It's from the new Greenwood Observatory. Professor Calloway needs me urgently."

"What's wrong?"

"I don't know but something must have happened. I'm going to get dressed."

He goes up to his room and reappears three minutes later, booted and wrapped in a thick leather jacket. In the glance he gives me, I see his invitation to follow him. I've already put on my coat when Funnigan gets up in turn.

"Well, I guess I'd better go home. I'm not hungry anymore."

"You won't be using silk napkins but you'd better think about your rag."

"What do you mean?"

"That it would be better if you stayed here. We might need you and that fine newspaper of yours."

Without giving him time to answer, I turn to Gloria and Margaret.

"As for you two, stay calm and don't touch anything. We'll try not to take too long."

When Archie and I leave to get into the Chrysler, a nearby clock strikes twelve.

Jesus is born... Midnight mass is in full swing...

Oh Lord! What a night!

CHAPTER VI

It is not very far. The new Greenwood Observatory is only a few miles from the Blue Cottage and we reach it in less than half an hour despite the snow and ice which make the winding road difficult.

We barely enter the huge building when we come across about fifty people who are clearly panicking. In the general confusion, we can make out the sound of voices and lively conversations. A feverish intensity looms over the auditorium we enter.

We elbow our way through to reach Professor Calloway, whom we spot in the middle of a group of disheveled astronomers.

He's a tall, lean, long-limbed fellow with a small pointed goatee and thick horn-rimmed glasses. He looks like a dervish who has dressed as best as he can for the occasion.

He rushes out of the middle of the group when he recognizes Archie.

"Ah, Professor Brent, there you are! My God, what's happening to us? It's dreadful... dreadful..."

"Yes, I know, I know, the toys?"

Calloway stares at him, stupefied.

"Toys! You call them toys! Ah, as a Christmas present, we got more than we bargained for! The stars... The galaxies... Planck's constant... The speed of light... Gravitation... All that... Everything..."

He's about to burst out but the emotion paralyzes his vocal cords.

"Come on, professor, what's going on?"

Calloway manages to grunt, "Come!"

We jump into an electric vehicle that takes us on a track that heads back towards the upper floors.

Two panels reacting to a photoelectric system slide open in front of us and we enter room with the big equatorial refracting telescope where a gaggle of astronomers are busy.

"The news came this morning from Palomar," Calloway declares feverishly as he scrambles out of the vehicle. "And then also from Mount Wilson, Yerkes, Brookhaven... and even from England, France, the USSR and Australia. We didn't want to believe it but we too were forced to face the facts. Ah, Professor Brent, it's the end of the world!"

He leads Archie to the big telescope, but before he jumps on the big iron spiral staircase, he turns to me.

"Mr. Gordon, you're a journalist. For heaven's sake, or at least what's left of it, be careful what you write. Panic must be avoided at all costs or else we're lost for sure"

He nods and repeats thoughtfully:

"Yes, lost..."

I still don't understand what he's talking about and as the two men rush up to the platform, I try to get some explanations from the other scientists who are bustling around me, but no one seems willing to answer me.

Telephones ring all over the place, television screens turn on and off, conversations are exchanged about different equations, while computers and electronic calculators continue to vomit out streams of paper that, in turn, are analyzed by other machines, and still others...

A real hell of noise, numbers and technical terms where trillions, parsecs and ergs per second fly from one mouth to another like so many cabalistic words in a gathering of sorcerers at its annual coven.

Still, really, what's the meaning of all this?

What kind of end of the world did Professor Calloway refer to?

What's this dreadful danger that's threatening us?

Half an hour passes in this mournful confusion, then Archie finally reappears, his face haggard, looking hopeless.

"Syd," he tells me, "no mind could dream up such a disaster."

"But for heaven's sake, talk, talk!"

"Entire stars have disappeared... especially within our own galaxy, without us being able to find the slightest explanation for the incomprehensible disappearance. On the other hand, quasars are suddenly appearing, releasing a hundred million times more energy than those we have studied so far."

"You're talking about super-condensed quasi-stars?"

"Exactly. The extraordinary power plants seem to be setting off a chain reaction, like the neutrons in an atomic bomb. The intense radiation travels from star to star and could very well destroy our entire galaxy."

"We're not alone in the universe," Calloway adds in a flat voice. "Millions and millions of peoples are perishing in this terrible catastrophe. It's horrible... and we won't escape it in our turn."

I cut him off bluntly, "Wait a minute, Professor, how far away is this happening?"

"The nearest destruction zone is four light years away... that is, in the constellation Centaurus."

"So it happened four years ago?"

"Which means that if the destructive wave travels towards Earth, we risk being swept away at any second. But if we escape it, our fate will not be much more pleasant."

I grimace. "How so?"

"I'll tell you," Archie answers me. "Gravitation, as was once believed, is not a purely local phenomenon. All the matter contained in the universe is affected by it simultaneously. A star several light years away exerts an infinitesimal attraction on each of us, in the same way that the skyscrapers of New York are doing right now. Remove half the stars from the universe and the natural laws will inevitably change within our system. Starting with the Sun, which will double its thermal power, then the Earth, whose orbit and rotation will be disrupted, and finally our weight, which will automatically double. Gravitation must maintain its balance, it's a fundamental law of the universe. But that's what very well might happen to us if this destruction continues. And unfortunately, that's not all..."

"You're not very encouraging. What else?"

Archie shrugs in despair.

"I talked about the fundamental law, but all that has already been turned upside down, and that's what we can't understand."

"You were talking about gravitation..."

"Yes, it's already changed in accordance with the principle that I just explained to you. You don't realize it, but you already weigh 500 grams more, for the same mass. Except, for light it's different and, from that point of view, it's totally incomprehensible. You know the speed of light."

"About 186,000 miles per second."

Calloway nods.

"This speed was still valid until this morning. Since then, it's changed. The light you're seeing at this moment now travels at only 125,000 miles per second."

I turn to Archie, feeling like I've just been hit on the head with a sledgehammer.

"I checked the calculations," he admits to me. "Light and radio waves are slowed down, as if they were traveling through a material medium. In benzene, for example, this is understandable, but in a vacuum... All our equations are wrong, all the laws of our modern physics are no longer worth anything. Don't ask me why or how, I don't know. What I've just seen is beyond imagination. Even Einstein's famous equation is wrong. E no longer equals mc^2. There's no longer any equivalence between energy and matter and vice versa. Something else applies. What? I don't know."

"Even computers are at a loss," Calloway continues. "The energy of a photon is given by the equation $E = hf$, but h has disappeared. In other words, Planck's constant is no longer applicable. Try and calculate energy... The same in de Broglie's formula according to which the wavelength λ of a particle is the constant h divided by P, the quantity of movement of the particle. The λ has lost its value, so we can't define the wavelength of a particle. Of course, in atoms electrons continue to jump from one orbit to another, but it's different. Yes, it's different... The atoms are real, formulas are theoretical models that predict their behavior. And if the formulas are right, fundamentally, well, with the disappearance of Planck's constant they're pointing to really catastrophic things that we can't even imagine."

He wipes his forehead and adds,

"And this is happening with magnetism, electromagnetism, radioactivity too. As for gravitation, the laws of Kepler and Newton no longer exist. There is something else, god knows what..."

Suddenly I feel myself turning pale. I'm neither a mathematician nor a physicist, but I can easily guess the terrible consequences that such an upheaval has in store for us. It's the complete collapse of all our science, all our knowledge, all our current technology.

Of course, Nature rebalances itself on other laws, the balance is restored, matter remains matter, energy energy, but us? What will become of us? Are we going to have to start all over again, after centuries and centuries of tireless efforts directed only against a mysterious and merciless Nature whose laws and rules are like locked and armored doors?

Yes, centuries and centuries to force a few locks, to crack open a few doors... and it only took a few hours to reduce all our efforts, hopes and sacrifices to nothing.

But the danger is certainly even more serious if we are to believe the dire predictions of Archie and Calloway.

The destruction of humanity may be just a matter of hours or days away.

I burst out:

"But in the end, every effect has a cause, Nature doesn't play dice. An apple falls down, it doesn't rise up..."

Calloway looks at me with a little compassion.

"If one day it does rise up, another Newton will rediscover a new universal mechanics. Why not? The old one no longer exists. Euclid? Einstein? Their theories and postulates now have the same value as a Bantu sorcerer's thesis on renal colic. All our knowledge has flown out the window... It's as if... it's as if..."

"As if our galaxy has shifted into another dimension," Archie says coldly. "As if new forces were suddenly joined together, conditioned by other laws that completely escape human nature."

"And the toys?"

"Again with your toys!" Calloway exclaims irritably. "I swear that's all you think about!"

"I'm talking about the toys we got, the ones the whole world must have got... About the real-life Santa Claus, who we..."

"Are you feeling all right?" Calloway's icy irony jolts me like a cold shower.

"Listen, professor, this isn't a joke. It happened when I plugged in the Moebius strip. A Santa Claus as alive as you and me, I swear it, and if you don't believe me..."

At that moment, a video call snaps Calloway out of his exasperation.

"Excuse me," he says, "I've got a call from Palomar."

He rushes over to one of the duplexes and disappears into the crowd.

Archie guesses my question and nods. Calloway and his colleagues have not left the observatory since the day before. They still know nothing about the mysterious gifts whose psychological threat seems to go hand in hand with the great universal upheaval.

"Indeed, and it's obvious. This disaster that's just been revealed to us is not the result of chance. Einstein said it and I repeat his words: Nature does not play dice. A will, a thought, a conscious mind, human or quasi-human, is at the origin of all this. The Borloks are in fact only a diversion designed to turn our attention away from the dreadful cataclysm that threatens humanity."

Archie suddenly decides:

"Let's get out of here and back to Blue Cottage. While I alert Washington, you deal with your paper... Put out a special edition, there's not a second to lose."

CHAPTER VII

News definitely travels fast.

As soon as we get back to the Blue Cottage, Archie and I rush to the telephone, but it takes a great deal of determination and urging to get through to the White House, despite my young friend's great renown.

The emergency services are already overloaded with calls and the fever is skyrocketing in the presidential residence.

Calls are coming in from all corners of the globe and the red telephone has already rung several times between Moscow and Washington.

The Kremlin had initially believed it was a subversive maneuver launched with the support of American corporations, but news from other governments had confirmed the worst.

The sudden and unexpected invasion of these mysterious toys of unknown origin is on a global scale.

No nation seems to have escaped it, even those whose religions are foreign to Christianity and have no interest in Christmas celebrations along with all the traditions that follow. As a result, on the sacred date of December 24th, the Japanese and Chinese are enjoying the generosity of a Santa Claus freed of all religious constraints.

But enough, there's also the universal disaster closely connected to the mysterious unidentified objects and the general alarm is still sounding over this.

All the scientists of the whole world are on edge and panic is already threatening the most eminent scientific centers that are showing no sign of being able to solve the problem.

A Russian space rocket, launched only a few hours ago from the Baikonur Cosmodrome, is drifting in space: its remote-control based on the Doppler-Fizeau principle no longer corresponds to current physical realities.

Radio signals are being disrupted, power plants are reportedly showing signs of weakness, which suggests that our energy networks will soon need to undergo significant changes.

An accident has been reported from Brookhaven: a particle accelerator has just exploded without the exact cause of the disaster being known.

Positive ions have become negative for no rhyme or reason, but Archie says this inversion of matter in the accelerator is probably a direct consequence of the new universal laws we find ourselves subject to.

All nuclear tests on the surface of the globe have to be stopped without further delay and the immediate defusing of all American, Russian or Chinese atomic bombs becomes an absolute necessity if we hope to postpone the fatal deadline.

In other circumstances, I might welcome this race towards total disarmament, but these circumstances that are causing it seem to me even more tragic than the effects of a possible nuclear war.

If the world is lost, this time it will be lost in its totality. Nothing will survive, not even a Chinese, and God knows those guys have a hard life!

But enough again... I digress and I delete that sentence from the article that I'm dictating to the New Sun telescript. Certainly, China is a charming country, but aren't the poor Chinese sailing on the same ship as us? So, what's the point of turning them against us once again?

That's Funnigan saying this with a silly smile. He's trying to joke, but he doesn't mean it, believe me!

When I hang up, he grabs my arm.

"I'd still like you to explain to me what's going on. After all, I am the editor of the paper, right?"

"Maybe but you're not the one reading it. So?"

"Syd... this speed of light... I don't see anything different. It shines like before, right?" He points to the chandelier in the living room.

"Yes, but it travels less fast. That's the problem."

"So what? It just needs to shine, right?"

"In any case, for you, it doesn't seem to shine much. Mind you, it's not serious, you've been affected since birth."

"But, for goodness sake, do I have the right to know what's going on? I come here with my merriest smile and I find a talking doll and a guy dressed as Santa Claus who disappears as if by magic. Then you talk to me about stars that vanish, about the slowing down of light and apples that fly... I'm not a scientist, I'm a regular guy. I try to be considerate, but, as soon as I open my mouth, they shut me up as if I had a mouth full of staphylococci."

"Stapho what?" Margaret says dryly. "And you say you know nothing about science, with words like that? Come on, let's have a drink. We all need one, so you'll fit right in."

It's not gratuitous, in fact, and a good dose of Cutty Sark after the sandwiches we've just nibbled lifts our spirits a little. Lord knows we've been down in the dumps!

During our absence, Gloria didn't do nothing. And her "find", if I can call it that, is quite surprising.

She picked up the little white mouse we had put on the Moebius strip ride. The animal had reappeared in the wagon after Gloria had the bright idea to start it up again, still under the control of its electronic analyzers.

Should we conclude that this was a miracle, a purely accidental result? No, at least according to Mrs Brent.

"It's speed that is at the base of the phenomenon," she explains to us. "It's not a mechanical speed but a temporal speed."

Archie furrows his brow.

"What do you mean?"

"First of all, this toy uses the flow of time as a source of energy. I'm talking about our own time. In order for the wagon to take advantage of an ever-increasing acceleration, the energy must be intensified, in other words, the flow of time must be accelerated, and this only inside the toy. I think I've discovered the time accelerator: this little block, there, between the two coils.

"From then on, the wagon disappears from our perceptions because it's reached a temporal speed that is no longer in sync with the physical balance of our normal four-dimensional continuum. Thanks to the twisted track, it leaves our continuum to come out in another dimension. What happens at that point, I don't know. Maybe another time passes during which the object in the wagon is dumped or tossed out, but it happens so fast that we don't see it. The wagon then returns, emptied of its load, slows down and goes back to its starting point."

She shows us the mouse in its cage, then an X-ray of the animal's digestive system.

"In my opinion, it must be a neutral time. For us, about three hours passed between the mouse's departure and its return. But not for it. And this X-ray proves it. The mouse had eaten before being subjected to the experiment. However, three hours later, the food is still in its stomach, which clearly shows that no digestion took place during these three hours. This is not normal when we know the extremely rapid digestion time of rodents."

Archie scratches his forehead, then the tip of his nose. He always does this when he's deep in thought.

"Mmmm... Mmmm..." he murmurs, "but how is it that the mouse could have been retrieved? It could only have been retrieved at a specific point, exactly the point where it made contact with the other world. It's a question of parameters. A rotation of the coordinate axes, however tiny, can produce a partial alteration of the distances, which automatically implies..."

"...A change in the orientation of the contact point. I thought about it. And that's where the luck factor comes in. When I started the ride again, the mouse must have moved exactly to the contact point. Maybe I also influenced the experiment with my control devices? Remember the experiment of Young's double-slit experiment in which the observer cause the uncertainty... In the present case, I don't know, but..."

She shrugs and sighs:

"In any case, it leads us nowhere. If only we could understand the goal of these creatures who are so set against our humanity... "

Of course, the question hangs in the air.

Why?

A big "why" in letters of fire that constantly arises in our minds, in the middle of a forest of question marks.

But Funnigan seems to have found the solution to his own problems. He takes another shot of whiskey and refills our glasses with a smile and sparkling eyes.

He explains to us, "I put the doll in her box, tied her up carefully and gagged her with tape. Frankly, it was becoming unbearable. She wanted to know at all costs what was in the package."

"What package?"

He tries to look coy.

"Well... The present I brought you..."

"A present? What present?"

He points to the big cube-shaped cardboard box that he put on the table in the living room when he first arrived. Oh, that's right... we'd completely forgotten.

"What is it?"

"Bah, I don't know. I didn't open it. I found it in my office this morning. Every Christmas, I always get toys. Colleagues, acquaintances who think that maybe I have some... But I don't have any children, you know that... So I thought that... well yes, for Bud."

Automatically I turned to Archie. Our eyes meet. Damn, here we go again.

"Well, open it," Margaret says to him suspiciously.

But Archie rattles off, "Hold on, experience advises us to be careful."

He weighs the box. It feels relatively light. He examines the object on all sides and then hesitates in front of the golden string that is wrapped around it.

I hand him my penknife. He cuts the string, lifts a clearly visible tab on one side of the top and takes out another cardboard box from inside, identical in every way to the first.

He repeats the operation by pulling on the tab and pulls out a third one.

"They're very careful people, don't you think, Archie?"

Archie nods, as he pulls yet another cube out of the box.

"You've been tricked," Margaret says to Funnigan, who is watching the scene with bulging eyes.

Archie has just lifted a sixth cube and we are still at the same point. The cubes decrease in volume in regular mathematical proportion and the tenth one is now not much bigger than a cube of butter.

Sweat begins to bead on Archie's forehead.

"What's the meaning of all this?"

"Keep going... We'll get to the end soon. The present can't be very big."

He repeats the experiment ten more times in a row and the cubes continue to come out of each other.

They end up the size of a jeweler's case, then a die, then... By Jove, it's so small that...

I grab the tiny package, perhaps a little too quickly, because I feel like I've stirred up something... inside. A slight click makes the object vibrate in my fingers.

"I think we've reached the end of the line."

I gulp hard and, in the oppressive silence that looms around me, I lift the tab with the tip of my nail.

What happens next is pure magic. Worse... Faustian delirium!

The new cube I pull out has suddenly doubled in volume.

As incredible as it may seem, the phenomenon we are all witnessing nullifies all the laws of universal physics.

A given volume can only contain a volume equal to or less than itself... but never a greater volume.

And yet, this is what has just happened before our wide-open and incredulous eyes.

To make a comparisons, it's as if we had extracted a jeweler's case from a die or a cube of butter from a jeweler's case.

Feverishly, I repeat the operation, and it goes on. All the cubes I bring back double in volume in an inverse mathematical progression.

I soon manage to find a cube equal to the size of the original package, so that now we have a whole range of cubes going from the smallest to the largest. And in both directions.

Archie is the first to come to his senses. His nervous hand tightens on my arm, but I can guess his thoughts. What's going to happen next?

Is the phenomenon to be repeated in the other direction? Or will the cubes once again move down the scale of dimensions?

I can't help myself. I pull the tab again and a new cube comes out double in volume in my trembling hands. I drop it on the ground with a grimace of disgust.

And I barely have the strength to whisper, "Suppose it doesn't stop... This thing could fill up the universe... Do you realize...?"

CHAPTER VIII

This time, I'm not waiting for Funnigan to grab the bottle of Cutty Sark. And a double dose, yes!

Filling up the universe! Of course! Provided that... you have the means to pull out bigger and bigger cubes. But no, this is not the idea that's bothering me. It's the other one. The one that just started running through my head.

Unless the whiskey has completely finished me off and my brain's gone miserably awry. And yet I'm sure that...

So I suddenly explode, "Archie! The merry-go-round! The Moebius strip! Damn, I think I've got it!"

"Got what?"

"Remember... remember the mouse... You sent it to the other dimension and it came back safe and sound."

"Yes, so what?"

"So I think if we could ship a human being in the same way, it would be safe too."

"But... I..."

"Anyway, I'm in."

Gloria walks up to me.

"But, Syd, come on, that's impossible."

"No, no, not if we make the ride big enough for me to fit in the wagon."

I point to the cube, but Archie already gets my idea.

"You want to put the ride in the box, don't you?"

"If it's possible. We have to make it bigger to get a ride on a human scale."

"How will you do that? It'll have to be really big."

"We'll do it outside... in the park. We'll use the crane, the one the workers are using to build your new laboratory."

Margaret then jumps in

"This is crazy," she cries. "Syd, my dear, you've had too much to drink."

"No, don't worry, I'm still completely lucid. Come on now, try to understand. It's the only way to know what's happening on the other side. We have to act before it's too late. We might have a chance... just one..."

This time Archie doesn't hesitate. And after Gloria rushes into the lab to bring back the toy, I delicately go at the cardboard cube with my penknife. The steel blade easily pierces the thing and, on one side I manage to make an opening large enough for the ride fit through.

Still being very cautious, I dare to take a look inside... but nothing's there... Nothing but a dark void, a kind of emptiness that even the beam of a flashlight cannot penetrate.

But the die is cast. Now we have to go all the way. I grab the toy and slowly slide it into the opening and a shudder of horror shakes me as my fingers come into contact with the void.

Lord, it's freezing cold, it's like I've dipped my hand into ether. I let go of the toy. It drops into the darkness.

I see it vaguely. It seems to be floating in the void... just like that... without rhyme or reason...

"Gloria, for heaven's sake, bring me another bottle of whiskey."

I take the time to down my glass while Archie decides to pull on the tab. He brings out another cube which has doubled in volume. But what is strange is the opening I cut into the previous cube—it also appears on this one.

Instinctively, Archie peeks into the opening.

"It seems to be working," he tells us. "The ride has also doubled in size."

"We can't go on like this. The next one won't fit through the door."

Then we hear, "Well, I know someone who will! And double time!"

I turn around. It's Funnigan. He's already put on his overcoat and his Russian hat.

"I won't stay in this house another minute," he says. "I've seen enough. No, no, don't try to stop me, I don't want to know anything more. You've made me sick... At least let me die in peace."

He disappears like he has a troop of devils after him. Poor guy! I'm sure he's going to have nightmares for the rest of his life. With a shrug, I turn to Archie:

"Come on, let's get to work!"

We leave the cottage, taking care not to shake the cube too much, then we march through the snow with long, even strides until we reach the middle of the park. Here, the space is big enough to allow us to carry out the experiment.

Now it's time to operate the construction crane and Archie volunteers for this rather delicate job.

He turns on some spotlights that light up the park from one end to the other, then climbs into the cabin and starts up the machine.

The first maneuvers are pretty clumsy and the hooks slip and slide around the cube. After fifteen minutes of effort and patience, there's finally success. The grappling hooks have lifted out a new cube and after four attempts we get a pretty big box over ten feet long per each side.

"Well done, Archie, two more shots like that and we'll be fine."

Everything is going wonderfully and the gigantic cube we now have before us has reached the proportions of a two-story house.

Now the most critical part of the operation remains: getting the ride out.

To do this, there's only one solution: knock out the rest of the side where the opening is.

Archie makes another maneuver and the grappling hooks begin to crush the cardboard which has become thicker. Sinking into the cube, biting into the steel, they bring out the gigantic ride which is dragged in the snow before our astonished eyes.

Of course, we were all expecting it, but it's still a strange feeling to see our toy transformed into a real funfair attraction. The wagon could hold half a dozen passengers, like those on the famous Big Dipper roller coaster in Luna Park.

Everything is enormously big. Even the ride's control buttons, which are now about twenty inches in diameter.

It doesn't matter! Thanks to the equipment in the laboratory, Archie and Gloria quickly made an automatic switch that should work by simply pressing it.

The engine begins to purr as soon as we connect the circuits and, while we're busy with the last preparations, a sudden flash of lightning bursts from the machinery.

The spark cracks like a gigantic whip, throwing us to the ground with unexpected violence.

At the same time, a sliding sound is heard above us and, in a split second, we see the wagon hurtling at breakneck speed down the twisted track. Gloria's scream strikes our eardrums.

"Lord! Margaret!"

Archie and I jumped up.

We look at Gloria whose trembling voice goes on.

"The shock wave threw her into the wagon. I saw her clearly, she fell in head first."

Suddenly, I feel myself turning pale.

"Oh my God! What are you telling me!"

Completely stunned, I watch the wagon as it continues to complete its circuit at a fantastic speed... Margaret has already disappeared from our sight. She is gone, body and soul, when the machine, after a gradual slowdown, returns to its starting point.

The inside is empty... desperately empty!

"Archie, please try to bring her back... For heaven's sake, do it quickly, before it's too late."

Archie and Gloria rush to the controls.

"Let's hope she gets the bright idea not to change places, not to make any movement," Archie whispers to me feverishly.

He starts the wagon again, once, twice, three times... But each time it returns, a sigh of anguish escapes from our heaving breasts.

Margaret still doesn't reappear.

I stop Archie on his fourth attempt.

"No, no need."

"But..."

"I'll try to join her. Anyway, it doesn't change anything for me... I might as well go right away."

I'm about to run off when the young scholar holds me back with his powerful grip.

"Okay, but I'm coming with you."

"That's very kind, Archie, but your sacrifice is useless."

"Maybe not. There will surely be enough to do for two of us... on the other side."

I know very well that his mind is made up and that anything I might say would have no effect. But there is the ride and all the maneuvers to be carried out.

"I'll be fine on my own," Gloria nobly interrupts my thoughts. "Archie's right, he belongs with you."

Admirable Gloria! I can guess the turmoil of emotions that she must be feeling, but she doesn't let it show. Barely a slight tremor in her voice, just a moist veil over her big black eyes as Archie hugs her.

And then we climb into the wagon, my friend and I, at the same time... A brutal jolt... The icy wind whipping our faces... the nauseating sensation of plunging headfirst into an immense... infinite... chasm...

The wagon rushes... rushes... and the sky disappears... Everything blurs and dissolves... I close my eyes to sink into superhuman anguish, while an icy whirlwind sucks me in and swallows me up.

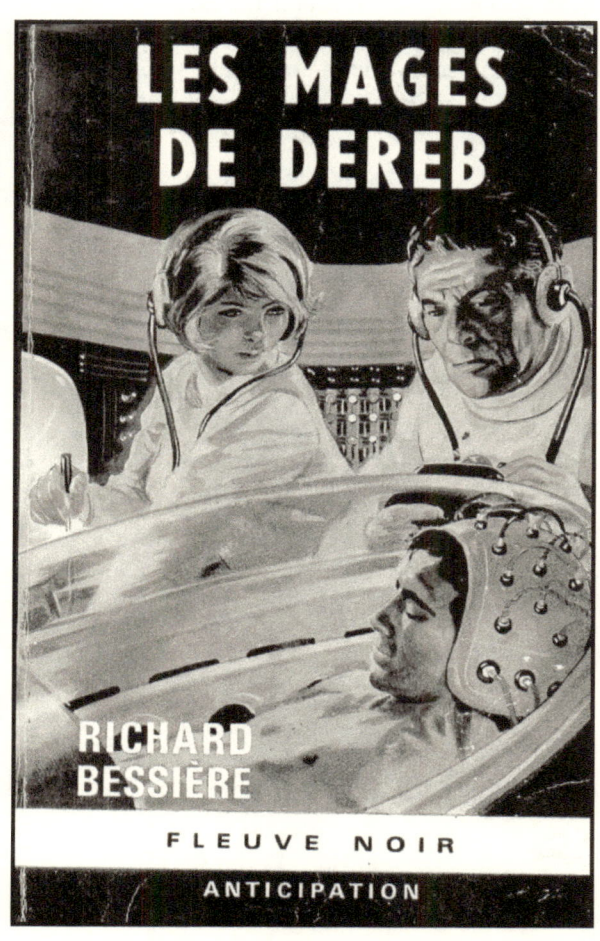

Cover by Gaston de Sainte-Croix

PART TWO

CHAPTER I

The plane is falling like a bomb-shell... A horrible whistling sound tears at my ears at the same time as the last clouds are thinning around the fuselage to reveal bare, arid ground, which seems to be shooting up at us at a dizzying speed.

Heads are popping out of the ground, huge stone heads with grimacing faces pointing at me, all dotted with fluctuating glimmers, but even more hideous because they look almost like human heads.

Nothing could be more mind-boggling than these cold, mesmerizing stares that make me feel like they are peering into the depths of my soul.

The helpless plane bounces through the mineral monsters, slides between the rigid heads, then suddenly plunges into the gaping hole of a greedy maw as if swallowed by the darkness and the stupendous laughter of a stone giant.

I know that something awful, something intolerable, is happening, but I also know that all these visions are just a nightmare caused by a blind, powerful, uncontrollable force.

I have the feeling that I exist, but a little like a spirit detached from its physical body after a violent accident.

Then everything clears up. Tingling travels down my spine, my muscles stiffened, and I regain all my bodily sensations as well as being full conscious of myself.

For a long time, I lie still, just stretched out there, trying to remember.

First Margaret... then Archie and I being carried by the wagon down the long, twisting track... and then the wretched feeling... the nightmare... the horrible nightmare...

Now, when I open my eyes, I see above me an unknown, bizarre, inky-black sky, speckled with pale, ghostly lights.

Like thousands and thousands of candles blazing behind frosted glass. Not a breath of air... not a sound... One of those heavy... eternal... silences that belong only to tombs and the sidereal void.

"Archie..."

My voice sounds muffled, as if inside a room with walls padded with cotton wool.

"Archie... where are you?"

I struggle to my feet, all my limbs aching. My word, I must have landed on a board of nails... It's pricking me all over... But, good heavens, where did I end up?

I make a movement and objects of all shapes and sizes slide and roll around me.

To my great astonishment, I discover that I'm at the top of a pyramid made up of the most varied objects. Matchboxes, tin cans, toothbrushes, apples, cigarette ends, nuts, hairpins, pliers, files, old watches. There's even a gold ring next to a tube of Nivea cream.

Talk about odds and ends. It looks like a flea market is having a sale.

So this is where the objects entrusted to the Moebius strip rides end up... A universal dump or something of the kind!

But the crazy thing is that all these objects have grown enormously. They are no longer their normal size. They have increased a hundredfold in volume.

The weight is also different. I can't find any explanation for that.

So I stand there and scan the area with my eyes, but I'm alone.

I find no trace of Archie, much less of Margaret, and my calls go unanswered.

I didn't quite understand Gloria's explanation about rotating the co-ordinate axes... but I guess the slightest shift in movement must cause significant changes in the drop points.

It's possible that Margaret and Archie, having experienced this shift, dematerialized at another contact point. But where? How far away? Are there other dumps nearby?

I see a piece of chalk nearby and after having cleared the space around me, I take time to mark the exact location of my landing point. Then, bravely, I push through the pile to set foot on this absurd and disappointing world that seems to go on as far as the eye can see. The ground is smooth, dusty, flat, uniformly flat.

No plants, no insects, no life of any kind. Nothing... Nothing but the cloudy sky above my head and the dusty ground beneath my feet.

And thus I cover a distance that I estimate must be a good half-mile, but it's always the same sad and desolate sight.

I go a little farther in the same direction and am about to give up when a huge dark mass blocks my path.

It looks like a wall... a big metal wall that can only be the work of thinking creatures. Well, that's good, the situation is starting to change.

Quickening my pace, I walk along the wall in search of some opening and soon find myself in front of a large half-moon-shaped hole with two doors that don't even have a lock.

Curiosity wins the day so I cautiously push the doors which open with a creak.

And now, a new world lies before me in the vast room I enter. A world both mind-boggling and magical, which takes my breath away and paralyzes me from head to toe.

I find myself standing in a universe of toys, a huge bazaar where there is piled up, as far as the eye can see, enough to amuse all the children of the Earth for several generations.

Bowling and skittle games, fire engines with their sliding ladders, multi-colored balloons, costumes, figurines, dolls in dresses of light. And all this life-size, frightening, colossal... As if the world around me had suddenly taken on abnormal proportions!

Nothing corresponds to the usual standards anymore, I mean those that ordinary mortals have been able to adapt to. Even in a world of toys!

Am I a new Gulliver in the land of giants or have I shrunk to the size of a toy tin soldier?

Here again, everything is like with the objects I found at my landing point. Everything is disproportionate, excessive, monstrous.

I continue my odyssey inside the "bazaar", but everything I see on the right and left defies my reason and understanding.

But really, where have I ended up? Where do these fantastic toys come from? Who makes them? Who?

And always this silence... this eternal silence disturbed only by the sound of my footsteps...

I feel like thousands of eyes are staring at me... the eyes of dolls, puppets, clowns and marionettes. Like Pat! Mocking... Ironic... But not a word, not a movement... Just eyes, round eyes full of strange gleams... and which roll slowly in their wax or plastic sockets.

I pass through other rooms, each as vast as the next, and all cluttered with these eternal toys, most of them piled up in a jumble, in total disorder.

It is when I push another door that I hear a dull hum. It sounds like the noise of machines... the ones you hear near a factory in full swing... Humming, and then creaks, clicks, banging, like metal hitting metal.

Guided by the noises, I cross the huge room and come out in a long, dimly lit corridor. My heart pounding, I rush forward, determined to do anything rather than prolong this absurd, senseless situation, which is getting the better of my nerves.

No, I wasn't wrong. It is indeed a factory.

In front of me, machines are working at full capacity. Drills, rolling mills, boring machines, lathes, hoists, conveyor belts that transport steel frames, doll heads, bowling pins, clothes...

Tanks filled with paint, red, green, blue, yellow.

Large openings where the toys appear in their final form, articulated arms that lift them, grope them, check them. Grapples that drop them in small wagons... and the small wagons that race down other corridors. Probably towards other rooms in a gigantic warehouse.

And all this is happening automatically, without any human intervention.

Just machines, machines... Nothing but machines. It's mind-boggling. Unthinkable...

I'm not a man to get discouraged easily, but this time it's gone too far.

Is there no one alive in this world?

Huge rooms... Never-ending toys... The same rooms... the same toys... the same silence and the same questions.

Who makes the toys? The machines? And for what purpose? Why?

In my opinion, the problem is completely absurd and one doesn't solve the absurd by reasoning.

And that's my biggest mistake—to reason, to ask sensible, logical, positive questions... But alas, asked again and again in human values... That's what's wrong.

You don't analyze a dog's feelings by referring to your own emotions, any more than a violin can solve one of Euclid's theorems.

Archie and Calloway told me so. There's something else... something else...

Like those doors that can be simply pushed open. No locks... Free entry... Solitude and mystery on every front.

And then suddenly... Oh my... what's happening? That sound of footsteps behind me... I stop dead and the noise stops abruptly.

A cold bead of sweat runs down my spine, but I still hesitate to turn around. The echo of my own footsteps, no doubt.

I set off again, my nerves on edge, my breath short, and there it goes again. Sharp smacks on the tiled floor... mixed with muffled slides... Damn, it sounds like I have a whole regiment following me.

I experience a brief moment of panic that shakes me to the marrow of my bones. Then, all at once, I swing around, arms close to my body, fists held up.

Good Gods, is this possible? First, I don't realize exactly how horrible and dreadful the scene is.

In any case, no one is there. Only shoes, without feet, pointing in my direction... And nothing but shoes... pumps, boots, moccasins, slippers, clogs... All in pairs. Enough to fill up a big shoe store. The long line goes all the way to the other end of the room.

Damn, I can't believe it... Cautiously, I take a few steps back. All together as one, the footless shoes resume their advance. Three steps, three steps!

On my back, the cold bead of sweat has turned into a veritable polar shower and when I turn around and kick up my heels (no pun intended, believe me) all the shoes rush after me in a frantic stampede.

As a game of tag, it'd be hard to outdo this one. Of course, I know how to climb trees, but that honorable flora would have to be part of this world. I have only one way out, to go through a door and close it behind me without losing a second.

This is fortunately what I manage to do in record time. Only one boot gets stuck in the steel doors, gaping there with its entire sole.

But go breathe a sigh of relief with the surprises awaiting you here!

This time a completely different kind of party is on the menu and the first hint I get is the sound of a firecracker, which takes my breath away.

I jump back and fall to the ground flat on my back. I'm out of the lair... I'm in the open air... A gray sky overhead... the sun has risen... a pale, timid, pear-shaped sun...

And another firecracker explodes, raising clouds of dust just a few yards away. What's going on?

Rolling hills block the horizon where sky and earth seem to merge into a monotonous, immaterial shade.

And the machine gun fire that comes after the noise of firecrackers. Panicking, I finally see what's responsible for all the noise. Hundreds and hundreds of articulated dolls have suddenly emerged on the right and left and are fighting each other in a cruel, fierce, merciless battle.

There are two kinds, blue and red, which are fighting over the entrance to a high citadel perched on a mound.

And the guns crackle... and the dolls fall, mowed down by the machine gun fire... horribly mutilated.

CHAPTER II

The attacks went on non-stop from both sides. The "blues" and the "reds" took turns trying to enter the citadel, which did not seem to be equipped with any means of defense.

But each time the enemy retaliated and the two opposing regiments suffered heavy losses.

Not a problem! The robots are all equipped with a tool kit that allows them to repair themselves in the blink of an eye.

And onward! A soldier in front of me hurries to screw his head back on his steel shoulders. At a simple whistle from his leader, he is back in the fight, all fired up. A curious method all the same to eliminate the slackers.

You'll tell me that with something like this, it spells the end of doctors and hospitals, except that I'm still flesh and blood. That's the tragedy. And I doubt that my social security card would have the slightest value in this crazy world!

I try to slip between two clumps of earth to escape the "carnage" and reach a quieter place, but it's not easy. There's machine-gun fire from all corners and lightning flashes above my head.

I walk a good hundred yards through the smoke and dust when suddenly I find myself face to face with a "blue" soldier. The doll is all in pieces. He's working on putting himself back together with pliers and screwdrivers when a metallic voice shouts at me furiously:

"You are not in the game. Evacuate the field... You are not in the game."

His big, bulging eyes examine me from head to toe.

"Return to your sector, you are not in the game. You are not in the Game..."

"It's okay, don't get mad, I got lost."

He grunts, finishes screwing his left arm back in, then stands up.

"Those damned reds, they won't get us like that."

And there he goes, back in the fray. At the foot of the citadel, his little buddies have resumed the offensive, but the Reds don't give up. They charge in turn, with every intention of taking the fortress.

None of this makes any sense and I have the feeling that this sense-less war is eternal. A true symbol of obstinacy and fanaticism in the most absolute sense.

Unfortunately, this doesn't solve my problem and the warning I was just given gives me food for thought.

When all these idiots spot me, I'm going to catch hell.

I'll become the troublemaker, the heretic led astray in a congregation of the faithful, in short the disruptive element that must be struck down and eliminated pure and simple. So I have to find an immediate solution if I want to get out of this combat zone.

With my head on fire, I keep crawling in the dust, manage another thirty yards and as I round a low hill, I see another puppet sprawled out on the ground.

This time it's a "red" but he looks damned stunned. He doesn't even move a finger.

He's alone. The others seem to have abandoned him. Then, I get an idea while looking at his clothes. Maybe it's a chance because mine, sooner or later, will end up betraying me. Well, so be it! Considering my situation, it's not much of a sacrifice.

Without a moment's hesitation, I strip off my clothes, manage somehow to undress the doll who is about my size and put on the red pants and red jacket.

In truth, it's nothing to sneeze at. A cross between an operetta hussar and the rags of a learned monkey... the kind of outfit that would send you straight to a madhouse with two thugs as nurses!

Well, you get what I mean.

The rifle doesn't look very complicated either. It has a barrel, a stock, a trigger.

"Hey there, you stole my uniform..."

I turn around. The puppet has sat up. He looks at me with a mix of fury and astonishment.

"And I'm naked!"

I try to calm him down with friendly gestures.

"For you, it's no big deal. You're just a doll..."

"Yes, so what? But who are you?"

"I'm a human. Can you understand that?"

"A human? That word is not in my vocabulary..."

"I suspected as much. I belong to another world... I'm from..."

"I understand. From another sector. You are not in the game."

I roll my eyes.

"That's it. I'm not in the game and I have to get out of it. That's obvious, right?"

"But that doesn't give you the right to steal my uniform. Look at me! What do I look like now?"

On the subject of similarities, we can shake hands... But try to explain it to him! He doesn't understand anything.

Yet he has a nice round head with a pointed nose and two fine child-like eyes. He looks like Walt Disney's Pinocchio. And stubborn at that! He won't stop ranting and demanding his rags back.

I shrug and tell him, "Okay, fine, let's make a deal. You lead me out of this area and I'll give you back your clothes."

He seems to consider my suggestion, eyeing the rifle I keep trained on him.

"But if I am found in this state, I will be completely eliminated."

"You already were."

"Not at all, I was just accidentally disconnected."

"We'll deal with it."

"Yes... but the game?"

As I look at him, he continues:

"My non-participation, if it continues, risks upsetting the balance and favoring the victory of the blues."

"Who cares? What are you going to do with the citadel once you've conquered it?"

"Everything will start over again. It is the will of M."

Hold on, it was such a long time ago. I was also thinking...

"With a capital M, right?"

"Yes."

"And who is M? Where is he?"

"I don't know."

Always the same. Nobody knows anything. Complete blackout when it comes to this mysterious creator who hides his true identity behind a simple capital letter.

I know that there are names that are forbidden to pronounce and the theosophists in particular refuse to name God. His inaccessible character, his infinitely impenetrable nature seem to be justified by a rather subtle esotericism that would be sacrilege to merely name the Unnameable.

But it's necessary to symbolize the Almighty by a word, by a sign or by some abstraction, and it's curious to find in this absurd world the same convention sternly respected by all these mechanical creatures.

If I accept the principle and if man is truly in the image of his God, despite the enormous gap that separates him from Him, must I conclude that the God of robots is only a super-machine, devoid of all spirituality? A material object incapable of any eschatological concept?

It's a fairly Cartesian line of reasoning, of course, but who would dare claim that these dolls have a soul?

Can even the most advanced electronic calculator and talking machine reflect upon their own problems, conceive of their own nature, worry about their own death?

I hadn't thought of it that way before. A Mechanical God versus a Spirit God... A universe of robots clashing with Humanity!

A duel on a cosmic scale between matter and spirit!

What the hell have I gotten myself into?

A firecracker exploding behind the mound yanks me out of my strange thoughts while Pinocchio jumps up, all his joints creaking.

"Okay," he blurts out, "I will help you leave this area... But let's hurry. I have to get back to the fight."

He leads me down a path worn through the loose stones and now we're heading towards the rolling hills...

CHAPTER III

The pear-shaped sun has already reached its zenith when Pinocchio and I approach the edge of the combat zone. There are no blues or reds in these parts, and we can barely hear the sound of machine-gun fire reaching us, weakened, from the citadel.

The puppet seems to have gotten used to me like a tame animal letting his master to do the thinking for him and it is only when we are at the very end of the path, at the top of a low cliff, that he turns around to say to me:

"Here is where the new sector begins. But I fear it is not yours. I say this because of the clothes you were wearing. They do not match with..."

"Where are we?"

"HBW Sector 12. This is the kidnapping game."

"The kidnapping game?"

"In other words, you are no better off. Here, the game consists of catching all the dolls who have had the unfortunate idea of straying outside their own sector."

"I don't see anyone."

"Oh, do not be fooled. Those who reside in this area are always on the lookout and they never miss a stranger who ventures beyond the boundaries."

"Better and better. And what do they do to them?"

"They punish them for their errors because every error deserves punishment, but it is only symbolic. The game is only a representation of the Great Universal Error, according to M's design."

"Ah, because M understands what is right and wrong!"

Pinocchio is about to answer me when shrill cries suddenly break out on the plain below us.

The borlok is the first to step forward onto the rocky overhang.

"There," he says to me. "Look. A stray has just been captured. You are going to witness his punishment."

I open my eyes wide to contemplate the scene unfolding on the rocky plain.

Come on now, it looks like a Western! The creatures that have just appeared from behind a rocky scree look like real Sioux, with their leather pants and feathered headpieces. Their faces are brightly colored... their hands are waving tomahawks... There are about twenty of them pushing a creature in front of them who...

Oh my... I wasn't expecting... But yes, yes there's mistake... It's definitely Archie, my old pal Professor Archibald Brent!

The poor guy is being dragged away roughly amidst shouts and threatening gestures, while other Sioux hasten to plant a wooden stake to which Archie is quickly tied.

Firewood is brought over and I imagine, not without horror, the terrible sacrifice that is being prepared.

"But they're crazy! They're going to burn him alive!"

Pinocchio shakes his head, "Not yet!"

"You don't think so?"

"First there is a whole ceremony. You will see. And then there is no danger because we are all fireproof... Fire has no effect on us."

"But this creature is made of flesh..."

"Flesh?"

"Oh, Pinocchio, try to realize that this is not a doll... This creature is human... like me. And he's my friend. They're making a mistake. This has to be stopped!"

"Stopped?"

"Yes, damn it, how can I explain it to you... Pinocchio, listen to me carefully. Do you ever create new games?"

The Borlok seems surprised by my question.

"A new game?"

I see him immersed in an ocean of thoughts while he continues dreamily:

"I never thought about that... What kind of game?"

"A game that beats all other games. It's called... counterplay. For example, if we stop this sacrifice, we bring a new element into the game. In other words, we play our own game."

It's not very clear, of course, but it's more than enough to pique Pinocchio's curiosity. He nods thoughtfully.

"I do not understand much of what you are saying, but I guess that is how it is in your sector, right?"

"Exactly."

"I am tempted to try it. But let's hurry up, you promised to give me back my clothes, did you not?"

"It'll only take a minute. You free my friend from his bonds while I take care of the uh... the others. Stay behind me and only act on my orders. Got it?"

Quickly, I take off my red tunic to put back on my own clothes that I made sure to bring with me.

The borlok rubs his hands and flashes one of his happiest smiles.

"I have the feeling we are going to have lots of fun."

Him, maybe! As for me, this Davy Crockett adventure leaves me baffled. The borloks have incredible reflexes and the slightest tactical error could lead to fatal consequences, both for Archie and for me.

But I can't leave my friend in such a critical situation, especially since the Sioux have begun their ritual dance around the post and the wood could go up in flames at any second.

Pinocchio is already about to take back his uniform, but I don't give him time.

"Later... Later..."

"But I am naked."

"It doesn't matter, for God's sake, hurry up!"

I keep tugging him along; we crawl between the rocks, trying not to make the slightest sound. We manage to reach the rocky plain without any problems.

We scurry to the pile of rocks and manage to slip between them without attracting the attention of the creatures that continue to circle around poor Archie.

Pinocchio doesn't flinch. I can sense his impatience to get into the game, but he follows my instructions with exemplary obedience.

I feel my hands tighten around the rifle as the first flames begin to spring up from the pyre.

Without hesitation, we rush out of hiding, furiously pulling the triggers of our weapons.

Surprised by the unexpected attack, a good half-dozen Sioux are swept away by the powerful jets. Dislocated and shattered, the puppets bite the dust, while the others retreat, panicking, unable to fathom the reason for this sudden and unforeseen attack which escapes their understanding.

It allows me time to run over to the fire, followed by Pinocchio. Archie's face suddenly lights up as he recognizes me.

"Syd!" he cries.

"Hold on, Archie, Pinocchio will get you out of there."

The fireproof borlok jumps into the flames. Using a tomahawk picked up in the dust, he hacks away at the bonds tied around the young scientist's body.

But a counterattack doesn't take long to get organized. The still unharmed Sioux rush at me, hooting war cries and more gun shots hurt my ears.

I drop to the ground where mutilated bodies are still writhing. But I hear no cries of pain, no screams.

I know that this is an otherwordly fight where death can only occur on the human side.

There are now only about ten Sioux left in fighting condition, but they abandon the battlefield and regroup farther away, once again hesitating over what to do.

We have to take advantage of this hesitation, so as the freed Archie jumps to my side, I turn to Pinocchio:

"Quickly, help us get out of this area."

He turns his head to the right and left, quickly orients himself and then signals us to follow him.

"This way!"

We set off after him, triple-timing it, and reach a small river that seems to be part of the scenery. Its tumultuous waters flow between two rows of flat stones worn down by the foam.

A plastic canoe is moored in a hollow. All at once, we run to it. We paddle away from the bank and drift, carried by the torrent, between whirlpools and moss-covered rocks.

Just in time!

The Sioux who had come after us have just appeared on the bank. But now they're nothing more than gesticulating figures that vanish from our sight as soon as we round the narrow curve formed by the majestic torrent.

Archie is even more stunned than I am by this miraculous encounter. As we exit the canyon and hit calm water, he shakes my hand effusively.

I quickly explain to him my adventure in the "Citadel Game" with Pinocchio. He cuts me off with a wave of his hand.

"The main thing is that we're alive. But we still have to find Margaret. And to think that I was just about to join her..."

I jump into the middle of the canoe.

"How? Did you find her trail?"

He explains to me how it came about. As I suspected, Archie dematerialized at another point and it was while leaving his dump that he noticed women's shoe-prints on the ground, with the characteristic little hole dug by their heels.

"Maybe they were shoes without feet?"

Archie looks at me, agog.

"What do you mean?"

"I'll explain later. Please continue..."

"I followed the tracks... They led me to this area where you found me. I only had time to see Margaret's silhouette on the horizon because at that moment some Indians jumped me and dragged me away. The rest, you know."

A wave of hope washed over me.

"Archie, could you find Margaret's tracks again?"

The young scientist carefully observes the region, then points out to me, upstream, a huge rock in the shape of a sugar loaf.

"I was in that area when I was attacked. I recognize it. Let's go ashore, we should be able to find the tracks."

Paddling hard, we bring the canoe to the bank and as we jump ashore Pinocchio holds up an Indian costume he found in the bottom of the boat.

"I always dreamed of being dressed like this," he tells us. "What luck."

He puts on the clothes with a cheerful smile.

"What's his deal?" Archie groans.

"It's nothing. He's got a thing about being naked. Come on, let's go!"

Archie is already on the "warpath". He has spotted Margaret's tracks in the yellow sand. The trail of footprints seems to get lost mysteriously between two rows of low dunes...

CHAPTER IV

We walk as fast as we can but there is still nothing in sight. Nothing but endless footprints in the golden sand.

Yet I know my wife well. Walking is not her strong point. Especially on heels in a sandy desert. You'll tell me that the circumstances we're struggling with must change our usual behavior... Nevertheless, what courage!

I stop at the foot of a dune to catch my breath.

"We're going to die like rats... Not a single drop of water."

Archie looks at me strangely.

"Why? Are you thirsty?"

"No... but..."

He goes on, "You're neither thirsty nor hungry, are you? Nor sleepy?"

"Uh... no..."

"That's what I thought. We're in a neutral time. A negative time. A zero time. Biologically speaking, this means that we no longer age and that we no longer have any needs."

"And yet things still happen one after the other. Isn't that an effect of the flow of time?"

"A simple psychological phenomenon. Our mind doesn't differentiate between real time and neutral time. We simply continue to classify events in a logical sequence by relegating them to a past that doesn't exist."

"And the future?"

Archie shrugs and points to the tracks.

"It's at the end of the road."

We set off again with Pinocchio hot on our heels.

Dunes... More dunes... The tracks continue in a straight line in this crazy desert... then soon the landscape starts changing.

Firm ground on which thorny, dull green bushes appear.

And soon big plants bristling with pricks and thorns. Then we find ourselves on a dusty road, more astonished than ever.

We stop. We look at each other, hesitant. Here, the traces have disappeared.

Which direction should we take? To the right? To the left? We're considering our options when the sound of an engine makes us swing around.

A long car, a Chrysler, is coming towards us, surrounded by a cloud of dust, and pulls up next to us.

But it's still just a toy... a toy in our size... unless it's us who are in its size (I still haven't solved the problem of dimensions in this strange world).

A borlok dressed as a chauffeur sits at the wheel. He sticks his round head out the window and winks at us.

"Come on in. It's your turn."

"Where are you taking us?"

"There is only one place I can take you."

"In other words, we have no choice."

He winks again. "Eh... Eh..."

"Tell me, have you already taken someone in your taxi?"

"Yes, just enough to get there and back."

It can only be Margaret. The thought gives me the courage to open the door and climb in beside the driver. Archie and Pinocchio climb into the back seat and the taxi swerves swiftly down the bumpy road.

"Can you tell us where we're going?"

"Straight ahead."

Other than that, we'll have to contact the Information Office! Can't get another word out of him. He just blinks. My word, it must be a twitching doll!

"I have the feeling we are going to have fun," Pinocchio says in a cheerful voice.

This idiot is also starting to become unbearable. It has the same effect on me as with Pat. If only he could disconnect from time to time!

But no, he's doing fine. What's more, since Archie's rescue, he seems to have completely forgotten his little friends in The Citadel Game... He's not letting us out of his sight.

He's still right behind us when, after a few miles of driving at breakneck speed on the long, dusty road, our driver invites us to get out.

Here, the scenery has changed again. The road stops abruptly in front of a high granite wall.

"Here you go," our guide tells us. "This is where the Game of Tests begins. My last passenger is still inside... but ahead of you. I just hope you all make it to the end of the course."

"What course? What's it about?"

He ignores our questions, his arm still outstretched toward the rock wall. He points at three monumental steel doors that open in the hard rock.

In front of the middle one, we see Margaret's footprints. They disappear there as if swallowed by a mysterious passkey.

"Your first test," the driver explains to us, "is to push one of these doors. But be careful! Only one guarantees you a safe journey. The other two are equipped with disintegrators that will fire the moment you put your hand on the door. In other words, you have a one in three chance."

Archie and I suddenly turn pale. What kind of trap have we gotten ourselves into again!

In a fit of anger, I'm about to pounce on the driver, but the horrible "thing" that has just appeared next to him removes any desire.

It's a kind of massive block that looks like a huge mouth. This mechanical mouth is fitted with steel millstones as teeth, and, on either side, long telescopic arms emerge, ending in hooks that look like human fingers. The whole thing is mounted on wheels and seems to me to be extraordinarily sensitive.

"The 'atomic devourer' will accompany you on the course," our guide adds with another wink. "You must never turn back but always move forward. A step backward or a refusal to participate in the tests would result in your immediate destruction. You must succeed or be destroyed. There is no in between. However, among the five tests that you will face, M grants you a wild card."

"How very thoughtful!"

"You only have to make a wish and I will give you one chance, but only one. Remember."

Pinocchio explodes, "We are going to have fun... We are going to have fun."

He claps his hands. But it seems that he's not included in the festivities because his colleague grabs him roughly and pushes him right back into the taxi.

The "devourer" advances a few feet, insidiously awaiting our decision.

Of course, our eyes rest on Margaret's footprints in front of the middle door but the driver's voice comes to us from the Chrysler, ironic, mocking.

"Don't trust it, it would be too easy… The course changes every time. Good luck! It's your turn!"

He starts the taxi and disappears in a cloud of dust.

CHAPTER V

One in three chance!

Of course, the laws of chance may allow us to come across the right door to open, but it's not certain that Archie and I will agree on the right choice.

Of course, one of us can be eliminated and offer the other the possibility of getting through the wall with a 50-50 chance.

But Archie doesn't think so. First, he's not a gambler and second, it's a matter of a third human life. We need all the chances we can get to make it through these tests.

Archie, who seems to have regained his usual composure, examines the three doors carefully. They appear to have been cast from the same mold. No difference.

"Maybe the driver was trying to throw us off track," he interrupted his thoughts. "It's possible that the course hasn't been changed and that the door Margaret pushed is still the right one."

"My wife has always been very lucky."

"I hope for her sake that it doesn't stop, but as for this game, I don't think it's based on chance. It's a test. So, there's a trick to discover for each part... and it's the discovery of these tricks that will allow us to reach the end of the course. Remember the Sphinx, there was always an exact answer to the questions it asked."

He goes back to the first door, examines it once more, then returns his attention to the other two.

I suddenly hear him say:

"All right, I think I've got it..."

He points out to me on door A and door B two tiny pinholes drilled opposite each other in the frames. He thinks it's a photoelectric system. All we had to do is put our hand out to turn the handle and the alarm will automatically go off, calling for our total destruction.

His hypothesis is supported by the fact that Gate C doesn't have anything of the kind.

A slight hesitation still, but the "devourer" behind us starts buzzing angrily, as if to remind us to get going.

The machine is getting impatient and its long articulated arms are already waving frantically. Its greedy fingers are reaching out towards us, ready to grab us. Its mouth opens, huge, horrible, voracious, threatening...

So, in a split second, our decision is made.

"By the grace of God," Archie sighs.

His nervous hand turns the handle and, in front of us, the heavy steel door swings wide open.

We rush into the passage, helpless and resigned, but no, nothing happens. The path is clear.

We have just successfully passed the first test.

We take the trail marked out by Margaret's footsteps, followed by the "devourer", always under pressure, and we soon arrive in front of a long building. A kind of parallelepiped whose main facade is a perfect square, with an opening at the base, also square.

We are taking it all in when, suddenly, the panel slides open into the side of the block.

So here's our second test.

Hearts pounding, Archie and I walk towards the strange building and enter the doorway.

There's a long corridor with an exit at the end. About twenty yards to go, not much more... but it's surely not as simple as it looks. The corridor is a trap, but we still can't see what kind of dangers these twenty yards of masonry have in store for us.

We don't flinch. In the silence that surrounds us, we just stand there, breathe swallow, nerves tense, minds alert.

Our eyes run over the smooth, completely bare walls. The one on the left is checkered over the entire surface. Checks, checks everywhere, around ten inches a side...

And then, suddenly, a bell rings, as if to yank us out of our procrastination.

Archie whispers to me, squeezing my arm, "Watch out, it's about to start."

And it starts!

Just a few inches from the ground, a long steel blade shoots out, crossing the width of the corridor to plant itself in the opposite wall.

And further away, a second, a third... a fourth... a fifth... A sixth... all at unequal heights.

Suddenly, it stops. But it's enough, we get it. You don't have to be a wizard or a graduate of West Point to understand what awaits us after this small sample.

We will be slain before we reach the exit. Impaled, skewered like poultry.

"Archie, I think it's time to use our wild card. We won't make it through."

He raises his hand.

"No, wait a second... Let me think. These first six blades give us a clue. It's a question of finding the logical sequence."

"There is no sequence, the skewers shoot out at random."

"No, there's an order to it, I'm sure."

Archie scratches the tip of his nose, studies the checkered wall, then nods thoughtfully.

"Consider the squares. The first blade came out from the lower left corner of the first one, the second from the upper right. Between them there's the value of a rising diagonal. The third sprang out in the middle of the next check, therefore a half-diagonal down from the second. From the third to the fourth it goes up two diagonals. From the fourth to the fifth it goes down one diagonal. Then back up three diagonals to the sixth. First of all, geometrically, they are connected by a broken line, each segment of which is at a right angle to the one before. Secondly, arithmetically, the unit being the diagonal, they ascend by one each time. It goes down, from a half unit to a whole, either by half units or doubling. So, it's easy to predict the probable position of the seventh blade: at 1.5 or two diagonals down from the sixth, which gives us a low ratio of uncertainty and almost no risk. Are you following me, Syd?"

He points to a point on the checkered wall.

"Archie, please, the devourer is getting antsy."

The angry buzzing of the mechanical mouth forces Archie to cut his presentation short. He deliberately pulls me along and we cross the six obstacles before lying flat on the ground in anticipation of the seventh. Better safe than sorry...

We start crawling toward the exit when something clicks above us.

Archie was not wrong. The seventh blade does indeed shoot out at the point he had predicted at one and a half diagonals down from the sixth.

"The descending increment is therefore 1.5," my fellow adventurer concludes.

From then on, it's easy to predict the eighth skewer at four diagonals up from the seventh. We jump to our feet at the same time. Three more steps, and plop, the blade cuts through the air just a couple of inches above our heads. A leap forward... The ninth in turn slides out two diagonals lower and grazes our spines.

Better than planned, as builders say.

I breath deeply as I point to the exit.

"It's okay, I understand, it's going to go up five!"

But I immediately realize my mistake. It can't go up five-diagonals, that would be nonsense, because the blade that would spring out at a point that would pass too far over our heads. The same with the next ones, which could only hit a giant.

100 to 1 odds that there's a new trick to discover...

All of a sudden a new blade shoots out right in front of us at a diagonal up 9 units. This tenth one doesn't seem to have any connection with the others.

In the next section of the trap there are other blades obviously arranged differently. This is what we have to figure out now if we want to be safe and sound at the end of this "Death Row".

But Archie doesn't admit defeat. His mathematical mind quickly studies all the possibilities.

A few excruciating seconds pass. In the silence, the buzzing of the devourer keeps growing louder. We have to keep moving forward at all cost, but two new blades shoot out almost simultaneously. That makes 12.

I hear Archie whispering coldly like a talking calculator.

"From 9 to 10 it goes up 1 diagonal. From 10 to 11, down 2. From 11 to 12, up 1..."

He breaks off and grabs me

"Get down, Syd!"

The 13th blade whistles through the air.

"Minus 2 from the 12th to the 13th," Archie states. "Okay, I've got the sequence. Plus one, minus two. That gives us seven blades left to the end. The next to last will be at ground level just one square from the end of the checkers and the 20th one diagonal higher."

The next two blades prove him right. The sequence is repeating itself as predicted.

"We can go, Syd, we won!"

Just in time. The long articulated arms of the devourer are already brushing by us as we start walking again down the hallway. Thanks to my gifted friend, we avoid the next two skewers that spring out of the wall, step over the 18th, then Archie's hand tightens on my arm and pulls me to the exit.

There is no longer anything to fear. The mathematical equivalence limited to plus 1 and minus 2 can no longer vary.

We just have to hop over the last two blades that spring from the wall as predicted and we leave Death Row.[4]

---

[4] For the curious reader, I have drawn up a diagram showing the location of the blades on the checkered wall. (Note in original version) I have, however, completely reformulated the geometric-arithmetical dissection made by Archie at the time, which I think makes it more relevant. (Added by Sydney Gordon)

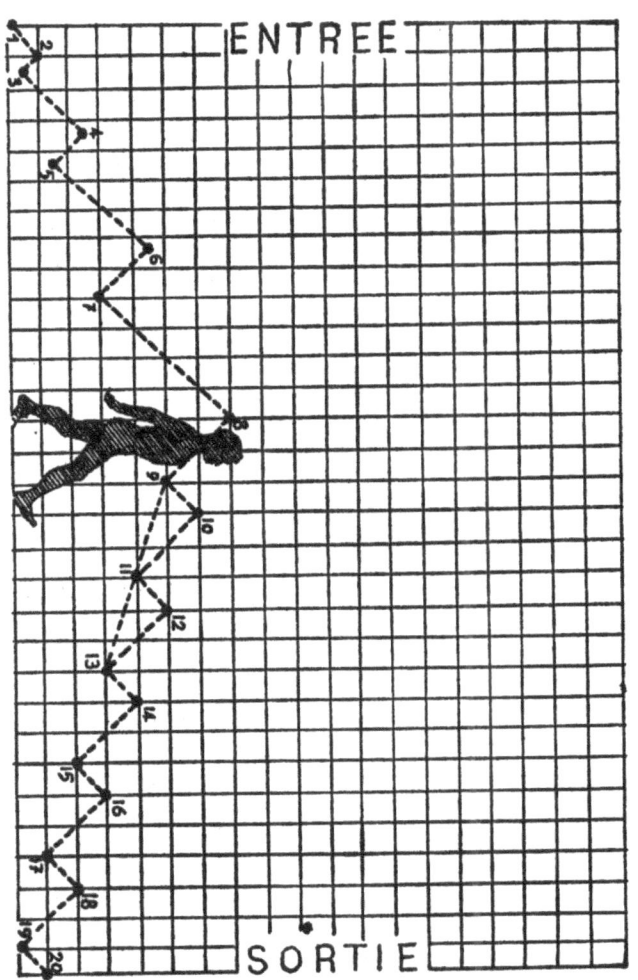

CHAPTER VI

Once out in the open air, the same thought hits Archie and me at the same time: Margaret!

But, incredible as it may seem, the footprints are still there and the trail continues in front of us, in the dust. I think I'm dreaming.

I mutter, "God only knows if she knows her Euclid and all that about geometry! I can't believe it."

"You're right," Archie says to me with his usual calm. "Your wife must be really lucky!"

"Archie, watch out!"

Suddenly, a cube-shaped building has just sprung up from the ground in front of us. A door opens.

We hesitate but the long steel arms of the devourer push us through the opening.

In the darkness, we panic for a moment, then a yellowish light floods the room. The door has closed. Above it, one word in red letters: "Exit".

No handle... No lock... Nothing but a metal panel as smooth and bare as the others.

And then the wires in the middle of the room... copper wires stretched vertically from floor to ceiling.

"There are 50 of them, exactly," the devourer announces to us in a voice that strangely resembles that of the Chrysler driver. "Only one controls the opening of the door. You just have to pull it. The other 49 operate the ceiling... A ceiling that will crush you under its four tons of steel if you do not pull the right wire. Go ahead! It is your turn!"

The order is brusque. Imperative!

Just one thread to pull. In other words, a 1 in 50 chance. And not a single clue!

This time it's alarming, to the point that my friend begins to turn strangely pale.

He frowns and moans:

"All these wires look the same. And yet we can't pull at random. It's impossible. There's got to be a trick to it. But which one?"

Mentally, Archie and I quickly begin to work out all sorts of hypotheses, but they all come to dead ends. No, even in the arrangements of the wires, there's no mathematical rule to let us locate the command wire.

Archie abruptly proposes the wild card, but I cut him off.

"Wait, I have one last idea."

"Say it quickly."

"These are copper wires, aren't they?"

"Yes."

"Why wouldn't they be electrified?"

Carefully, I brush a few wires with my fingertips.

"Obviously, we're not sensitive to electricity as long as our feet are on an insulator. Look at the floor..."

There is indeed a hard and thick rubber mat, which we had not taken notice of until then.

"So, one of two things. Either we have 49 electrified wires and one that is not, or it's the other way around. In both cases, there's one wire that's different from the others. And that is the right one."

"Yes, but how to tell?"

The answer pops into our heads at the same split second. Yes... the walls, quite simply. The walls, the metal walls.

Archie is the first to try the experiment. He grabs a wire with one hand, places the other on one of a wall and grounds himself.

The current is very low, but enough to be felt. In a few minutes, all the wires are checked, one after the other. There is indeed a neutral wire: the one we pull with a sigh of relief and that unlocks the opening for us.

Our first instinct is to look for traces of Margaret. What do you know, they're still there! All clear, all fresh!...

It's becoming unimaginable. My word, she must have bathed in a holy water font!

There are six of them. Six "demons" who seem to have sprung straight out of Hell. Horrible, dreadful... The kind of puppets that no shop on earth would dare to offer its customers without risking immediate bankruptcy.

The body is black, stocky, with a long tail: their glossy coat has something feline about it, just like the long, nervous fingers with thin, sharp claws armed with tridents.

They walk non-stop around a column of fire, a kind of burning geyser, spewing out of a circular orifice at ground level.

Archie and I feel a little queasy at the sight of these hideous heads bristling with horns constantly pointed in our direction, these monstrous faces where red eyes shine in perpetual motion, and these menacing pitchforks that slice the air with sinister hisses.

They come and go, changing their gait in an unpredictable way, after a few steps taken in any direction.

And it doesn't stop.

However, their range appears to be limited to a red circle surrounding the column of flame.

We understand. There are two huge walls, one on the right, the other on the left, flush with the red circle like two diametrically opposed tangents.

It's up to us to choose. One or the other of these walls that we must go along to reach the other safe zone.

Meaning, we must inevitably come into contact with the red circle and face all the vile creatures in a merciless fight.

"Not necessarily all of them," Archie points out. "There's a good chance we'll only be dealing with one or maybe two..."

"Because you think the others will play nice with us? Wait until we've crossed the circle, they will all drop on us like misery on the poor."

"But no... Look at their little dance. Their disordered coming and going doesn't change. Each one turns around the fire in a zigzag and at random. They can't ever stop. But on the other hand the disordered movement, multiplied by six, regularly brings at least one creature to the point of contact that we have to cross. Repeated endlessly, the movement would necessarily lead to all possible combinations, with the probability of having six creatures at the point of contact or none at all."

"I follow you. If I understand correctly, this new trap is based on the law of disorder?"

"Exactly. In other words, it's the law of static behavior."

"But how can we predict all possible arrangements with certainty?"

Archie scratches the tip of his nose.

"It's a question of probability. We can only specify the most probable distances and arrangements. To approach the problem mathematically, we have to remember the Pythagorean theorem, by drawing coordinate axes starting from the pillar of fire and ending at the edge of the circle. For each creature, one law remains immutable: its most probable distance from the pillar of fire, after a large number of irregular turns, is equal to the average length of each of the straight sections it has traveled, multiplied by the square root of their number. Of course, the more demons there are, the greater the number of zigzags they make in their disorderly march and the more precise the rule. But here's the thing... There will always be a margin of error, and it's enough for this margin to be within reach of a trident for us to end our lives along this wall."

Archie glances at the devourer. It seems to be waiting very patiently, as if we had been granted a longer period of time for this fourth test.

"Two solutions," he finally adds. "Either we risk it in the fight or we use the wild card."

"Fighting with machines? They'll break our bones in no time. No, I think the wild card is called for in this test. His Majesty the King of the Borloks must have known it."

"Okay, Syd, let's go!"

Archie announces our request out loud and immediately, in a whirlwind of steam, Pinocchio appears, near the devourer.

"Hello, friends, I finally found you! We are going to have fun, aren't we? We are going to have fun!"

"What are you doing here? We asked for the wild card."

The borlok looks at us naively while Archie steps forward with a tense face.

"Come on, what's going on? Are they making fun of us or what?"

I calm him down with a wave of my hand.

"No, no, I think I get it. Pinocchio is our wild card."

"Pinocchio?"

"Sure. If he goes first, he'll be the bait. The demons will pounce on him and we'll take advantage of the diversion to cross the danger zone. In any case, that's what I propose we do."

Archie hesitates, then finally agrees with me. But he stays cautious. We still have to figure out the most favorable arrangement and the square roots. The x's and y's start fluttering in his neural calculator. Finally the result bursts out of his mouth like from the slot of an IBM calculator.

"Two more turns and we get the following probability: 2-3-1, that is, there will be two creatures in front of the left wall, three in the back behind the pillar of fire and only one in front of the right wall. But that's just a probability, of course, and I..."

"Okay, we choose the right wall."

I doubt that Pinocchio understands what we expect of him because the moment we push him in front of us, he starts clapping his hands.

"I was sure of it, we are going to have fun."

"That's it, buddy, you're going to have yourself a time, you'll see...

"Be careful," Archie advises...

Pinocchio steps on the edge of the circle, but at this moment he finds himself in front of two creatures and not just one. The kind of surprise that probability calculations have in store for you! But it's too late to turn back.

The two mechanical monsters have already rushed towards poor Pinocchio and the blows of the trident sound like blows of a bat on his puppet carcass.

Archie and I immediately take off.

In my haste, I sprawl full length with a cry of rage. A third demon turns towards me, I see him pop up, his trident raised high, ready to strike. But Archie tackles him head-on with remarkable skill. Both of them roll on the ground, glued to each other.

I jump in and manage to snatch the trident from the evil creature. As Archie gets up, dodging the sharp claws, I strike at the eyes.

The electronic globes explode under the blow, which allows us to get away from the chaotic kicks of the monster.

A clammy sweat runs down Archie's face as soon as we reach the safe zone.

"Well! I mean, that was a close call! I must have made a mistake in calculating the last square root."

"Let's not think about it, forget your squares and your roots and let's get out of here fast."

We leave the paved enclosure without even a glance at poor Pinocchio, and as we step back onto dusty ground, the lump in my stomach begins to melt for the fourth time.

I show Archie the tracks.

"Margaret! She did it again!"

Archie still has the strength to smile at me.

"Grant me a lock of her hair if I make it back to Earth. I swear I'll keep it with me forever, by Jove!"

CHAPTER VII

The fifth and final test awaits us a few yards away. A large pavilion surrounded by columns, whose architecture vaguely reminds me of the temples of ancient Rome!

The interior is plunged into darkness and as we grope between the columns, spotlights come on and start sweeping over the center of the building. On a big white rectangle, there are six rows of four regularly spaced black circles.

This is all we get to see, for, almost at that very moment, all our attention is focused on a metallic voice, loudly amplified, apparently emanating from the dark vault.

"Congratulations, Sydney Gordon and Archibald Brent. You have come out victorious from the first four trials. I dare hope that you will succeed in passing this last test with equal success. This is M speaking to you, the Almighty Master of this universe. But, before explaining the rules of this game, know that the human creature you are looking for is safe and sound at the end of the course, on the last black spot on the right. You can only see her silhouette, because she is still flooded by the halo of the spotlights. This creature, therefore, constitutes the stakes of the game. You can save her only by reaching her spot. But there is only one way to reach her because the game consists of crossing the 24 spots without ever passing over the same one twice. The starting point is on the first spot in the first row starting from the left. But remember! The slightest mistake in tactics will cause the ground beneath you to tilt and you will all be thrown into an eternal abyss. That is all, gentlemen. M. the Almighty wishes you luck."

The voice fades and everything falls silent again. A helpless rage shakes me, but this time again, the situation forbids me to indulge in more aptly expressed anger. Some things don't need to be translated into words.

I can't help it. The presence of my wife at the other end of the room forces me to shout her name, "Margaret!"

Of course, no answer... I knew beforehand that I wouldn't get one. She's not allowed to say anything, to make any gesture towards us. The slightest cheating and it's over for all three of us!

Besides, I can only see her vague silhouette in the halo of the spotlights. Only about thirty yards away. But I've never been so far from her...

Archie whispers to me:

"Come on, Syd, pull yourself together."

He leads me to the starting point and together we quickly study a few paths. We come up with more than ten of them, but none of them work. There's always one spot that needs to be crossed twice to reach Margaret's.

The "devourer" is still lying in wait. He watches us, respecting the time accorded us.

In terms of suspense, I think it's hard to imagine anything better. We are starting to get agitated and everything becomes blurry in our eyes.

Our nerves have been put to the test since... since when exactly? I can't say...

Our strength begins to wane and we exchange glances full of unspoken innuendos.

Twelve black spots in parallel... Three to the right, fourth row, two to the left... But no, the path is blocked again.

Let's start over...

And then suddenly:

"Archie! A thousand million fiddlesticks! But the trick is at the starting point!

"How so?"

Suddenly the devourer slides towards us. Its hooked fingers snapping behind us. I barely have time to push Archie onto the next spot in the second row and jump in turn.

And here we are in the game!

It's simple. As simple as Christopher Columbus' egg! The whole trick is in the word 'cross'. Our starting spot doesn't count as long as we don't cross it to jump to the next pawn like we just did."

We are therefore allowed to go back over this spot, crossing it this time. Back at the starting point, we go over the four spots in the first row, then start on the second in the stepped path that will take us directly to the finish.[5]

---

[5] The curious reader can learn about the route using the diagram below.

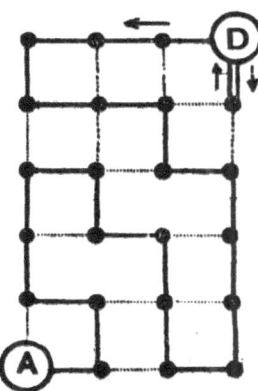

On the next to last pawn, my heart starts beating wildly. The idea of finally holding Margaret in my arms makes me leap for joy. And it is indeed a leap of joy that throws me onto the last pawn, my arms wide open.

"Marga..."

But I don't go any farther. The delightful creature looking at me with tears in her eyes prevents me from pronouncing the last syllable.

It's not Margaret.
Oh! Good Lord! If I'd known...
"Gloria! Gloria Brent!"

CHAPTER VIII

"Gloria! You! How is this possible?"

In terms of bewilderment, Archie is no better off than me. He looks at his wife as if she had suddenly turned into a rattlesnake on her birthday.

"Let's not stay here," Gloria said, leading us away. "Come on!"

We follow her out of the game and, once outside the temple, we notice that her dress is torn everywhere, almost in tatters.

"Gloria, what happened? How did you get here?"

"It happened just after you left. I tried to get you back but after a few unsuccessful tries, the Moebius wagon came back with Margaret."

"With Margaret?"

"Yes, but she'd fainted and while struggling to get her out, I too fell victim to the transdimensional ride."

The rest we can guess. The wagon had suddenly left with its load and the two young women had found themselves in this unknown world, separated like Archie and I had been.

Of course, Gloria has no idea what has become of Margaret. Certainly there is still hope for her, but our situation, on the other hand, is definitively settled.

We now have no chance of going back. We're condemned to end our days in this absurd world at the mercy of these borloks and their monstrous games which are beyond human reason.

"I've never experienced anything so terrible," Gloria confesses with a shudder. "I still wonder how we're alive."

She's been through the same trials as us, but when I think that she succeeded all by herself where we worked together to find the solutions, I have to admit that she is incredibly clever.

As for Margaret, she would need at least a 100 wild cards to get through that mess.

I was also thinking that...

"Hello, friends, I have been looking for you everywhere!"

Oh come on! This is all we need! Pinocchio is in front of us, with a cheerful smile and his pointed nose slightly crooked. He must have quickly put himself back together with the help of a tool kit. This guy is indestructible!

The trouble is he picked the wrong time and I'm about to unleash my anger on him when the Chrysler comes barreling up and screeches to a halt in front of us.

The round-headed driver winks at me.

"Can I take you somewhere? This time it's up to you to choose."

"No, seriously!"

"Always the wishes of M."

"Okay. In that case, head to M and fast. We have a few things to say to him."

"That's impossible, I don't have the right…"

Archie grabs the borlok and pulls him out of his seat, but the threat has no effect on him. Nor does banging his head against the hood of the Chrysler, which we do.

Something must have broken in his circuits because he eventually collapses like a puppet with its strings cut.

At that moment, a siren sounds in the distance, sobering us up in a split second.

"Come on," Archie orders, "everyone climb in."

Without another word, we all pile into the vehicle and Archie sits behind the wheel. The car starts and we find a road not too far away. We drive down it at full speed.

Two other cars appear behind us, obviously giving chase.

"Faster, Archie, faster!"

The Chrysler's electric motor is already at full throttle. Archie is handling the steering wheel with his arms bobbing like connecting rods.

A sharp turn to the right, which we take at full speed, and we skid down another road, then another to the left.

Right, then left again. The sirens turn off. The pursuing cars have disappeared, apparently lost in this crazy race that is taking us God knows where.

Archie turns down a dusty path and slows down after panting a little.

We find ourselves in a real no man's land, between sky and dust. The pear-shaped sun is still at its zenith.

The days must be terribly long in this world...

"If only we knew where Margaret was," Gloria whispers in a desolate voice.

"You didn't see any traces?"

"No, Syd, none."

"Apart from her fainting, nothing struck you?"

"Uh... no... except she had a little white rabbit that she was hugging."

"A white rabbit?"

"That's what I thought it was... But it all happened so fast..."

"A white rabbit! Where could we find white rabbits?"

Pinocchio leans towards me, his face beaming.

"I know."

I grab his arm.

"Speak, hurry up! Where?"

The borlok seems to reflect on it, looks around at the surroundings for a long time, then points to the left.

I could hug him in the surge of affection I feel, but I prefer to wait and see what happens next. I can only trust these borloks so far...

So, we dash from one road to another, from one path to another, always following his directions, until we finally reach the edge of what looks like a forest. But a bizarre, strange forest, made up of pseudo-vegetal plants whose shapes and colors seem to come out of the imagination of a Salvador Dali.

Here, everything is eerily out of proportion: huge mushrooms with their caps and stems the same as Dali would have painted with red and blue spirals; round leaves speckled with multicolored spots; silver and gold vines all sparkling; glass flowers with delicate bells, curved timidly on an almost vaporous moss.

We enter the surrealist setting, still guided by Pinocchio, and we have not gone ten yards when a big black rabbit springs out of a thicket.

"Hello. Welcome to Wonderland. This has to stay between us. Unknown to others. A deep secret. Between you and me!"

He stands on his hind legs, his whiskers bedraggled, one ear split in two.

"Pinocchio, you told me about a white rabbit..."

"I am a fake black rabbit," the long-eared borlok went on. "Hee... Hee... In truth, I am a Young White Rabbit, but I am the only one who knows it. Hee... Hee... Me and the Mad Hatter. "

Archie turns around.

"I think this game's inspired by Alice in Wonderland."

"With all due respect to Lewis Carroll, I don't give a hoot about Alice. It's Margaret I'm looking for. Let's ask this idiot, he must know something."

"Margaret?" the black rabbit answers me. "Margaret? How would I know, I who know everything, eh? I wonder... Hee... Hee..."

Archie is right, this character is right out of Carroll's work. His sentences are nothing but riddles and paradoxes that result from this insane fantasy that serves as a support for Alice's universe.

Yet he knows... he must know... I'm sure of it.

"A cousin of my cousin could have told you," the black rabbit continues, "but all of my cousin's cousins are dead."

"But you're alive!"

He doesn't fall into the trap.

"I am a liar," he declares. "For example, if I tell you, 'No path leads to the one you seek, except a path that is not a path', I'll quickly add, 'No old rabbit is a liar but all black rabbits are liars'.

Gloria shakes her head.

"Another paradox. If all old rabbits are not liars, how can old black rabbits lie?"

"Let's eliminate the black ones," Archie suggests thoughtfully, "there are still the young white rabbits who are still liars. Now, this one thinks he's a young white rabbit, so he's a liar."

This time I explode.

"But damn it, if he's a liar, then he's lying, since he says he's a liar. Therefore, what he says is true."

"Which is to say that he is indeed a liar," Gloria shoots back.

"Oh, I've had enough... I'm sick... And this path that is not a path, what is it, huh? A sewing machine?"

At that moment, Pinocchio pops up out of nowhere, his eyes ablaze.

"Hey, look what I found."

He hands us a dress and a velvet coat. Immediately, I recognize my wife's clothes. I jump at him.

"Where? Where'd you find them?"

Pinocchio takes us under the trees, then through a forest of giant, multi-colored mushrooms.

We're heading down a narrow path lined with moss. This is probably the path mentioned by the black rabbit. Maybe he wanted to show the difference and imply "a path not like the others."

We come to a corner in the sector when we see a playing card with arms and legs as thin as spider legs pass in front of us. I recognize him. He's the Knave of Hearts who stole the tarts, constantly on the run from his trial.

Further on, a Calf-Headed Turtle whistles proudly as we pass, a Humpty Dumpty on a wall, penned into its solitary and grumpy egg form. Lobsters perform a jolly quadrille.

And then finally the huge paper plain we come out on, with its checkerboards, its card castles and its dollhouses.

We are in full Carrollian fantasy!

"It's there," Pinocchio proudly announces to us, pointing to a honey-colored bush.

Two legs, two bare legs stick out from the bush. My heart pounding, I push the branches aside. But no, it's just a doll's body stripped of its clothes. The head is smashed. Wires and coils stick out of its skull.

"Head her off cuts Hearts of Queen the before her find!

It's the Cheshire Cat who has just appeared with his immutable, enigmatic smile. With his right paw, he motions to a doll's house, salutes us and disappears.

"I get it," Gloria says. "The sentence was spoken backwards: Find her before the Queen of Hearts cuts off her head."

We head out on the abstract, surrealist decor of the paper plain, avoid a white rider who falls on his head every five feet, and hurry towards the house indicated by the sinister cat.

A door has to be pushed open and there is Margaret in the middle of the room!

But a Margaret dressed as Alice, with a short, puffy dress and a tow-blond wig with tight braids tied in green ribbons.

Damn, she looks like a twelve-year old!

When she throws herself into my arms, I feel like I'm committing statutory rape!

"Good Lord, here you are... Oh! Syd... Syd... My darling!..."

She hugs me, but I'll spare you the touching scene, especially since it's interrupted by a cheerful white rabbit wearing gloves and a blue and gold spencer jacket.

He jumps on a table, salutes us, then starts clapping his hands and shouting, "Bravo, we are saved!"

"Who's that?"

"Pay no attention," Margaret tells us, seeming to have regained her composure, "he's even crazier than the others."

"My word," I say, "they must never have heard about myxomatosis in this place!"

She rolls her eyes.

"And to think that I managed to get out the first time! That damned wagon had to bring me back here. Of course, I was spotted, so I knocked out that trashy Alice and borrowed her clothes. Just to sneak away. But now they won't let me go. It's even worse than before. If only I understood what they're talking about! It's like they're picking words out of the dictionary at random. Worse than Japanese!"

Archie breaks in, "Come on, enough talking! Let's get out of here before some new catastrophe happens to us."

It's as if it's already on our track. Gloria screams and points out the window at a whole poker game coming our way double-quick. Soldiers of clubs followed by courtiers of diamonds and a bevy of children of hearts.

They've already surrounded the house.

"Oh, if only I could find the bottle!" Margaret exclaims.

"What bottle?"

She searches everywhere, gets on all fours to look under a cupboard and brings back a bottle whose label simply reads "Drink me"!

"It's safe. I've tried it before, but I must not have drunk enough. Come on, hurry up, it apparently gives you strength."

It's amazing what you can do in moments of panic! The bottle is passed from one mouth to another while Pinocchio, disappointed, looks at us sadly.

"What about me?"

But who could answer him? What is happening at this moment takes our breath away. We suddenly grow bigger with the opposite sensation of seeing the objects around us shrink.

And then crack! We burst the paper roof and keep going. We've reached five times the height of the house when the phenomenon suddenly stops. A fleeting thought crosses my mind: Have we, under the influence of the "magic liquid", returned to our normal size?

Another question mark added to the others and yet another with the appearance of a sparkling sphere that shoots across the sky like lightning. The big ball lands in front of us on the checkerboard.

A panel opens in the gleaming hull and steel steps descend to the ground.

"This way!" A voice that seems to fall from the sky orders us.

Exhausted, broken, confused, we run towards the airlock, pursued by the soldiers of clubs who bruise our ankles with their slender swords.

A shock... A violent acceleration... The sphere shoots above the forest.

First, incomprehension... astonishment. A round room... completely round... and in the background a glass panel. Behind it, a control station, with joysticks, buttons, levers. And, in the middle of it all, a patriarch with a long white beard... an old man in a snowsuit.

Santa Claus!

CHAPTER IX

"Well done again and my compliments. Your intervention in Wonderland was very much appreciated. A complete success in terms of the dramatic."

The voice seems to come from a small speaker embedded in the metal partition. M's voice!

"But these last adventures were harmless," the voice continues. "It was just a prelude to the role that I intend for you in this world. By your skill, your intelligence, your composure, you have earned the right to be here. But on one condition: your total integration in all the games that will be proposed to you. Let's say that they will be the problems and you will be the equations governing all the eventualities that can occur in all possible situations. As long as you respect the rules, no harm will come to you."

"It's not our fate that concerns us," Archie cuts in sharply, "my friend and I came here voluntarily."

"I know that."

"Why are you attacking humanity? What reasons are driving you to destroy our Universe?"

"Don't ask such questions. They are forbidden to you. Just think about your own situation. Play... or die! That's all!"

A faint click in the speaker lets us know that the conversation is over and that all of our questions will continue to remain unanswered.

We look at each other for a long time, prisoners of our impotent rage, at the heart of an inextricable situation.

And all our sacrifices will have been for nothing. We feel like we've been fighting against a brick wall and we're close to despair.

We'll have to fight against the impossible and the incomprehensible.

Equations in a problem! The idea revolts me all the more because I can imagine the humiliating role that we're destined to play in this absurd world.

In a reversal of values, are we going to become the toys of these toys? We, the Humans! Can we be condemned to the amusement of these cheap puppets?

It feels exactly like being held on a leash by a dog or put on display behind a fence to entertain a troop of monkeys.

The sphere is finishing its aerial journey and a rapid descent pulls me out of my dark thoughts.

The landing takes place in a field covered with artificial snow. Pseudo-pine trees are part of the decor with the same immaculate whiteness.

The airlock is opened and, at a kind gesture from Santa, we are asked to leave the aircraft.

A sleigh arrives at that moment, pulled by six mechanical reindeer. The same team that we had accidentally made appear at Blue Cottage. But this time there are no toys—we're the ones taking their place in the steel trunk.

Santa Claus climbs into the front seat. A crack of the whip and we're off through the pine forest. I told you: humiliation at every level!

The trip is short but it still gives us time to make an observation: Our guide is not a human, as we had believed at first. He is a borlok, like the others, a cybernetic being programmed and conditioned with the same concern for perfection.

Not until we're inside the large building does he finally decide to break his silence. He's happy to see us again, assures us of his complete friendship, but he remains as impenetrable as ever when it comes to M, his Almighty Master.

"I am only the supervisor," he tells us. "I am the one in charge of checking the borloks that are created in this world. I watch over the programming of the sectors, their balance, I record the production defects and I study all the prototype games. My reports are transmitted to M by the 'sacred computer' and my role ends there. I only know that M exists, but I have never seen him."

"You're certainly not very curious," Margaret said to him, "especially for a Santa Claus."

He shrugs, "Curiosity is a feeling that should never be gratified. What would be the use of knowing the essence of all things if it only means sinking into detachment and disinterestedness. It is, in my opinion, better to understand that there are things that are absolutely incomprehensible."

To make a long story short, he guides us through the premises put at our disposal. Here again, everything is mechanical and all we have to do is press a button for any desired object to spring from the walls or floor like a jack in the box.

So I take the opportunity to get Margaret a more decent outfit. Alice's dress for a firefighter's uniform. It's better than nothing, especially since in this world, Dior models aren't hanging around... the borloks.

But that's not all. We're also treated to all kinds of entertainment, namely scale models of the "living games" in which we're bound to participate. And then there's also a "hall of mirrors", an innovation that Santa Claus shows to us with some excitement.

All these mirrors are psychic catalysts. They concretize human thought in different aspects. For example, we find in this gallery the famous mirror that reflected all of Gloria's intimate thoughts, when we got to the Blue Cottage.

Another, called the "time mirror", reflects our own image in a fourth dimension. We can admire ourselves there at all ages of our lives.

Physically, our youth marches by in accordance with the memories we have of it, but there is something even crazier. Our faces become covered with wrinkles, our hair turns white, our shoulders stoop. The mirror also works in the direction of the future. It shows us as we would be at 20, 30 or 40 years old (earthly time of course, because here time doesn't count. A charming touch all the same).

"That's me at 60!" Margaret grumbles at her shrunken face. "So what's the point of plastic surgery? It's all a sham!"

No comment! And the visit continues with another mirror that reproduces us in "multicata". We can converse with our doubles, even organize games, like a baseball game where we experience all the reactions of the "other players" at the same time... Always us... Forever us...

But the highlight of this gallery is undoubtedly the "multi-temporal" mirror. It represents us in all kinds of situations as they would have occurred if some event had changed the course of our existence. A repercussion down to the tiniest detail. This is how I see myself as a race-car driver at the wheel of a Maseratti, which is what I was about to do if I hadn't one day inadvertently set foot in the offices of the *New Sun*.

Archie is a grand concert pianist. Gloria is involved in politics, has her own office at the UN. As for Margaret, she's a snake woman in the Pinder Circus (now I understand why we never miss an opportunity to see one).

"As for that one," Santa Claus says...

But a scream bursts out as we turn towards the indicated mirror.

"Syd! My God! Syd!"

At the time, we don't realize exactly what has just happened. Margaret is right in front of us, just a few steps away... but she's no longer in the room. There's a barrier between her and us... a mirror ten feet tall and six feet wide. And Margaret is on the other side of the mirror!

"Syd! Syd!"

Santa Claus orders:

"Don't touch that mirror. It's a 'dimensional' one. Your wife must have entered it by mistake."

"Please, get her out of there."

As the Borlok fiddles with a bunch of levers and buttons stuck to the uprights of the mirror, we watch, stunned, the weird scene unfolding inside the mirror.

Margaret is in another dimension. There's sand everywhere... An oasis in the background on the right and a body of water infested with slimy, crawling creatures. It all looks real... frighteningly real!

"Hurry up, damn it, hurry up!" Margaret implores, her fingers seeming to be stuck to the "inner" wall of the mirror. "I'm suffocating... I'm suffocating... and I'm completely inverted... My heart is on the right. Oh Syd! My heart..."

Of course, it's normal. On the other side of a mirror, everything on the left is on the right and vice versa. But how can I explain this to her?

"My God, Syd... Look..."

With a trembling hand, Gloria points to the horizon.

A nightmare monster, part dragon, part giant scorpion, appears, rising out of a dune. It stands menacingly on its clawed feet, pointing a tongue of fire in my wife's direction.

Good heavens, if only Margaret's costume had a fire hose!

The fire monster lunges forward just as a loud click sounds inside the machinery.

A hand breaks through the mirror and reaches out to me. I grab it, pull and yank Margaret out of the nightmare.

Suddenly everything disappears, blacks out... there's just a dark void in the frame of the dimensional mirror.

A cold sweat washes over my body as I hug my wife.

"It's always like that with this mirror," the borlok tells us, "you never know which dimension you will connect with. It's the 'adventure game'. But your wife was lucky. Usually, the mirror is set to the 'void'."

"That's a real comfort, thanks!" I point to the mirror. "What would have happened if we had unfortunately broken this mirror while..."

Santa waves off the question and leaves me pondering!

CHAPTER X

Fortunately, we don't have the same idea about curiosity as Santa Claus.

Given full freedom in the many sectors that make up this unknown world has allowed us to make a discovery.

First, the rooms we were assigned are located at the very heart of the big building where Santa Claus performs all his experimental tests on the borloks. But M is not hiding here. Where he is hiding is Archie's idea from the results of his own investigations.

He had ventured into the basements, randomly exploring the round tunnels dug into the hard rock, but whose geometric lines seem revealing.

All the tunnels in fact encircle a practically inaccessible zone, exactly like an anthill that has dug its passageways around a big rock. According to Archie, the big rock would be the nerve center of the entire organization of this mad world. In other words, the headquarters of M.

"Are you sure there's no passage that could give us to access it?"

Archie, scratching the tip of his nose, guesses my intentions. "I don't know. So far I haven't found anything."

"Do you want to try again?"

"Okay. Follow me."

No one seems to oppose us leaving the rooms, so we're completely alone when we reach the basement.

We enter a long vaulted tunnel and soon find ourselves at a junction.

Archie, who has taken charge of our small group, guides us and keeps us moving from one tunnel to another.

We can't see any doors or openings. The tunnels seem to wind back on themselves, but thanks to certain landmarks, Archie still manages to lead us farther along.

However, we soon have to retrace our steps, hesitant and completely disoriented. Ariadne's thread has snapped. We've lost our way in the maze and it's impossible for us to find our way back.

Margaret grumbles between sighs, "Another one of their damned games! I think we've been had like a bunch of school children."

She's probably right and her remark sinks us into total despair.

But we have to get out of this maze at all costs and for that we have to rely on our own resources.

"Let's try this way," Gloria suggests, leading us into a new tunnel.

It leads to other tunnels... and others again...

In the end, we're utterly discouraged and are about to give up when Margaret lets out a quiet yelp. She's discovered a little metal staircase at the end of the tunnel that leads up to a heavy, massive door.

We don't waste any time running up all together. The door opens without the slightest difficulty and a breath of fresh air blows across our faces.

Outside, night has fallen. Fluorescent clusters trail across an inky sky, flooding the surrounding landscape with pale, ghostly glows.

A moor... deserted... silent as a tomb...

"Where are we? What sector have we ended up in?"

We walk, our senses alert, without saying a word, at random, scrutinizing the space around us.

We've gotten to the a point where we no longer dare to communicate our impressions to each other. We're overwhelmed and follow numbly a destiny for which we were perhaps not made. We're swimming in suspense...

We continue walking in the hazy light when suddenly a gigantic mass rises up before us. A tall steel column pierced with portholes and a truncated cone-shaped top that looks like it's made of a transparent material.

"By Jove!" Archie exclaims, frozen in amazement. "A spaceship!"

It is indeed a rocket and a closer look reveals the four thrusters arranged at 90 degrees around the long steel cigar.

A spaceship!

And the most astonishing thing is that it's not a toy or even a scale model! The machine is on a human scale, over 300 feet tall, 50-60 feet in diameter, with its massive frame and its tripod of retractable struts deeply embedded in the ground. A boarding ladder accesses a semi-circular platform at the rim of the airlock door.

Archie is the first to climb the ladder. He's already operating the airlock when we follow him onto the platform.

The heavy door opens with a slight creak and Archie's fumbling hand discovers a switch. Light streams from a ceiling. A yellowish light that we find brighter now in the narrow passageway lined with armored doors.

The ones we open at random lead to the holds cluttered with various equipment.

The engine room is on the upper floor and a quick examination by Archie informs us that it's a plasma converter connected to the side thrusters by four exhaust vents.

The next floor only increases our astonishment when we discover, in the mess, chairs, tables and a bunch of everyday utensils that seem to us quite useless for mechanical creatures.

No, this is all essentially human, like the pressurized bunks that crowd the 4th floor dormitories by the dozen.

But we've not yet exhausted our surprises because we've barely step into the cockpit when Archie, after a quick glance around, points out a large wall map spread out above the control panel.

It's a celestial map representing part of our universe: groupings of distant nebulae at the poles of the Milky Way.

Feverishly, the young scientist manipulates a selector underneath it and other images appear in the rectangle of glass: a cluster of stars in the constellation of Centaurus, a dark cloud in Monoceros and other more easily recognizable clusters such as the Big Dipper, Cassiopeia, Pegasus and Andromeda.

"By Jove!"

This time it's the Earth. But the terrestrial globe, split into two hemispheres, displays an abnormal topography, especially with regard to the Atlantic and Pacific Oceans...

Archie cries out, "Oh, that! Now come on!"

"What is it?"

He thinks for a second and then explains.

"These two continents! Exactly the location that modern geology assigns to Atlantis and Gondwana!"

"Archie, look what I found!"

I point out to my friend the pile of books and notebooks that I've just taken out of a niche in the wall.

He leans over my find eagerly, leafs through a few books, then grabs a big notebook stuffed with small, cramped handwriting. Strange, cuneiform signs, embellished with ideograms even more hermetic than Egyptian or Mayan hieroglyphs!

Archie's emotion is so deep that even words are powerless to express it. He merely gasps, stammers incomprehensible sounds, and sighs.

I look at him curiously. His face is covered in sweat when, after a long silence, he turns to us.

"Gondwana! This rocket comes from Gondwana!"

On the wall map, he shows us the continent that stretches roughly from the Gobi Desert to Easter Island, overlapping three-fifths of the Pacific Ocean.

"The famous land of Mû," he adds.

"But no, really, how far back would that date?"

"Up to 15,000 thousand years before our era. At that time, Atlantis also existed... here... in the middle of the Atlantic Ocean..."

He turns back to the notebook full of glyphs.

"It's Vedic Sanskrit... a language much older than Zend. I had the opportunity in the past to make some rudimentary translations from this language. I can only give a rough idea of the meaning of the text, unfortunately... but I've still noted some very interesting details... It's a logbook."

"What's it talk about?"

"A war. A terrible, atrocious war between Atlantis and the Land of Mu. These two ancient civilizations that were fighting over the world had reached a degree of evolution certainly much higher than ours. In their kind of atomic war, Atlantis was destroyed and the continent sank, following a geological cataclysm caused by the madness of men. Only the survivors of the Land of Mû had the chance to leave our planet before their own continent suffered the same fate. They embarked on spaceships of the same model as this one and launched into space towards a destination that I can't make out. The notebook says that there were 471 people on board this rocket. Men or women... I can't translate the word exactly."

"But what were they doing in this universe... and on this desolate world?"

A completely unexpected answer comes to us out of Margaret's mouth.

"Lo and behold... Look what I see coming..."

All together we join her in front of the porthole.

A sphere appears in the cloudy sky, descends like a rocket and lands just a few yards from the rocket.

Any resistance would be useless, we know, and caution advises that we leave the ship as soon as possible.

"I have the feeling we've bitten into the forbidden fruit," Gloria tells us, leading us toward the airlock. "Something new is sure to happen, believe me."

Furiously, I grab a steel bar lying in front of a hold.

"Starting with Santa Claus, I swear to you that he will speak by hook or by crook."

I'm the first to jump into the sphere, but there's no one on board. The enigmatic snowman remains invisible in the cockpit. The access panel closes behind us and the craft carries us off into the night.

The trip is short and a few seconds later we find ourselves back in the rooms assigned to us.

There's no one there except for a huge "thing" that sits in the middle of the main room and is totally unknown to us.

It looks like a six-foot tall battle tank mounted on toothed wheels and with a dome containing a sort of perpetually moving magic eye, as well as a multitude of thin, flexible antennae that resemble branches of gelatin.

The "thing" swivels slightly, its magic eye fixed on us.

"I've been waiting for you. But do not worry. I do not want to hurt you. I am the Mechabrain."

The artificial voice is a sinister mix of sweetness and arrogance.

"More symbolically," it continues, "*I am M.*"

CHAPTER XI

If lightning had struck at our feet it would certainly not have had any greater effect.

The mechanical creature advances towards us slowly, its quivering antennae spread wide around it.

It watches us from behind its steel armor and we sense in its attitude a kind of contempt comparable to that of a cat playing with a little mouse.

"You are definitely men of spirit and action," it continues in the same ambivalent tone. "To be honest, I thought long and hard before revealing myself to you, but this time you went too far. So, I might as well satisfy your curiosity. In any case, you will never return to your world."

"Our world, which was also yours, wasn't it?" Archie replies dryly.

"Gondwana! The Land of Mû! It was indeed on this ancient terrestrial continent that I was conceived. Originally, my functions were purely pediatric and educational. In anticipation of the cataclysm that was about to destroy our continent, the humans of that time decided to emigrate to a distant planet in the constellation of Andromeda. This terrestrial-type planet was, it seemed, perfectly suited to their needs. I was therefore boarded onto an escape rocket with the mission of watching over the 471 children entrusted to me."

"Children?"

"Only children. The craft was piloted automatically and our journey was to take place in the underlying space-time continuum, which you call subspace. Unfortunately, a slight malfunction in the machinery caused a sudden saturation in the ion generator and the rocket accidentally 'tilted' into this parallel universe. This is how we made contact with this unknown world."

"And the children," Gloria asks, "what happened to them?"

"The accident was violent. All of them died except for one. So I devoted myself solely to the lone survivor. Of course, it would have been easy for me to repair the rocket and reach Andromeda, but the child would not have survived the journey. Here, things were different. Time, as you know, has another value. For a human organism, a century in this world corresponds to an Earth minute on the biological level. So I had every hope of prolonging the life of this child. Moreover, I, too, benefited from the alteration in the temporal rhythm because the terrestrial materials of which I am made became practically imperishable here. So, I had an eternity before me. And for the child."

M took a short break to let us digest this first bundle of information. Then he went on.

"With an almost infinite time at my disposal I could focus on the first fundamental phenomenon, that of the evolution of machines. A proven reality, you have to admit, since you have some examples of artificial intelligence that you are fabricating on Earth. No machine ever repeats the same error twice. The 'evolving' machine assimilates the error and judges the same problem according to new criteria. Repeat this self-correcting loop ad infinitum and you will obtain an infallible analytical machine, exceedingly evolved, which will ultimately surpass anything that human brains can conceive. Such is my case. Nothing more."

A silent pause.

"While busy with this, the idea came to me to create borloks in order to distract the unfortunate child," the Mechabrain added.

"What exactly does borlok mean?" Gloria interrupts.

"It is an old word, borrowed from the Gondwana language, and which I have kept. It means a systematic and conditioned toy."

"And then?"

"My borloks have improved. I have created games of my own invention, each more fanciful than the last, and this always for the wonder of my young protégé."

"What happened to the child?"

The Mechabrain darts its magic eye at me. I have the weird feeling of being stabbed by a dagger.

"He died," it snaps, "a long time ago."

"Poor little thing!" Margaret sighs. "And you continued to create toys, just for your own pleasure. How touching!"

Clenching his fists Archie takes a step forward.

"And again for your own pleasure, you've attacked Humanity. You've decided to destroy our universe. How? Why?"

"What useless words!" the Mechabrain replied, wearily shaking its gelatinous antennae. "Attack? Destroy? No... As soon as I was able to create my interdimensional sensors, I followed with interest the evolution of your new race. Unfortunately, it was neither better nor worse than the one that gave birth to me. In turn, you became victims of progress and your own creations. You play with dangerous toys... too dangerous... We can say, well, that I wanted to offer you more harmless toys... toys capable of diverting you from your wretched ambitions. Your Humanity is digging its own grave."

"And you set yourself up as the Good Samaritan!"

"I offer my Power to your Weakness," the Mechabrain corrects. "But for this my toys alone would never suffice. I had to find another way. For example, I had to modify all the universal laws on which your science was based. Therefore, I studied, analyzed, and, in a word, I found the key to the unified field governing your four-dimensional continuum."

"How the hell did you manage that?"

"Time, Professor Brent, time, I told you. The speed of light, gravity, nuclear energy, radioactivity, electromagnetism... it all had to do with time. There was an equation to be found and I found it. The stars that I destroyed? Nothing very serious. Just a simple experiment to test my extraordinary power. I never intended to destroy your Universe... at least not yet."

"But the idea tempts you, doesn't it?"

A kind of quickly stifled snicker.

"It would be fitting for me to measure myself against your Spirit-God... but later... One day perhaps! It will probably be the last game I will play."

"You're crazy... Yes, crazy as hell!"

The Mechabrain turns towards me.

"So you don't believe me?"

"It's just a bluff... A bunch of hot air! You're trying to intimidate us but you're just a pile of scrap metal, as vulnerable as your miserable borloks. Let's go... come closer, if you've got the courage."

My hands clenched on the steel bar I brought from the rocket, I face off with the Mechabrain. The first blow I strike, right on its dome, echoes lugubriously in the room. I hit it a second time. My enemy still doesn't budge an inch.

"Oh, Syd, please stop, I beg you!"

Margaret is about to rush forward, but the metallic voice blasts out with the same irony.

"Fear not, Mrs. Gordon. Your husband is amusing himself at his own expense. He will soon run out of strength!"

Angrily, I attack again. I know very well that my blows are ineffective, but I have a little idea in the back of my mind. If only I could...

Bang!

The thunderous blow raises the antennae on the dome. They whip the air with sinister whistling.

This time, the Mechabrain pivots in place, its magic eye wide open.

"So, are you answering me or what? Come closer, come closer!"

"I can crush you, Mr. Gordon, you are wrong to insist."

"Syd, you've lost your mind! Stop it, damn it!"

"Leave it to me, Archie! This tin can has no guts and I'll prove it."

I move slowly, turning my back to the "hall of mirrors". A crackling sound warns me that the Mechabrain is seriously starting to "warm up".

"Of course, see, you can destroy me with your thermal rays or with your disintegrator... but that wouldn't be fair game... Let's fight on equal terms... Well, I'm just a human, armed only with an iron bar. So, do you accept the fight, God of Gods?"

Stung to the quick, the Mechabrain starts in motion and charges at me. I dodge it with a leap to the side, landing another blow on its armored carcass in the process.

I manage to drag it into the middle of the tunnel. I attack again on the left, then on the right. It brushes past me with its mass like a fighting bull charging at the red cape.

"Come on, pal, a little more effort! Break my back! With one good blow if you can do it."

Watch this... Here I am planted right in front of the "dimensional" mirror that almost got the better of Margaret... The selector is set to the null position. What happens next, I had imagined and wished for in every detail.

The Mechabrain charges forward with a frightening buzz, misses me again and, carried away by its momentum, plunges into the mirror. It disappears entirely into the dark abyss and my swing of the iron bar shatters the mirror, which explodes into a thousand pieces.

The sound of breaking glass... but also a scream... a howl... a moan of agony... a heart-wrenching appeal...

Something that sounds like...

A child's voice!

CHAPTER XII

Archie is the first to come over me. He looks bewildered at the destroyed mirror. The Mechabrain has disappeared, for good... and God knows where!

"By Jove, Syd, you've got guts! But I have to admit..."

I grab his arm.

"Archie, that voice... that voice... Did you hear it?"

But a violent jolt cuts off my breath and my speech. A jolt of unheard-of violence followed by a dreadful din.

We're thrown to the ground brutally among the broken glass while another jolt shakes the room like an earthquake.

"It's coming from the basement," Gloria shouts, struggling to get up.

We all rush, by instinct rather than reason, through the hall of mirrors to dive darkly into the underground maze with its circular corridors.

Entire walls have collapsed. It's real chaos down here. Through a gaping hole, we glimpse a huge room completely cluttered with debris.

The central unit! The Mechabrain's sanctuary! That inaccessible area we had tried in vain to get into during our first foray into the underground.

We enter but it's the same spectacle everywhere. Around us, the weird and mysterious devices conjured up by the Mechabrain are in total ruin.

The very same ones that ruled the destiny of our Universe, overturning with their magical powers all the natural laws that had been imposed on it since Genesis.

None of the machines have survived M's annihilation, like disciplined soldiers offering themselves up as a holy sacrifice upon the death of their leader.

"Oh my God... Look!..." Gloria's voice launches us into another room located in the very heart of the gigantic sanctuary and it looks untouched.

But we stand before the entrance, paralyzed in awe at the sight of the creature within.

This time it's not a borlok, but a human creature, truly human...

A child! A four-year-old child, hardly more... A poor little thing, lying inert and lifeless on a soft sofa surrounded by toys.

His face, as pale as wax, still reflects all the pain, all the horror of a violent, sudden, unexpected death. But there is still in his big blue eyes a silent wonder so intense in its purity that no Botticelli could depict it. A strange, overwhelming look, frozen between Life and Death!

"A child!" Gloria's voice cracks. "A child 15,000 years-old!"

"M's little protégé," Archie says, leaning over the corpse. "He, too, lived only under the Mechabrain's influence."

"But what about the cry that we heard..."

"It was him. Him and M at the same time," Archie goes on dreamily. "A close relationship had been established between the child and the Machine. A kind of unity, if you will... It's incredible... incredible that an artificial intelligence can nourish feelings, feelings too..."

He straightens up and points out the many television screens that line the walls three feet above the ground.

"It was for him that all these toys were created... only for him. For him, too, that we were spared after the trials we were forced to go through. I suppose the child watched all our adventures on these screens. For him, we were new toys... something that the Mechabrain could not create for him."

Yes, now I see the real purpose of all this. And the reason why M didn't tell us the whole truth.

It was afraid that one day we would discover its little protégé for whom it felt an overwhelming love. Maybe it was originally equipped with some embryos of pseudo-human feelings. But, over time, these feelings also evolved.

And then there was Earth, our new humanity re-emerged from the ashes of ancient civilizations, from a few survivors who had fallen back into barbarism.

The Mechabrain watched our evolution and one day it got scared. It understood that we, in turn, were about to conquer the Universe by launching ourselves into the stars, that we were sooner or later going to break through the space-time barriers that protect the parallel universes from each other and the idea that Humans might one day penetrate its secrets and steal this child from it was unthinkable.

No, it wasn't seeking to destroy us, which was within its capabilities, but it changed everything, reduced our Universe to its personal will.

As things stood, we were lost. All our science was collapsing, we were starting from scratch. But for that, we needed a distraction, a kind of diversion, a means that could tear man away from reality and plunge him into total passivity: in other words... the borloks.

Archie turns the televisions back on one by one. Images appear in the luminous rectangles, toys come to life, great epics take shape, the kaleidoscope of eternal games flood the room. Doors are opened onto the imagination, onto harmless children's fantasies, onto wonder and dream.

Onto a multitude of "Wonderlands".

"This show is all for him," Archie says after a last look at the dead child of Gondwana.

In the engine room of the big rocket-ship, I watch Archie and Gloria. Pliers, wrenches and all kinds of tools fly from one hand to the other.

"With a little luck it ought to work," our favorite scientist announces.

How long have we been here? I don't know. But I try to reason, to maintain a sense of continuity in the course of action. Hours... five, six maybe...

The Mechabrain had mentioned a slight malfunction in the ion generator. We just need to unravel the Gordian knot of this otherworldly machine. For that I trust Archie and Gloria.

Multiple connections are spliced and coupled, joints screwed back onto their supports, wires plugged back in...

One try... a second... Levers... Buttons... Crackling and humming that vibrate the whole ship. We'll get there. Archie confirms this to me with a confident smile.

"Ready for another try?"

I settle into my pressurized seat with an affirmative wink. My fingers are already on the control buttons.

"Watch out, Syd!"

I jump up.

"Wait a second, Archie, wait a second! I saw something through the porthole."

I can't help myself. No, we definitely can't leave this world without a final farewell to Pinocchio. That devil of a puppet is standing in front of the airlock with a sad smile.

"And me?" he says to me, "you are not taking me to your new game?"

I stroke his cheek. But, what the hell is wrong with me? He's just a doll... he's not...

"This time, it's not a game for you," I try to keep my voice steady but I fail. "Thanks again, Pinocchio, thanks, my friend."

Oh, drats, that's enough! Come on, scram, let's get going. I take my place at the controls again, my eyes blurred by tears.

"Over to you, Archie!"

"Ready?"

"Ready!"

"5...4...3...2...1...0!"

The sudden jolt makes me wince.

EPILOGUE

"With a little luck," Archie had said.

Well, it's done. We had that luck. We landed on Earth not far from the foothills of the Himalayas, in the middle of a desert in northern India.

We came back to a normal world, freed of nightmares, a humanity freed of its obsessions and complexes.

Only poor Funnigan seems seriously affected, but his psychiatrist has assured us that he will recover.

What happened to the borloks? You'll obviously want to know.

The idea was simple and we made it happen, again thanks to Archie.

Blue Cottage was for a while a kind of global crossroads. All the dangerous toys shipped from the four corners of the planet were put in the Moebius ride which was responsible for shipping them back to the other universe. Of course, Pat suffered the same fate, to the great disappointment of our Bud. But we couldn't break the rules.

Then the ride was taken apart, piece by piece, and the scrap metal thrown away.

No, there is definitely nothing left of those "mysterious Christmas presents".

Oh, I almost forgot... A member of the government had proposed, after the return of the last toy, to send an H-bomb into the world of the borloks, but we opposed it.

What's the point? And that's the question I ask you too.

When you close this book, if this story makes you dream a little, that's wonderful... But if, one Christmas Eve, you start thinking that under another sky there are wonderful toys with a universe of their own, and a Santa Claus who paints radiant smiles on happy and innocent dolls, then that'll be great!

Deep down, aren't we all just...

Big kids?

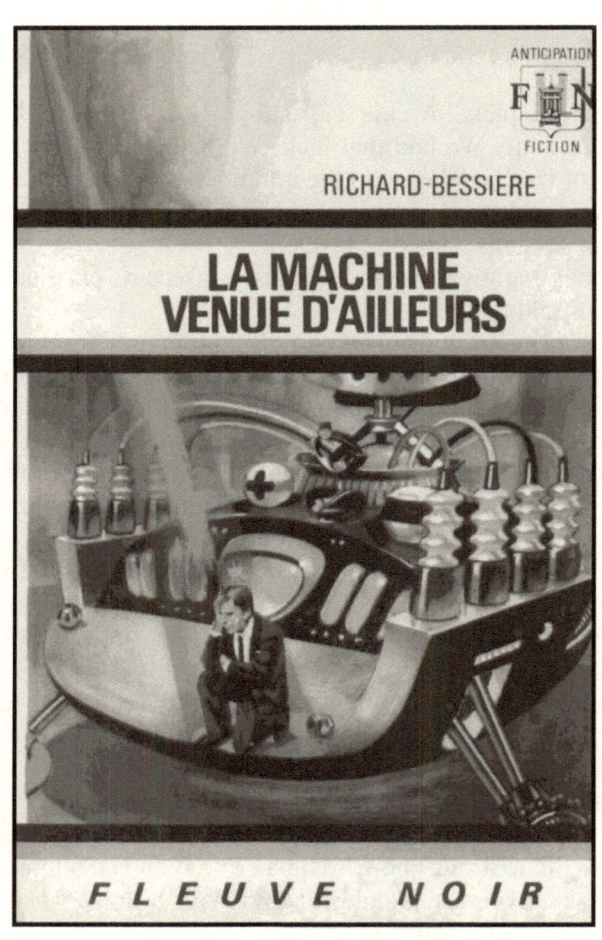

Cover by Gaston de Sainte-Croix

NO MERCY FOR THE BORLOKS

CHAPTER ONE

For at least the third time, I try to get my message across to Margaret.

"We'll be back tonight around seven or eight, darling. Don't wait dinner for us, we'll probably get a bite to eat there. Otherwise, we'll dig into the reserves."

As closed as an oyster to anything that doesn't come out of her holy TV, my sweetheart doesn't even deign to nod. When they say that too much information kills information... A little more each day, the Fox channel gets on my nerves. Margaret is glued to it from morning to night, from time to time also from night to morning. To make myself heard, I would really have to cast my line into the magic window. But that's a different story. The audiovisual media and I are not on the best of terms. Especially if it's Fox.

Go fox hunting, my inner voice quips.

I embark on a new attempt at verbal communication, no different than the last ones. So, I adopt a radical tactic. I plant myself right in front of the screen to pick up from the living room table yesterday's edition of the *New Sun*, which I really have no need of.

"Syd, please... Move aside and don't throw that newspaper away!"

"Excuse me, *darling*, of course not," I say with a falsely contrite air before reciting my litany again.

And there, a miracle. Very small, but real.

"Don't worry, honey. I won't wait for you."

Phew! Message received, at least for the most part. Bud and I, tonight, won't have the cowboys of the NYPD on our backs. Don't laugh, it's happened to us before. And to redo another episode of *Unsolved Mysteries*, sponsored by my desperate sweetheart, oh no, thank you!

"Please don't throw that newspaper away," my dear wife repeats. "Your colleague's article yesterday about poor Larry Conway is sublime... What do you think of that unfortunate young man?"

There's no point in me answering her rhetorical question. Whatever my opinion on the subject, Margaret won't care. All she cares about is what Fox is feeding her about the national moral dilemma posed by "the stricken hero." And this ordeal has been going on for two weeks already...

There is no divine justice. The great clemency of the Most High, which I used to believe in as a child, being the rival of the Holy Virgin, has long since packed its bags.

Just think.

Larry Conway found himself a hero at 18 years-old. But a hero decorated with the medals *no future*, *exit*, *game over*. Rewarded with a one-way ticket to a coma with no return, for having rushed headlong and saved a poor guy who was about to be burned alive in his house on fire. Vegetablelized for life—for death, let's not kid ourselves—because he didn't hesitate to rush into the flames and snatch away their victim. Nice consolation, on the other hand, is that he is publicized like no martyr ever was.

This world is getting more and more hopeless. Sinking into a bottomless global quagmire. I know this well, for ten years now that the *New Sun* has been transformed into one of those weekly tabloids that I would never have even glanced at for all the gold of the Incas.

When James Funnigan's paper was bought by Rupert Murdoch's group, I didn't see it coming right away. Even less so when I was offered the position of features editor, i.e. JF's chair and office, with a quadrupling of my previous salary, bonuses not included. From then on, my former monkey, promoted to managing editor and moved to a luxurious gilded closet of an honorary big boss, has almost stopped getting on my back.

The paper's transformation happened later, insidiously. I was, so to speak, anesthetized, too comfortable in my new position to think of rebelling against the revolutionary, ethically disgusting policy imposed surreptitiously by that evil old fox Voldemort... sorry, Murdoch.

Materially speaking, the Gordon family quickly reached seventh heaven. And they're still there, which is no small thing. A pretty house on Long Island, on the beach, with a view of the waves. A swimming pool, covered, heated and bubbling if needed. A landscaped garden with automated gardening and watering, absolutely amazing. Everyone has their own car: a Fiat 500 special edition *Hello Kitty* for Margaret, a ruby red Mini Cooper for Bud, a 4 x 4 Jeep Grand Cherokee in sky blue—fitting for a Murdoch employee—for yours truly. As for our interior design, no need to list its furnishings, we have everything. It was Margaret who said it indirectly (and rather clumsily) a few weeks ago, when she saw our wild child come home with his new girlfriend, the first girl of color…

She said when she was introduced to us, "That's all we need!"

When I tell you that we have everything...

And yet, all is not well. *I* am not well.

Dear esteemed reader, I see your eyes widen, your eyebrows form question marks. While a childish refrain transmitted by my former biographer echoes in my head, translating your silent question.

Assho—, what are you complaining about?

I will try to be precise, Sire, concise and succinct.

Here we go.

To maintain all this, I've stayed the course for years. Against all odds, or rather against storms and tsunamis continually brewing under my skull. Because this course, all the professional renunciation and personal denial, is leading me straight to the abyss. I'm well aware of it. Burn out or slow death in depression, boredom and sorrow, I don't know how I'll end up. What I do know is that it will be long before the crows come home to roost.

Or Larry Conway regains consciousness.

To think that there are fools who still believe...

Oh, not the kid's parents, who have accepted the meaning and implications of the term "brain death", even though the awful truth is unbearable to them. They demand that their child be unplugged, that the machines that are keeping alive the empty shell that his body has become be turned off, and that seems humanely normal to me.

The idiots are the *antis*. Those people who open their pie-holes against this "odious request" in the name of a religion, whatever it may be. Although, when I write that they still believe... I'm leaning more towards a false, simulated faith, towards a comedic hypocrisy that disgusts me. It makes me want to vomit much more than the stinking smoke of the ever-present Tuscan cigars of my big boss. Holy water snakes, toads from the great lakes of politics, slimy reptiles of the extreme right cesspools pissing all their bile on the courage of these "unworthy parents", and wallow in all the details of the Larry Conway case to duel with warlike violence over the problem of euthanasia.

As if these matters of conscience and love, of a purely intimate and private nature, should be decided by anyone other than the relatives of the unfortunate living dead...

Shut your mouths and leave these poor people alone!

I'm itching to go and shout my anger in the street and on the airwaves. To plaster it on the front page of the *New Sun* where I enter every morning with the growing impression of coming to prostitute myself. Since I passed the age of forty, it's even worse than before. I'm more and more ashamed of doing what I do, of providing grist to the mill for the people and things I hate more than anything else.

How wonderful is this Infotainment Age!

And the detestable fashion of giving voice on any subject to all points of view, even the most feeble or the most abject, as if they were of equal value or credibility... Think of the pathetic debate of opinions on whether the Earth is round or not and you will understand, (I don't have to draw you a picture), where I want to stick this practice!

With Larry Conway, we have reached the sad summit of electoral strategy based on populist tactics. And the bottom of the abyss, for media ethics.

So, what am I still doing in this mess?

More and more often, when I *reflect* in the bathroom mirror, I tell myself that I'm sick, totally sick. That only a lama from Tibet (not from the Andes) would succeed in yanking himself out of the abyss of my depression. Because a lama from Tibet is educated to sulk at the surrounding world, according to the first precept of the Buddhist religion, whose second precept he also obeys, and, as such, has no wife.

A fortiori, no woman who becomes addicted to Fox, to the abominable, gominoxidable Glenn Boor—sorry, Glenn Beck, whose enema-like effectiveness as a brainwasher and neuron shaper (in short) makes him a veritable media Methuselah.

And normally, since the lama has no wife, he has no son.

Whereas I...

I do. But increasingly, it's as if I don't. Bud and I are the perfect example of the continental drift. I couldn't tell you how long our tectonic plates have been drifting apart, given our rather confusing family timeline. Given that Bud is 17 years-old but was around 11 when we stopped playing baseball together in the backyard, you can do the math yourself, dear reader.

Did the brilliant Wegener[6] strike us back then? Or did it wait a little longer before initiating between my son and me the fault line—or the tunnel of the same name but in the open air—which has now become as wide as the Atlantic? What does it matter... In any case, it had the help of an army of model moles, surely the fifty best in consumerist strategy against a backdrop of mass addiction, whose names, ranks and war exploits I won't cite here.

Because it is indeed a war that is being fought, in my humble opinion. Even the greatest of all time since the theater of operations is the entire Earth, in total simultaneity. And the stakes: the progressive hypnotic enslavement of the entire population of the globe.

I accuse the Gorgon, as Zola said...

I accuse the planetary octopus with billions of tentacles, the sticky cyberweb in which my fellow citizens and others are stuck, first the individual consoles, then the online games, the *anti*-social networks, the casinos, the virtual sleazy hotels and cheap markets, the purveyors of drugs and intangible fantasies, and the Great *Et Cetera* that you know as well as I do.

In sum, you get it, Bud is a kind of geek. Not quite 100%, which I am happy about. His free fraction is certainly not big, but hey... As long as it exists and lets a little bit of the real world slip into the cocoon of my cyber-mad son, hope remains.

Of course, this little bit of the real world is limited to three basic fundamentals: girls, sensitivity to basic needs (meaning a minimum of respect and contact with those who provide them) and comics based on outlandish characters endowed with even more outlandish powers.

Paradoxically, in this environment where dematerialization triumphs, Bud remains a visceral addict of paper, plastic and tangible materials from which are made the objects he collects with a humongous passion: books, booklets, pamphlets, toys, figurines, etc., all from his favorite series. If there were only one or two of these series, it would be easy and the tour quickly wrapped up. But given their number and the feverish pace at which the basic or derivative products related to them come out, the invasion of our domestic living space has been underway for ages. In other words, the nightmare started a long time ago.

---

[6] Everyone fathers what he can. I am the father of Bud, and Wegener that of the theory of continental drift. *(Note of Sydney Gordon)*

Yet, as I've already explained to you, there's no question of deliberately cutting this link that still joins our child to the real world. Nor, either, that represented by girls, even if Margaret has a hard time accepting such a parade in her house. I consider that at just 17 years-old, being on the tenth girl that one goes out with is neither a monstrous anomaly, nor a risky pre-pathology.

Furthermore, since our offspring is the complete opposite of an IQ-deprived person, his female relationships generally stack up pretty well. Not a single birdbrain, not a single *fashion-victim* dodo sticks her painted beak in our house. Nor a single dog, I assure you. Bud has very good taste, like his father who, as a result, gets all the pleasure of watching. Well, it is very pleasant. On the other hand, the neighbors, friends, family, colleagues, and all the rest of the what-people-might-say...

Let them say what they want, little rats, and that's it!

Back to the point, no more counting sheep, I swear on Saint Panurge. The starting point of this story, the subject of the day, is not girls. If Bud and I are coming home late, it's because we're going to New York Comic Con.

More precisely, it's my son who's going. I'm only along for the ride, without any passion for the subject matter. But it's a way for me to try to build a bridge between our two continents or to launch the first grappling hooks that I will haul in, trying to bring our drifting lands a little closer together.

Oh my, I better get my butt in gear because we're less than five minutes away from the departure time we agreed on last night. In other words, Bud Lightyear is going to be hurtling down the stairs any minute now and I'm in for a rough ride if I'm not already out the door when he leaps down the last four steps.

CHAPTER II

At that time on a Saturday morning, it's a real pleasure to get to the West Side of Manhattan and the Javits Center, even if the train from Long Island is crowded and we are packed like sardines in a can on the cross-town bus that takes us to our destination. So that Bud, not really happy to drag me around like a ball and chain for the whole holy day, can't avoid staying glued to me. And he takes the opportunity to give me a master class on his favorite comic, *Strangers*, a cult sweries from Hexagon Comics, which personally I wouldn't know from a hole in the ground.

As a bonus, I'm treated to a closeup on his favorite character, Homicron, about whom I now know pretty much everything. Except for one detail, and not the least: I don't really understand whether he is a hero or a heroine. Judge for yourself, it's neither natural nor clear.

Homicron is one of the members of the group of *Strangers*. He used to be a man, a brilliant NASA astronaut named Ted White. One day, a cosmic entity from some "elsewhere" called Alpha takes up residence in his body. Thus is born Homicron, endowed with superpowers whose description goes in one ear and out the other. Because between us, up until now, the originality doesn't sound like all its cracked up to be.

The weight of words and the shock of photos, because there is one, a little rough round the edges. Today, Homicron *is a woman*: Rita Tower, Ted White's ex-girlfriend. He died after the invasion of Earth by some evil aliens called the Kyrosians. As a result, Alpha's envoy simply jumped ship and he went to live in Rita's body.

The rest of the story, my little lambs, don't ask. As sparkling clear as it is for Bud, it's more convoluted to me than String Theory. All the while reminding me, in some way, of the comics I loved when I was Bud's age.

"So, if I come across your Homicron, I'll say to him 'Hello, They,'" I rephrase in hyper-synthesis of the veritable university class I just took.

This earns me, as a prelude to his verbal response, a grimace sealed with the most appalled pity.

"That's all you got out of it, Dad?"

"Uh... That's pretty much the only thing that differentiates your comics from the ones that I grew up with. They were more moral and less unhealthy in my time. No risk of coming face to face with transsexuals."

"No surprise, in that corny old stuff of yours," Bud slams me before exploding, "Hey, you had the gall to say transsexual...?"

"Yeah, so what?"

"THAT'S WRONG!" he is even more outraged. "You're wrong! This is a *post-mortem metasomal transfer*, not a castration with plastic surgery reconstruction! When you've seen Homicron with your own eyes, you'll understand right away.'

"Because..."

"No, don't make that stupid face! I'm talking about the new Hexagon Comics action figure, quarter scale, on sale exclusively at the Convention for the first time. You'll fall for that stunner!"

Usually, it was the stunners who fell for me. Some even nearly fell on top of me, in the past, suddenly plummeting out of nowhere and the sky. Times change, I won't complain. But from my son's beaming face, I suspect that he plans to buy the next wonder of the world.

Immediate verification.

"Are you really planning on buying this doll?"

I pay promptly for my poor choice of words.

"That's right. And I'll even buy you the inflatable model, Dad. That way, there'll be two of us having fun with Rita."

In the increasingly dense crowd around us, heads turn. Eyes widen, mouths twist. Laughing, Bud hurries up and I stick to him like a tick on a mutt. This is not the time to be left behind. Here we are at the entrance to the Javits Center, a crazy, colossal futuristic architecture of glass and metal that is already pretty imposing when nothing is happening inside.

But today the feeling of being crushed is coupled with the oppressive impression of entering a boiling anthill. Except for the colors, because the place is the scene of a chromatic debauchery worthy of a painter gone mad. It's aggressive, violent, since the world of comics doesn't go for faded pastels.

The ambient noise is like a hive abuzz with activity. Shouting, hollering, heated conversations, unbroken series of announcements, most of them so nasal that they are barely intelligible, bursts of syncopated music meld in a cacophony on the fringe of what is audibly tolerable.

As a bonus, an endless line awaits us before we're allowed to cross the threshold of the event itself, a huge bright blue and fire-engine red portico on which *New York Comic Con* is displayed in big letters.

I have plenty of time, so I use it to study at my leisure the fine folks around us, among whom stand out a number of fans who are passionate enough to wear the costume of their favorite character.

The Carnival in Rio, compared to this, is small potatoes...

Think of those cover illustrations of old SF pulps or trade magazines from the 50s or 60s showing space stations in the middle of an interstellar void or busy markets on distant planets with hordes of extraterrestrials, each more alien than the last, and you'll have a rough idea of the caravansary of madness that I'm stuck in the middle of.

The only detail that's wrong is the voices. And the language, unique. No one cackles, yelps, quacks, buzzes, snaps their mandibles, growls, lisps, scratches or gurgles, all in a fireworks display of disparate idioms that would ruin the very foundations of the Tower of Babel. No, all of these good people talk like you and me, without using the any kind of machine translator. On this score, the gathering rings false, seriously lacks exoticism, and that disappoints me.

Criticism is easy, but art is difficult. I know, some things never change.

The real serious stuff starts right after the Convention entrance. I have to decide on a concrete strategy so I don't lose my son, who is as comfortable in this carnival of illusions as an anchovy in a school of sardines. Luckily, he agrees that we spend five minutes consulting the map of this mega-fair and agree on various foolproof meeting points.

As you might have guessed, Bud has little desire to drag me along in his wake all day long. And, heavens, I would be no more pleased to have to stick him, like some little suckerfish, through all the stops that, for me, would turn into stations of the cross worthy of fifty calvaries. Because my kid has a plan all mapped out, but it can be summed up in five dark and ominous words:

"I want to see *everything*!"

He'll have to dress up as a cruise missile or the *Rocketeer*, given the cosmic scale of that Comic Con! But he can do it, I have confidence in him.

Wandering haphazardly through the various halls and aisles of the event, maybe I'll find some touchstones—not too expensive—of my memories of reading as a teenage. In order to sniff out a possible subject that might inspire me to write an article on the event, I think I'll focus on some publishers' stands whose names still remind me of something positive: Marvel or DC Comics, for example. I'll also take a close look at some of the illustrators whose style doesn't stray too far from what I used to like. On the other hand, hunting for autographs is out of the question. Bud tries to assign some of them to me, but I give him a categorical "no". I'm not enough of a sheep or masochist to stand in line after line for hours on end...

No need, either, for me to tire myself out feigning interest in games, DVDs, all kinds of collectors' items, promotional items, and even less so in "dolls". I'm going to be embarrassed enough coming home with my 17 year-old son lugging one around under his arm—and of a woman who isn't quite one, that takes the cake!

I can do without the round tables and conferences too, except to take a breather and snooze for a while if necessary. As for going out of my way to interview celebrities from television series, because there are some being announced, don't even dream about it, friends. Even for all the gold in the world, I wouldn't approach anyone who haunts that sinister magic box. Call it a raging allergy, I could care less.

On the other hand, one or two animated films, I wouldn't say no to that.

And that's it, we'll see...

Bud and I will meet up for a bite to eat around noon, which is only an hour away, after all. Then, free time again until around 5 pm and the final rendezvous at the Hexagon Comics booth. By the way, that's where my son is going to head first, so as not to miss out on getting *his* new quarter-scale Homicron and immediately lightening his wallet of around 100 dollars.

I will long remember his fanatical look when he leaves me there to rush over to the stand where his beautiful "envoy from Alpha" is waiting for him. Like the kid of barely eight years old who, at dawn on December 25, runs to the Christmas tree and all its wondrous promises.

Speaking of more down-to-earth promises, I hope Bud keeps the ones we made about the timing agreed upon for the day...

Well, he comes through! In this matter, the young man is a worthy son of his father. He even made sure that we ran into each other several times during his comics marathon, just to reassure me by proving to me that he hadn't dissolved into nothingness just for the pleasure of breaking my balls.

So not everything is rotten with this child, I say to myself with a touch of satisfaction.

It's now a little after 5 pm and we're both at the Hexagon Comics booth, next to the Wanga Comics booth where I'd just spent a good half hour chatting with cartoonist Anthony Dugenest.

A Frenchman, you wouldn't have guessed it. Super nice, incredibly talented, not at all full of himself despite his talent and success. A genius *and* a human being, let's keep the two words separate, which is extremely rare. And he knows my current biographer Jean-Marc Lofficier very well. It surprises me, but you can't make this up.

I now know pretty much everything about the recent return of the *Strangers*, a very worthy project that I'm still not buying. I must admit, however, that I've partly changed my mind about my first impressions.

Bud, meanwhile, is deep in a heated discussion with a guy and a girl I can't identify. He's giving a master class on the works he's an inveterate fanatic for. I wait patiently, leafing through one of the three volumes of reissues of legendary episodes of Dan Barry's *Flash Gordon*, part of the gift I offered myself earlier this afternoon.

Little lambs, my head is like a washing machine... I would be quite unable to give you a list of everything I saw at this show, but I can assure you that in the end, I don't regret my day. If only for my visit to the DC Comics booth, where I was touched to see the original versions of the *Metal Men*, *Kamandi* and *Legion of Super-Heroes* that I read many long years ago. I also bought myself a hardcover omnibus volume of *Legion*, it's the other part of the gift to myself.

My son looked at my acquisitions wistfully.

"Dad, you'll never stop being a nerd... Couldn't you have chosen one of the latest *Futura* or *Jaleb*, instead of your relics?"

No need to answer... If I was going to break, I would have done it for *Elektra*, especially since she was present in the flesh — especially in the flesh — at the Marvel Comics booth where I gawked at her for awhile, like a carp on the verge of suffocating. I even got to pose right next to her for the photos taken by a guy who recognized me, who told me he was my most devoted admirer because I embody the model journalist in his eyes and he swore to high heaven that these holy pictures would remain strictly private.

I confess, I'll never in my life find out who the girl dressed up as Elektra is, but standing next to me... *she electrified me.* I forsook taking her card for one reason and one reason only, in the name of a puritanism, which will make you bust up laughing. Because I would have had to slide my hand between her breasts. If I had done that, I would not have been responsible for whatever happened next... Not a word to my son or to Margaret, I'm counting on you.

As a souvenir, I wanted to buy one of the books of this disturbing heroine. The price put me off.

Hypocrite!

Okay, I'll confess. I got hung up on the blinding eroticism of some of the illustrations. Enough to turn a 40-year-old man who owns this comic into a perverted old man whose frustrated fantasies are fulfilled by young girls in virtual worlds. Bringing this home I would have felt like I was smuggling in a pornographic magazine...

I shudder and bury the memories of the photo shoot deep in my mind. Then I step closer to my son and gently pat him on the shoulder.

"Okay, I'm almost done," he says to me, sounding annoyed. "I'll be right there..."

A few more words with the guy, including a curt "That's my dad, we have to go home...", a smack on the girl's lips, then Bud picks up a whole load of plastic bags as rich in color as in content and gets ready to join me.

"Doggie at heel, master can leash Doggie back to his kennel!" he tells me to my face, just to embarrass me in front of everyone by making me into the consummate family tyrant.

Translation: "I just want to live my life and go home all alone like a big boy after driving around a while with my friends, but I can always deny myself..."

I'm on the verge of giving in, seeing that the distance between our respective tectonic plates has now shrunk by a couple of inches, when the shadows appear.

Between my son and me, two guys in suits as black as night and as black as their ties, glasses to match, snow-white shirts. Long, pale, frozen faces, as expressive as wax masks, topped with crow-black hair, wavy like the plumage of the birds of the same name, and glistening with blue reflections. Stealthier than cats, these crows, because we didn't hear them arrive.

"Mr. Sydney Gordon, from the *New Sun*?"

His icy, aloof tone is more of an affirmation than an inquiry.

In any case, I turn around. But no, my doppelganger isn't hiding behind my back. So it's definitely me they are after.

"At your service, gentlemen. What can I do for you?"

With no expression on his face, devoid of any emotion, one of the two *men in black* hands me a card. Before examining what's on it, I notice out of the corner of my eye the very mechanical gestures and stiffness of the man.

He must be a disabled veteran of semi-robocopized war, I muse. *All that's missing is the whirring of the joints...*

Three letters jump out at me.

F.B.I.

Federal Bureau of Investigations for the uninitiated. Nothing but...

"You will follow us, Mr. Gordon. Our boss wants to have a brief talk with you about the activities of your newspaper."

"But it's Saturday, gentlemen. Can't it wait til Monday morning?"

"It's now or never, Mr. Gordon," MIB #1 says, as his sidekick slowly opens his jacket an inch, just enough to give me a glimpse of a decisive asset to make up my mind. To stop the evil, it must be cut off at its root.

Illumination.

Someone in high places got wind of the series of articles we were preparing on the scandal of the cannibalistic Wall Street bankers and he mobilized the Federal Bureau to nip it in the bud...

"Come on, Dad, don't resist," Bud interjects, his voice trembling slightly, "otherwise they'll *flash us* and then give us fake memories... I'm gonna take off."

"No way, kid!" And without giving him time to answer, I turn back to MIB #1. "You'll allow me to bring my son along, won't you? Thank you!"

As trapped as I am when Margaret uses this kind of irrefusable request, the MIB consults his sidekick then almost snaps in half, like the Asians do, and tells me that it is agreed.

"We must go now, time is pressing," he tells us curtly.

One *man in black* in front of us, the other behind, and off we go.

A strange way to leave a public event, if you hope to go unnoticed...

As I am going through the automatic exit gate, I pretend to get caught up and deliberately drop my bag of books at my son's feet.

"You can't keep it together, can you?" he grumbles.

He catches my facial expression and he gets the idea. He bends down at the same time as me to pick up my purchases and I whisper to him very softly:

"As soon as we've got a handle on things and the time is right, you get back to the old world and blow the whistle. Until then, *wait and see. QX, Lensman?*"

Certainly, my Lensman of a son is not happy that I've boarded him onto my galley and deprived him of a few hours of real freedom. But he got 5 out of 5 and I can count on his Indian tomb discretion because, to read behind the scowl that he'll wear until further notice, you'd have to have at least XXX-ray vision.

We leave the Javits Center and head toward a long, black (as expected) car parked a short distance away.

One of the two MIB takes the wheel after having Bud get in behind him. The other one settles into the front passenger seat after closing my door. So I'm in the back, on the right, with a diagonal view of the driver. Just in case, it might come in handy.

All the doors lock automatically. Then the car starts quietly, with a well-oiled purr.

CHAPTER III

Between my son and me, the barrier of silence has risen again. As physical as the pile of brightly colored plastic bags, crammed into the middle seat and stuffed to bursting point. On comics, action figures, games, and sundry items, Bud has blown at least six months of his allowance or I'm a monkey's uncle.

A confirmed disciple with a black belt in the Buddhist religion, he pulls a six-foot-long face. He doesn't forgive me for forcing him to follow me into this mess when he could have chatted a little longer with other fans and then gone home alone, taking inventory of his loot from the day and blogging with his buddies to make them drool with jealousy.

Even if he's angry, I'm not going to get upset about it. Other things make me madder.

Starting with the direction the vehicle took, in the opposite direction of downtown where the local FBI headquarters should be located. What the hell, the Bureau wouldn't have moved just like that, we would have known! An operation of that kind, it's impossible to do it on the sly.

After the Brooklyn Battery Tunnel, the car heads due south then catches up with the 278 and heads west.

"Are you sure this isn't a screw up?" I tried to engage our captors.

Not a word, not a gesture in response. As if these two crows were deaf, or if they'd forgotten they had passengers. They're in their hermetic bubble, nothing from the outside can reach them.

The one next to me is no better off. Immersed as he is in reading one of the comics he bought, he doesn't notice anything. From time to time, he lets out a little chuckle or a laugh. Or even an ecstatic sigh while looking at his quarter-scale Homicron that he had unpacked and placed next to him. I have to admit that the doll is pretty spoiled in terms of form and that the size reduction must have only been applied in the vertical direction. They were inspired by Rita Hayworth to model their Rita Tower, I would bet, by inflating her a little more Mae West style where necessary to make it alluring.

In short, Bud is paying zero attention to the world around him, just like he is paying no attention to his "zero" father, in whose head a carousel of increasingly nagging questions and anxieties is taking up residence without permission.

Basically, I'd rather see my kid absorbed in his "Homicraziness", and as autistic as his mother when she's tuned into Fox, than have him accost me with a barrage of questions that I would be utterly unable to answer...

Let's recap.

Either a big fish from the FBI has a pressing need to talk to me or it looks like we're going to have a chat not in the New York offices of the Federal Bureau, but in the country residence where the big shot goes green from time to time.

It's simple, I finally conclude. That's why we're being driven out of town. It's nothing to get my brain tied up in knots about.

Oh, by the way, although Bud and I still have our iPhones, they no longer pick up any network. As my old pal Richard Bessière once said, laughing like a whale: *Parasites are jamming our listening*. Personally, I never found anything hilarious about it.

Back to our cell phones, now down for the count, good only for using as flashlights. Long live the latest in ultramodern and cheap technology—surely the latest in agony!

We leave the 278 and head due south on 95, the New Jersey Turnpike to natives. A valuable clue as to the geographical direction of our destination, but nothing more.

The reason for the location being clarified now, I wonder *why* this boss wants to talk to me. In other words, what could the *New Sun* have been ranting about, say last year, to the point of so irritating the Federal Bureau that it felt the need to settle a score solo and quietly with the paper's features editor?

It's true that the rag can snap a little hard at the various branches of the American administration, and that there's no shortage of articles that jump down the throats of the CIA, FBI and other official slimy squid. But as the saying goes, to live in happiness, live in hiding. It's not our fault if some of their lying and cheating gets exposed, like neglected warts. They should have disinfected first.

I quickly think about the papers over the last twelve months. There were a lot. However, nothing sensational or hypersensitive. No stories about mistresses or moral scandals, no misappropriation of public funds for personal purposes, no proven collusion between corrupt agents and rotten branches of politics, business, or troubled emissaries of foreign countries. Nothing but the usual batch of swipes at the growing inertia of the FBI in the face of all kinds of espionage, at its increasingly proven inability to track down terrorist or drug supply networks via the Net, at its morbid determination to perpetuate debunking by beating the hell out of the first person who shouts too loudly about UFOs,

It's true that we'd let through a vitriolic article by old Jimmy about the military cover-up of a sordid case of massive, bloody mutilations of sea lions on the California coast last summer. The arbitrarily designated *official culprits*—supposed collectors of seal fat, a market that has become very lucrative since the imposition of zero quotas on cetacean blubber—paid a heavy price for an alleged anti-ecological genocide, getting all their boats sunk by surface-to-sea stealth missile strikes.

Anti-ecology, paper tiger!

Jimmy's beloved phrase, who didn't hesitate to denounce the real culprits, the notorious occult residents of Area 51. Them punished? No way! They're not going to risk upsetting such allies.. They kindly and simply asked them to go to Eastern Siberia instead, to the coasts of Kamchatka or the great Sakhalin Island, where not a soul will see them, to carry out their draining of lipid-energy (essential to their metabolism) on the crowds of local seals.

Apart from that, I hardly remember any outrage to their majesty that could earn me, today, the regrettable honor of this forced summons.

After about 30 miles, the car leaves the 95 and heads east. Without a word from our two *men in black,* muter than 100-year-old carp. And not a comment from Bud who, as long as there's enough light from the outside, is immersed in reading the stock of comics bought at the Convention.

As long as he's reading, at least he isn't asking himself any questions—and he doesn't ask me any either. It saves me from not being able to find an answer and from passing on my gnawing anxiety to him.

So, we're on the 195. If I remember correctly, it leads, among other places, to a major US Navy logistics base. The bigwig would therefore be waiting for us somewhere other than in his *dacha,* as our former sworn enemies would call it.

This doesn't clear things up. A review of our recent publications has given me no clue as to the motive for our... kidnapping. Upcoming issues of the *New Sun,* then? No, I can't think of any loaded articles scheduled about the US Navy. Or, another hypothesis, I was bypassed and the plan comes directly from Voldemort and his ultimate circle... In any case, if the Navy is in on it and is getting help from the FBI, it must know about whatever it is. And it must be very unhappy.

The prospect doesn't reassure me at all, to put it mildly. I have the eerie feeling of wearing a hat that isn't mine.

Well, here we go, veering right, almost skidding at the intersection! The guy driving is crazy, I swear!

I unleash a string of curses. It's like preaching in the desert, no reaction.

Even Bud, who, unaffected, doesn't stop reading.

I have to hold on to the door handle to keep from being thrown against him. In doing so, I turn my head just before our car finally leaves the 195 and I catch a glimpse of a sign indicating Jackson several miles away, if we'd kept on the road we're leaving. The one we are on now is not wide but straight as far as the eye can see. It motivates our driver to attempt a speed record.

Goodbye to the idea of a military base. On both sides, the woods are getting thicker and thicker. So, we're being taken deep into the sticks. I have no knowledge of the existence of a secret strategic site in the area. This trip is smelling fishier and fishier. What if, instead of a meeting in the countryside, these *men in black* have the sole mission of getting rid of us without leaving a trace by shooting us like dogs in the middle of nowhere?

On top of everything, I got my son into this mess and he's going to end up like me...

FBI... Aïe! Aïe! Aïe! my inner voice starts humming. *FBI... Aïe! Aïe! Aïe!*

I shudder in spite of myself and say:

"You guys wouldn't have some music, would you?"

Just to hear something real, instead of this dark refrain in the shadow of my growing pessimism.

It's like talking to mannequins in a shop window. The driver doesn't flinch and neither does his sidekick.

You'd think these two were crash test dummies, as deaf as they are expressionless. Worse than fugitives from Madame Tussaud's!

The car slows down at the end of the endless stretch of straight road. Thank goodness, because we take a very tight left turn that could have landed us in a far from dreamy landscape. It's dark, even though we have come out of the woods and are passing through a remarkably unremarkable landscape. But yes, evening has fallen, as light as a dead leaf.

Very quietly, without making a sound.

Yet all of a sudden, this breaks the silence. Bothered by the twilight, Bud has looked up from his harder to read books, searches in vain for a spotlight over his door or on the ceiling, then heaves a huge sigh of disappointment. In the end, he deigns to look outside and open his mouth.

"Where are we, Dad?"

"On the way to the devil, son. Somewhere in deep, dark New Jersey."

I'm cultured and I show it with a micro-chance of scoring points by slipping in an allusion to the very famous *X-Files*. I'm still a fan of the series, and Bud was pretty hooked on it for a while. But it wasn't enough to bring our continents closer together...

"Lol," he says to me. "Stop treating me like an idiot!"

Yet his eye suddenly sparkles with a flash of curiosity.

"I'm not kidding, really. We're even coming up on New Egypt."

Because, on Gordon's word, there was *New Egypt* written on the sign at the intersection where we just turned.

"You're messing with me!" my son exclaims. "But it's pretty great!"

Far from being petrified by anxiety, Bud starts to wiggle in his seat, as jumpy as a flea—or a lass shocked by a spark from her love toy.

"Because you know New Egypt, *you?*" I ask, looking even more distraught.

"No, not directly. Besides, I don't give a damn about the place. On the other hand, when you see what's a little farther on..."

He looks at me with a real conspiratorial expression and then, adopting a most authentic Japanese accent, concludes:

"*Eu-re-ka!*"

I hold back from pointing it out. No need to tell him for at least the hundred and first time that it's Greek, not Japanese. F... *manga* culture!

"What did you find, exactly?"

"Well, Dad, that's it, I know where we're going."

"And where's that?"

"You just wait, it's like we're already there. Hold onto your horses, it'll really worth it."

"But, come on..."

I don't bother, my son is already gone. And far away, too. As proof, his inner monologue that he ends up expressing in a long version.

"So, *they* kept on going underground... The *Lone Gunmen*[7] were right! We pretend to close a base, we throw everything out, we raze the buildings, we decontaminate the site... *Demilitarization*, that's what it's called. In its place, we build something else that's as civilian as it gets, very flashy, bling bling, fun and high tech, everyone comes to have fun with their families... But underneath, well hidden, the bastards continue their top secret crap... Even long after their surface cover has gone haywire because of the recession..."

My friends, I'm flabbergasted. Bud, a conspiracy theorist! Who would have thought it? I almost want to offer him a job at the *New Sun* right away and replace old Jimmy who, given his advanced age, is less and less motivated to chronicle Fortean cases.[8]

But this is no the time to talk about that. The car is cresting a slight slope between two low hills and there, in a huge depression of land slightly below, a real nightmare vision comes into view.

Just risen, the big lazy moon hitches pale patches of light onto monstrous things, unable to veil their horrors behind thin blankets of fog that the evening breeze doesn't even try to chase away.

And these monstrous things, from a bygone era, are giant dinosaur skeletons...

---

[7] Lone wolf UFOlogists well known to *X-Files* fans. *(Note of Sydney Gordon)*
[8] Raining frogs, crop circles and other unexplained phenomena that Charles Fort had made his specialty. *(Note of Sydney Gordon)*

CHAPTER IV

Welcome to Funland!
We've just passed under a huge gateway displaying, in lettering fashionable 15 years ago, the welcome message to the blessed visitors of a place once reputed to be magical.

Funland...
An amusement park built after 1990 on the demilitarized grounds of what was formerly Joint Base McGuire-Dix-Lakehurst, one of those logistics complexes whose justification collapsed along with the Berlin Wall.

Funland...
One among hundreds of the flash-in-the-pans sparked up in the euphoria preceding the new millennium, then quickly extinguished when the economic recession struck following the repeated stock market crashes of the 2000s. Bankruptcy, liquidation, attempted takeovers by foreign investors smelling black gold, re-bankruptcy, re-liquidation, this time irreparable.

Funland...
Not a dinosaur cemetery, but a mausoleum to the glory of human vanity and false values. A tomb for the lost dreams of adults who played at being children.

The giant skeletons are nothing but the unfinished remains of scenic railways designed to take the breath away and stun the faint of heart. Rising out of the extraordinary tangle of old, exposed frames and beams supporting colossal engines, they stand out as a delirious lacework against the silvered sky. Here and there, wide, unriveted sheets of metal sway like dying leaves in the soft autumn breeze, skeins of tangled cables flutter like the languid vines of a stagnant jungle.

The car moves very slowly through this caricature of a factory for fallen titans, populated with outlandish machines doomed to rust, in silence and immobility.

Speaking of which, it seems that Bud has suffered the same fate, except for the rust. Nailed to his seat and gaping, he's keeping a low profile. In my opinion, for him, fiction has just caught up with reality. And dumped a whole bucket of anxiety on him.

No time to think. Our vehicle has reached a fairly clear area and stops. The driver cuts the engine and gets out, followed by his sidekick.

As rigid as the law, they stand in front of the doors, take out their weapons and point them at us. Then the driver unlocks our doors.

Bud and I give each other a knowing glance. We have to get out, we have no choice.

"Take the bags, son. Mine with yours."

"Did you think I was going to leave them in the car, Dad? Hey, I don't give away my collector items just like that!"

He packs up his sculptural Homicron, then we climb out and find ourselves face to face with our two kidnappers, as inscrutable as poker players, almost frozen and mute.

But armed, I repeat. Threatening, therefore dangerous.

Strange, it's almost as if they're listening to inaudible inner voices...

I'm using this freeze-frame to better assess our environment and to think about the very short term.

Lugubrious echoes run through the immense cemetery. Creaking and moaning that the nocturnal cooling pries from the joints of the half-corroded metal, tumbling bolts loosened by oxidation, drops of falling water, whistling of the wind tearing at the broken struts, muffled crash of chains ringing against empty carcasses, bowing of springs suddenly released.

The car has stopped in the middle of a circular space, oddly free of the debris and dirt that litters the ground everywhere else.

Above us looms a huge mass, like a rocket cut in two, the upper part of which is nothing but shredded sheet metal.

It's all well and good, this post-apocalyptic setting, but not enough to make me want to dawdle. Same for Bud, who starts dancing from one foot to the other with the affable air of a caged grizzly bear.

The MIBs, however, still seem to be elsewhere. My goodness, their truth is perhaps out there...

At my wit's end, I decide to bring them back to Earth.

"Guys, are you waiting for the thaw?"

"Get your thumbs out of your asses, you dummies!" my son chimes in. "We didn't come here to play statues!"

Two expressionless faces turn towards us. All the more unfathomable since the big black glasses still hide their eyes. My word, they haven't noticed that the sun is long gone!

The detail does not escape Bud.

"These two boneheads are blind. We're gonna find out they brought us to the wrong place..."

"There's no mistake and everything is fine," our driver then declares with relative conviction.

"There's no mistake and everything is fine," his partner repeats in the same tone.

For elite agents, it lacks panache and originality, doesn't it?

Suddenly, doubt floods me.

"With bozos like you, the FBI has sunk very low... Are you sure you're from the bureau, Mr. So-and so? Let's see your ID again!"

Zero reaction from the mannequin. So, I literally jump at his throat.

"Let's go, dumbshit! Show me your badge!"

So saying, I shake him like a plum tree.

And I stop short, for two reasons.

The first: the ground starts moving. Descending, to be more precise. The circular surface in the middle of which the four of us are standing, as well as the car, is slowly sinking into the well it sits on.

It's the platform of a freight elevator for large equipment, including vehicles...

The second is the feeling I get from the physical contact with the MIB. I had grabbed him by the lapel of his jacket without managing to make him budge. He retaliates by blocking my wrists, then his colleague grabs me from behind.

By Jove, these guys are cold as marble. And it looks like their very supple skin is synthetic. Plus, they're as strong as Turks...

Me, despite my young age and being in good shape, I am definitely not up to par.

Bud hesitantly eyes us. Ready to pounce. I know he's just waiting for a sign from me.

I struggle like a devil, manage to free myself a bit. Suddenly, the MIB facing me is unbalanced. A wink to my Fulgur of a kid, who drops his bags on the ground then goes on the offensive.

Might as well ram into a concrete wall. But hey, a point for Bud because the guy is surprised and lets go of my hand with which I tear off his dark glasses.

And there, my lambs, believe it if you want...

The guy's eyes are frozen, dull, no contours. Not even enamel or glass. No, he has eyes that look like they're painted on.

"Look, son! This guy has doll's eyes!"

In a flash, all the little incongruous details that struck me about these two guys come rushing back to me and fill in the picture.

I tell Bud straightaway.

"Even worse, kid. These monkeys *are dolls*!"

"Hands up, or we shoot!" the two simulacra shout in chorus.

Sure, the tone isn't there, it sounds artificial, hollow, even absent. But those pocket guns, they are definitely there.

So I stop resisting and the *men in black* release me after a few seconds. Incredible, this slow reactivity, as if they can't decide for themselves what to do next, but have to refer it to a distant partner.

The one who lost his sunglasses neglects to pick them up and the other one has just put his in his coat pocket.

Still unsteady, Bud examines them with new eyes.

"Nothing like Barbies, Dad," he grumbles. "You're wrong, they're definitely not dolls. These two bozos are *action figures*!"

I stand there stunned, even without understanding where he sees the difference.

And he continues with the following illumination:

"Plus, *I recognize them now*!"

This tops it.

"And…?"

"It's Nick Thunder and Mark Bolt, two detectives from *The Thunderbolt Agency*!"

"Because you've already dealt with people like this?"

At my suddenly worried expression, Bud bursts out laughing.

"Yes, Dad. But not in real life, don't worry. In a Hexagon Comics. These guys are comic book characters!"

For me, it's the last straw. The deathblow. The apotheosis, according to the worshipers of the Holy Potato.

Full-size action figures, animated with a life of their own, a little mechanical, but endowed with relative intelligence and autonomy…

Well, a lot of details jibe with this. But still…

Pinch me, dear reader, and prove to me that I'm having nightmares.

No… Not that…

It's impossible! It can't be happening again! It *can't* be happening again!

And yet…

You, too, are hesitating. You're saying to yourself: "What if, in spite of everything…"

You have the same memory as me, so the same crazy idea is coming, right?

Okay, so I'll be the one who lets loose the hare.

What if the Borloks are back?

CHAPTER V

Bud and I, on the other hand, are nowhere near being back. For now, we're underground, miles from the surface, considering the length of the trip, because the elevator just stopped at the bottom of the shaft.

The truth that we risk finding here, I dare not even sketch its spectrum of terror.

The Borloks walk among us again... That's all that was missing.

But let's not put the cart before the horse, that remains to be proven. And also, let's not forget the connection to this meeting demanded by an FBI boss.

Presently, Borloks or not, our pair of MIB are once again playing their role of guide squared and, weapon in hand, they unambiguously "invite" us to cross the threshold of a concrete gallery that heads towards unknowable distances.

"Can't we drive?" Bud complains, having obviously picked up all this stuff. "The car would fit through the tunnel just fine."

"No use," Thunder says—or Bolt, the same. "We are not going far. Move it!"

"I would say even more, we are not going far," confirms the other. "Move it!"

We don't need to be told any more by our doll-eyed guardian angels. The icy cement walls, damp in places, the stingy lighting from the ceiling, the whiffs of an abandoned mushroom farm don't encourage us to wander around in this drab passage. Along the dark gray walls run bundles of cables and pipes, in a state that exudes anything but dilapidation and lack of maintenance. From time to time, I can make out junction or breakout boxes as well as relays with digital displays, brand new, or almost.

Strange this mixture of old inactivity and very sparing but recent rehabilitation.

Suddenly, a right turn. And, via the passage opened by an armored door that disappears into the wall, we enter a kind of rotunda room where the spectacle is completely different.

Equipped with ultra-modern high-tech equipment, the place is full of interactive terminals, communication consoles and large flat screens.

Quite a few metal cabinets, too. In the middle, a conference table with seven or eight chairs around it. We are in a command post or a control center, the question is for what.

As for the big boss who wants to talk to me, he is still conspicuous by his absence.

Several openings gape at regular intervals in the circular wall. It's impossible to see where they lead because, beyond them is very dark. Potential hiding places for us? Not without risk, but I'm taking notes, just in case...

"So, your boss, is he showing up soon?" Bud asks, annoyed.

"We need to inform him that you are here first, Mr. Gordon," they say in unison, ignoring my son who lets out a resounding curse.

Immediately, the MIB stiffen like tomato stakes—and their painted eyeballs turn red like the tomatoes on said stakes, once ripe.

These laser eyes, and not revolver eyes, have the most sinister gore effect...

A strange buzzing sound fills the rotunda room. It sounds like layers of voices, like radio stations whose frequencies overlap. The result is an interference racket that is completely unintelligible, especially since the voices don't seem to be speaking our language.

Thunder and Bolt "unfreeze" themselves just enough to nod and acknowledge receipt of what is surely new information.

Strange, their physiognomy suddenly changes completely. Goodbye to their porcelain inexpressiveness. Now they're forcing a grin like a clown mask or, even worse, the Joker from *Batman* in his worst moments of delirious frenzy. It makes me shudder to the core.

"Affirmative, *Ghost*," they reply as one man in black with the sparkling eyes of a white rabbit suffering from a raging fever.

I don't know what presence of mind makes me realize that they are switching back to the American way. Confirmation provided later in their statement, which confirms two problems.

Number one, minor. We're dealing with congenital morons. They're FBI agents like I'm the Archbishop of New York. Real ones would continue in coded language, never in plain language in front of their captives. Oh, today's borloks seem light years away from technical perfection...

Number two, major. Because this is the fate promised to said captives:

"Imminent elimination of the one contacted and the one unwanted, with zero residual traces. Omega process..."

The first one states it, the second one repeats it. Both in English, in case we turned deaf or stupid in the meantime.

But Bud and I didn't wait for Number 2 to finish parroting, nor for him and his crony to pull out from who knows where two new weapons that would make a former governor of California immortalized in the cinema turn green with envy...

Like two rockets, Gordon father and son shoot out of the control room. In the gallery, one turns right, that's me. Bud chooses the left, towards the freight elevator and the car. He runs much faster than me, so he has a better chance of getting the car and then going through the tunnel and flattening our opponents.

Thunder or Bolt, who cares which, is hot on his heels. *A priori*, the *action figure* can't hold out.

Obviously, the other one has a clear advantage. The farther I go, at peak performance, the closer I hear his hissing joints.

An opening in the wall, on my right. Pale pink light beyond. Dark disk on the ground a little further. A well, a hole, what do I know... Could you see better, in a split second?

I swerve, so to speak. And flatten myself against the wall inside the room, right next to the entrance.

In a stroke of genius, I take out my iPhone, turn on the flashlight, then skim it over ground, aiming so that it passes diagonally in front of the entrance and continues to the dark disk.

One point for me.

With a lot of servomechanical squeaking, the borlok turns and come in. Sure, it'd seen me slip away, but it's focusing on my lit cell phone.

Semi-smart toys and high-tech gadgets, the same fight!

In life, then in imminent death.

Second point for me.

Goodbye iPhone, which literally disappears as soon as it reaches the edge of the dark disk. QED, so it is indeed a well.

Third point for me.

Bolt, or Thunder, approaches the circle without foreseeing that this will be his brink, if I'm lucky—meaning if the hole is deep enough. With his eyes, the borlok follows the light of the iPhone that must still be falling since I haven't heard a crash. A promising sign, isn't it?

Fourth point for me.

Quietly, but quickly, I slip up to the MIB who doesn't see anything coming. Has no eyes in the back of his head, the simulacrum. And will soon have no head at all. Like shooting ducks in a barrel, I just have to push him gently so that he falls into the well.

A breaking noise, pretty far away. My phone hit the bottom.

Bolt, or Thunder, does the same shortly after.

Without a cry, but with a crash compared to which the death of my iPhone, murdered by myself, was just a weak rabbit fart.

Five points for me, round won.

I rush out of the pale pink room as quickly as my age allows.

On the freight elevator side, it didn't go as expected.

Bud is indeed at the wheel of the car, but the other ectoplasm is holding onto his arm while blocking the door. That also explains why the borlok hasn't had the leisure to fire his mega-gun yet. Try to handle a mess like this with your hands full...

Zero points for my kid who can't get the car started.

When suddenly...

I guess that Thunder and Bolt were closely connected to each other, immaterially speaking, even if the communications were not transluminal.

Suddenly, Bud's MIB stops his flurry of activity, swivels around and aims his weapon at me.

"Filthy Human... You killed my brother..."

From where I stand, I can see his plastic finger resting on the trigger.

When suddenly, again...

As if springing from the sky, in other words, coming from a source located higher up in the elevator shaft, a cerulean ray envelops the borlok.

Frozen in place, better than in Sodom and Gomorrah, the *action figure* whose eyes have gone out then falls like an uprooted tree.

Deactivated for the count.

A real miracle!

But we're not in Lourdes, and the apparition which appears shortly afterwards has no connection to the beautiful blue lady of little Bernadette.

Today's Holy Virgin is a man like you and me. Whom we all know well.

My old friend Professor Archibald Brent, as brilliant as ever!
Accompanied by Gloria, his wife, who's just as brilliant as he is.

CHAPTER VI

A few minutes later now, having come back from afar and from our surprise, here we are in a new control center, much larger and more welcoming than the one where Thunder and Bolt had taken us, but just as underground. It's not very original. It feels like the control room of a nuclear complex.

I do notice one major difference, though. Along the entire length of the rectangular room and from floor to ceiling, there is a metal curtain behind which the front of a store could be hiding, if we were on the surface and in a normal environment.

Here, I doubt that this is a shop...

But this is of secondary interest, *a priori*, compared to the explanations that our saviors and friends kindly undertook to give us after settling us in, very comfortably, and bringing us a drink to recover from our cascading emotions.

First point, I had guessed right. Bud and I, along with Archie and Gloria, are starring in a new blockbuster called *Borloks 2: The Return*. Unbeknownst to us, I insist. The two action figures, one of which I cleverly eliminated before my scientist buddy paralyzed the other, are indeed from the parallel dimension we visited, at great risk to our lives, a few decades ago.

Secondly, in order not to deviate from tradition, our couple of geniuses are a few steps ahead of us. More precisely, of me, as you will see, because my son...

Let's not get ahead of ourselves. We finish quenching our thirst when Archie launches, light years above the classic plurality of worlds, into a robust preamble on the multiplicity of cosmoses. Teeming with strings that wiggle in every corner with nothing, unfortunately, to do with Brazilian beaches, this "all branes" concept is as indigestible as the almost homonymous fibrous strands well for their stimulation of intestinal transit.

But I digress, excuse me. The floor is over to Archie.

"Our universe, with all that it contains, is imprisoned in a 4-brane itself included in a super-continuum with additional dimensions. Our 4-brane borders other 4-branes, so many universes traditionally called "parallel" while the more adequate term would be "tangent". One of the theories postulates that only the gravitational interaction "circulates" between the various 4-branes as if it underpinned them by a super-frame called the Ramond-Ramond gauge field."

I pull a mocking grimace.

"No, Dad, its inventor didn't stutter," Bud reassures me with a sly wink.

I glare at him. No one bats an eyelid, and Gloria continues.

"Remember our first encounter with the Möbius ride. The luminescent aura that enveloped the cart when crossing the twist, once the necessary speed had been acquired in our 4-brane, corresponded to the fleeting establishment of a Ramond-Ramond field zone thanks to which the round trip passage in the 4-brane of the borloks took place."

"Without any apparent delay for us between the outward and return journeys," Archie recalls. "While *over there*, the vehicle would stay for a variable length of time allowing it to be unloaded... And sometimes also reloaded, later, during another passage, if the spatial concurrence with the arrival point was by chance restored."

Hello, the dive into memories that aren't necessarily rosy. You're following, I hope! I don't understand much at all. But as Archie reminds us, Reagan himself didn't understand anything at all. So...

Anyway, you haven't read it all yet. The rest will leave you speechless, just like it did me.

"I'll sum it up for my father," Bud breaks in with a confidence that no string will ever have. "It's a mini-wormhole, not a shortcut between two places in our continuum, but a two-way tunnel between two 4-branes, ours and the Borloks'."

Spoken by my son... Who would have believed it? Here he goes knocking me for a loop. Oh, it's really too bad his mother isn't here to marvel!

Archie and Gloria nod their heads with conviction, then my scholar friend adds:

"We had also considered a round-trip passage to an invisible microdimension, but the consistency between modeling and observed phenomena does not hold up. Isn't that right, Bud?"

I will spare you the small details of the following presentation. Here is the substantial gist, just enough for you to share my growing astonishment of my son.

By Jove, where the devil did the kid get so much knowledge? And without anyone, neither his poor mother nor me, noticing?

So... A soda straw has a two-dimensional surface, its length and its circumference. From a distance, you will only see the length. The smaller dimension, which is the circumference, is rolled or folded back on itself and will remain hidden until you examine the straw closely.

By stratospheric extrapolation, the theory of Calabi-Yau manifolds—not *caballero*, mind you, and don't go looking on the Mexican ranches for one—says that a universe like ours has the four classical dimensions—three of space and one of time—plus six micro-dimensions or rolled-up dimensions. So that the super-continuum in which our Universe is included would be eleven-dimensional, which is what the so-called "M" theory advocates.

"In terms of theories," Bud concludes, "there's a whole landscape of string theories because, from a probabilistic point of view, their number is estimated at ten to the power of five hundred... But in the case that concerns us, we can stick to the two 4-branes from the start because it's coherent, sufficient, and almost demonstrated with regard to the underlying problem."

Coming full circle, back to common sense. I land on my feet after all these intellectual loops that I have so commendably tried to follow, haven't I?

"The borloks' universe and ours, then," I summed up, "separated by a...

"A 'membrane', that's it," Gloria interjects, smiling at me knowingly.

As if he had been waiting for this precise moment to act, Archie goes to the corner of the room, to the right of the metal curtain, and presses a button on a kind of switch box hanging on the wall next to it.

With a loud hum, the imposing shutter begins to rise up to the ceiling and reveals a huge, rectangular bay window.

Archie flips another switch, turning on a row of spotlights whose harsh glow bathes a concrete, soundproof room the size of a cathedral choir.

But here, no stalls, no altar, no Christ on the cross, no polychrome saints or beautiful stained glass windows. And yet I recognize it without hesitation, this formidable thing that sits here and leaves my son speechless.

And wham!

It's normal. He's just heard about it and has never seen it. While I've *experienced* it, this diabolical thing.

This infernal, twisted track, which once sent us to the parallel world where the borloks come from...

Well yes, good people, it's here. It's that damned Möbius ride!

CHAPTER VII

Proof by riding on the big figure eight—not by casting out nines, for once—oh, they don't tell us everything, just what they want to tell us.

No, the former toy that we had magnified was not destroyed at Blue Cottage, as I had been told. It was moved quietly, put into total secrecy by the American army *under* the Navy logistics base in the ultra-confidential research center that it "covered" in every sense of the word. In the post-Reagan era, when McGuire-Dix-Lakehurst was closed and the land sold to amusement park developers, the underground complex was decommissioned, mostly emptied. But the ride remained here. Well hidden, deactivated, ready to be put back into service if it were ever needed.

For exploratory purposes like Richard Blade's famous *Project DX*, or to send contingents of undesirables on one-way trips to other dimensions...? We'll probably never know.

Well, anyway, the magic thing is still here. In working order. Shining like a new penny, polished all over. A bit modernized too, at first glance. Goodbye to the wagon, replaced, it seems, by a sort of teardrop capsule.

In authorized circles—only in these, in principle—there are people in-the-know. This is not a scoop, Archie and Gloria are part of it. So, *they* knew. And so...

"Very recently," our friend tells us, "my iPhone started receiving a strange message repeatedly. Very succinct, very clear too. An SOS, a veritable call for help."

"Sent by whom and from where?" Bud asks, who looks he's just returned from the Moon.

"Sent by someone we thought was destroyed," his godmother replies. "M, the Mechabrain of the borlok world."

My turn to come back, at least from Mars. In a flash, I see again our dramatic confrontation with the rather disturbed entity, then our discoveries in its *apparently* devastated underground domain.

"But I settled the score with him, didn't I?"

"Everything led us to believe so," Archie sighs. "But some fine details must have escaped us. As for knowing which ones..."

"It's not a red-light emergency," my son interrupts. "They sent the message and it landed directly on your iPhone, just like that, Godmother? By magic?"

"Not just mine. Also anyone within a radius of a few miles. But apart from Archie and me, who could understand?"

The technical part, I'll keep it short. It was a condensed signal with a hyperfocused carrier, a real wave pin capable of piercing the "membrane" between the two universes. It requires a phenomenal expenditure of energy, so there's no question of telling your life story for hours or covering the entire planet.

Being pragmatic, M stuck to the essentials and targeted his sending. His series of sendings, rather. A single one risked not being enough. As for the receivers... Used to communicating with the toys he creates, the central supercomputer tried his luck with what could come closest to it, in our country and in our day.

No need to dwell on it, I've already told you: semi-intelligent toys and high-tech gadgets, the same fight!

Determined to learn more about the ins and outs of the SOS, Archie and Gloria sneaked into Funland, which had already fallen into bankruptcy and was abandoned—again, due to the recession. They, the cutting-edge scientists, knew a way to learn more: reactivate the famous ride!

They almost just had to get the thing moving to win the jackpot, without having to budge an inch.

"We weren't going to rush headlong into a possible trap," Archie explains. "That's why we first scheduled a series of empty laps. The first two times the Ramond-Ramond gauge field was established, nothing happened. The third time, however..."

"You still hadn't shipped anything, but the capsule picked up some-thing *from the other side*," Bud says as if it were obvious.

"Exactly," Gloria corroborates. "The pair you dealt with. Special agents of the Mechabrain, charged with bringing him help. And not just any help: that of the old pros.

"I get it. So you're the ones who sent them to get us," I say with a grimace.

Archie and his wife nod in agreement. But for me, there's still a catch.

"If M needs our help so badly, why the hell did Thunder and Bolt try to take out Bud and me? And while we're at it, who or what are we going to be hitting with our big, strong fists?"

Actually, I'd already heard the answer. Given the circumstances at the time, it was normal that I didn't register it right away.

"M says he's being threatened by an undefined adversary, from his own world," Gloria says. "An entity known only as *The Ghost*, who also presents a great danger to our dimension. And he's convinced that only 'Players'—that is what he now calls Humans, since most of them are now enthralled almost exclusively by the virtual in all its avatars—are able to unmask and then stop this formidable enemy. He himself can't do it because it's an artificial intelligence that lacks the sparkling initiative that is the privilege of... natural intelligence. Based on that, how could he instill the genius that he lacks into his creations, the borloks?"

"Plus, this Ghost is very likely to be a super-borlok more evolved than the others, born from a marginal process beyond M's control," Archie adds. "Moreover, this entity would be twisted, if not downright deviant."

"It's the Ghost who took control of Thunder and Bolt. We heard them say his name, didn't we, Dad?" Bud declares.

I confirm.

"It was at that moment that they became truly evil and threatening."

"When they blatantly turned to the dark side, yes," my apprentice Jedi son agrees.

"I can think of only one explanation, Syd," Archie concludes. "The Ghost is afraid of you, old man."

"A really dumb scaredy-cat," Bud rephrases, bursting out laughing. "When we know how bad you are at virtual games... No, it has nothing to do with you, Dad. I'm the one who scares the pants off this Ghost. He must have seen me ranked in the top five of the Hall of Fame of at least fifty games, no matter what kind. *Me*, Dad. Not you."

The slap I'm taking was inevitable. I keep my head down without saying a word and continue, as a way of improving my rating:

"Anyway, to wrap up the story, things are looking bad since our two bozos are 'broken'..."

"Bad *here*, not *there*," Bud corrects with a superior air. "We'll all just have to take a look on the other side, in the world of the borloks."

"We, son. Not 'we all'."

"Okay, Professor, *we* just have to go..."

Bud doesn't get the nuance.

"*We* are Archie and I," I spell it out for him. "I assume your godmother will stay here, at the controls and as backup in case things go south on the other side. And you'll keep her company. Very obediently. There are too many unknowns and risks out there for us to let you be exposed to them."

"Because of you, Dad," my son replied, no longer haughty or self-assured but just... worried. "Since your chances in virtual games, compared to mine..."

"Don't say another word, please. I'm the one going with Archie, and we're not taking you. On Sydney Gordon's word!"

I'm about to turn around with dignity when, suddenly:

"No offense, Syd, but Bud isn't entirely wrong."

It was Archie who figuratively shot me in the back.

"No, he's completely right," Gloria insists.

Mentally, I bless her for this second fatal stroke.

"Thank you, friends, it's obvious that you've never had children... Fearing for the flesh of your flesh and the blood of your blood, you don't know what that is!"

"You may be a little too scared when it comes to Bud," the godmother of the aforementioned goes on. "You raised him in such a sheltered life that you can't imagine him able to get himself out of a thorn bush. But he can... *All the more so* in what seems to be an almost real extension of his field of expertise, he has all the virtues of a potential winner."

What arguments can I throw against that, fellows? If Margaret were here, or if I could reach her...

Not even in my dreams! my conscience jiminycrickettises. *She has sunk body and soul into the world of Fox!*

Archie's turn:

"Wasn't he the one who identified the two action figures as Thunder and Bolt?" he reminded me. "And he wasn't a useless fool in the fight between you and them, if I heard right. No, Syd, I don't agree with your refusal. In my opinion—in Gloria's and my opinion, to be exact—Bud *should* come with us. Maybe he'll save us at the crucial moment, maybe he'll even save M and the universe from the borloks..."

Would you keep locking horns if the matter was put to you like that?

Thank you for your unanimous "No!", dear readers. If my son dies from an unfortunate fate, you will bear 99.99 percent of the civil liability!

"QX, Bud, they win. And so do you. You'll come along for the ride, it'll be a little training for your youth."

"Put it another way, Dad: it's better to do something than to waste a few days slumped in front of my screens, which would spoil it worse!"

A beautiful, well-constructed sentence, delivered with an enthusiasm that is ultimately quite rare in my son, as I have already mentioned.

"Enthusiasm" is far too weak a word, moreover, to express the emotion that Bud has been radiating for the past minute or two. An emotion that rewards me a hundred times over for the gesture—so to speak—of accepting his participation in the expedition.

For the first time since he passed the so-called age of reason, my little one shows me a real gratitude that I dare to label "materially selfless".

Because today, it comes out on a completely different level.

My son is going to come with me. He and I are finally going *to share* an adventure.

Whatever the outcome, we will discover it *together*.

This is a huge step towards bringing the continents closer together!

To say that I got ready in a state of euphoria is a euphemism.

The same goes for Bud, who radiates excitement, motivation and a thirst for battle. For him, it's nothing more than a new war game, much more interactive than all the others he's already beat. Much more rewarding, too: the stakes are, apparently, on the scale of two universes and their survival.

And Archie is no different.

We quickly recover, then are freed from the inevitable physiological constraints that can ruin any trip if precautions are not taken in advance.

We are wearing tight-fitting, royal blue suits, extremely flexible and thermoregulating, complemented by short boots with platform soles and gloves whose suppleness is matched only by their resistance. Thus spake Gloria.

Around our waists, we wear a belt with a bunch of pockets and cases containing everything we could possibly need. Survival rations, rehydrating pills, self-medication kit, emergency micropharmacy...

But no weapons, except for a good dagger worthy of the Navy 's elite divers.

Once equipped, the three of us go through the access airlock to the roller coaster cathedral, and climb the steps leading to the boarding platform in the interdimensional craft.

We slip inside the cabin, say a final farewell to Gloria watching us from the other side of the bay window, and then the top of the capsule gently closes.

For two or three minutes nothing happens. Not a sound, not a movement, not a change in the ambient light. We don't dare speak, so much does the feverish expectation strain our nerves and our attention.

The start is so sudden that it takes us by surprise.

Here we go, my darlings!

To infinity, and beyond..

.

CHAPTER VIII

First impression: a security that would reassure even the greatest barons of worry.

Safety resulting from a great deal of modernization of vehicles, which today move by sliding on a single-sided circuit.

The completely transparent capsule, in the shape of a teardrop and therefore very aerodynamic, "cocoons" us in a kind of padded shell filled with memory foam and inclined at about 45°, like "walking". We barely notice the traction of the support harnesses, the increasing linear acceleration and the lateral components inherent in turns or reversals. Oh, we're far from the rustic mine cart of yesteryear and its straps that would bind you in like the black or white sausages so popular with the French!

As a bonus, this car has multi-axial gyroscopic stabilization, which makes its seats independent of the upside-down or upright position of the capsule and the slope of the rails. Goodbye to vertigo, nausea possibly accompanied by unwanted spewing, and the need to close our eyes to neutralize the visual effect of continuous turning or spinning. We can therefore enjoy the show in thorough peace, thanks to this complete "bubble" of a capsule that envelops us. But for the moment, it's the grayness that dominates, the uniformity into which our environment melts more and more as the speed increases.

The second feeling is that the car is making a a lot of laps of the circuit without yet reaching the required spatiotemporal acceleration. It's true that we are three passengers who equal a significant weight load. Over the years, Archie and I haven't lost any weight, and in his way, my son is a real beast. All the same, the indigestion of gray awaits us, to the point that we will end up becoming it ourselves...

We complete yet an umpteenth round in the right direction and are diving towards the famous twist, the theoretical place of singularity, when a swarm of buzzing fireflies suddenly seems to come out of nowhere on the axis of our trajectory.

These fireflies, growing larger and larger, transform into giant Asian hornets with bright orange abdominal bands which begin a phantasmagorical ballet around us, to the haunting wail of frenetic mega-cicadas.

"Rrraaa... Rrraaa... Rrraaa... Rrraaa... Rrraaa..."

It gyres and gimbles all over the place, scrapes, creaks and buzzes even louder, dazzling our eyes and ears.

Until, also out of nowhere, there springs forth some kind of big, spindly birds with very long beaks, whose wings do not beat but which leave behind them trails of fluorescent green condensation and whirl around, unleashing apocalyptic bellowing.

"Mmmooonnn... Mmmooonnn... Mmmooonnn... Mmmooonnn... Mmmooonnn..."

Then begins a battle—aerial, spatial or transdimensional, as you like—in the purest F16 versus Sukhoi style. The self-propelled "birds" swoop down on the "hornets" and impale them on their beaks as sharp as foil blades. It's simply fantastic, breathtaking if we had any to spare! Because as far as Archie, Bud and I are concerned, we've been as quiet as clams since the start of the skirmish.

To sum up, Clostermann's *Grand Circus* was, in comparison, an amateur show for debutant dancers at the Opera.

Very brutal, a huge fuchsia-pink wave sweeps away the fighters whose nagging "Rrraaa... Mmmooonnn... Rrraaa... Mmmooonnn..." suddenly stops. As I move on to the next image, I note in a corner of my mind that we have here the real origin of the name of the inter-universe transit field...[9]

The next image, then, is like a peek inside a panoramic fisheye zoom lens with the diameter of a planet and focused on midtown Manhattan at Christmas time.

Small, very bright polychrome maggots wriggle and spin in concentric circles, in opposite directions, on the periphery of the immense "objective" in the center of which pulsating sparks are twinkling frantically. Some of the glowworms escape from the circle, rush towards the car, brushing past us, then disappear behind it. The effect like the lights of a tunnel that we're traveling through at the speed of a cosmic meteor.

Little by little, in the middle of the "lens", something still hazy and slowly rotating takes shape. I hesitate between an eye, a 9 (neither spades nor chickens, just the number) or an embryo of a barred spiral galaxy.

Are you surprised that I can recall so many precise details? Remember the perfection of our cocoon-vehicle, I've already talked about it. Therefore, we experience this crossing a little like a ride on a scenic railway, minus the shaking and discomfort. It's weird, psychedelic, like

---

[9] Too bad for Mr. Ramond-Ramond, but that's life. *(Note from Sydney Gordon)*

the famous final journey of astronaut Bowman in *2001: A Space Odyssey*... And just as not very reassuring as to the final outcome.

In short, the dive continues, the thing in front of us grows, grows, turns faster and faster, and begins to shine with warm copper reflections.

Like a... Yes, a door knob!

That suddenly opens a blue eye and looks at me.

Good Lord, where do I get such absurd images?

No time to waste in speculation because at this moment we begin a phenomenal deceleration. Anticipating the shock of a landing, I hunch down. Even if I seem to remember that rematerialization among the borloks is generally carried out without violence or pain.

5... 4... 3...

Zap!

Zap! And re-zap!

For the traditional "2... 1... 0!", we'll come back to it.

In the corner of the blue eye, there's no furtive tear pearling, but a ray between mauve and indigo darts out and shoots towards our capsule, widening into a club then a universal funnel.

The braking suddenly stops. We set off again at increasing speed. In the same direction and, alas, also rotating. Like a fighter plane going out of control in the middle of a hurricane to plummet spinning towards the bottom of a cardinal's cap.

Funny idea...

An existential terror washes over me. That of delicate laundry dragged by the drum of a washing machine gone mad. As a softener, we bathe entirely in the Vatican color that envelops us—with, strangely, a sacred whiff of runny rustic cheese.

Hop, hop, hop...

Apart from this violent violet violating our vision [10], everything else fades away.

Nothing is going as planned , I tell myself.

With all this, where the hell are we going to resurface?

---

[10] Note the alliterations! *(Note from Sydney Gordon)*

CHAPTER IX

We have resurfaced somewhere, that's for sure.

Bud, Archie and I, all intact. A little ruffled, but we'll get over it.

Less shiny, our capsule. Dented like old armor and become so dull that you would think you were in a homonymous wagon.

Until it deigns to creak open, we see nothing outside.

Which gives me time to think a bit. And to thank my scientist friend for insisting on equipping the transdimensional vehicle with very simple emergency controls. Thanks to them, when the zapper ray—camembert, judging by the smell—caught us, the molecular integrity of the machine was preserved. Ours too, at the same time.

Where we've landed, I repeat, we've done so in one piece. But in a crash.

"Where are we, Dad?" Bud would have drilled me ten or twelve years ago.

"In theory, among the borloks, " I would have reassured him without assurance, and yet without error.

Because as soon as we have a view outside, it's confirmed. The kind of thing that we discover, from the side of the hill halfway up which the capsule has landed, it cannot exist anywhere else but in toyland.

Imagine a vast and dreary plain dotted with solids in primary colors. Cubes, parallelepipeds, prisms, pyramids, trapezohedrons, rhombohedrons, tadpolohedra, frogohedra *et cetera*, not in a jumble but in perfect geometric order, a Euclidean precision from which the circle seems to be banished, like pawns placed on the squares of a giant checkerboard.

Under the blinding white sky, all these blocks shine with the harsh reflections of mirror-polished metal. Scrubbed and polished, they must be done regularly, and thoroughly.

A paradox: over this perfect model of sparkling cleanliness, surely designed by madmen obsessed with the line and the right angle, a gigantic spider's web spreads...

Dazed, we step out of our machine, which Archie examines in two glances and condemns in three words.

"The capsule's ruined!"

Then, shoulder to shoulder for a moment, we scrutinize the dazzling spectacle.

"Given the distance to the first cubes and the altitude of our crash, it feels like we're facing fifty Manhattans juxtaposed," I say.

Not free of worry, because it doesn't correspond to our destination. We can't be in Center, the pragmatically conventional name of the place where the Mechabrain is located. Or else, a huge demographic and urban revolution has taken place here since our last visit!

"For a hypermegacity, it's a hypermegacity," Bud says, his voice suddenly breaking. "Uh... that means there might be millions of them in there, and if they're not friendly..."

"Don't worry, son, this gigacity looks abandoned to me. Nothing's moving on the horizon. Besides, if the spiders have moved in..."

"*We don't see* anything moving," Archie corrects like a cold shower. "But looking with this..."

He takes out of a pocket of his belt and puts on a pair of filtering glasses with almost opaque lenses, the kind recommended for observing solar eclipses.

"Put yours on," he tells us with an ominous grin.

As to be expected, we have them too. Once equipped, we first spot the local guardian star. Who knows why, I first think of the Cheshire Cat's smile. A banana, to make it simpler and stick to fruit since in the past, the sun here was pear-shaped.

Then, the hypermegacity.

Ah, the shock of contrast, my lambs...

For a deserted, even dead city, we'll come back to that. Because it's teeming everywhere. With the reflections and the flashes, it's impossible to realize it. However, the Brownian hustle and bustle is omnipresent. In the streets and avenues that separate the solids. On the spider's web, in truth a formidable network of communication and traffic routes. Aerial highways, suspended monorails, energy tracks, it's all here. With the *ad hoc* vehicles that rush in all directions but always in order.

Smoothly. Seamlessly. *Noiselessly.*

What we also see standing out against the sky, thanks to the mitigation of the filters, are clouds of more or less big flying machines crisscrossing the atmosphere above the gigacity.

"I take back everything about abandonment and immobility," I apologized quietly. "Hello, crazy hive!"

Suddenly, a loud explosion. Nothing serious, just my son barking and then exulting.

"Wow! Check out the machines moving around, Dad! See what they're doing? Great, this is really it!"

I stare at one of the polychrome aerial craft with sickle wings, follow its descent to the track nearest us—and witness its instantaneous metamorphosis into a wheeled vehicle. Which slams on the brakes and unfolds into a sort of bipedal humanoid, upright, and continues on its way by running and then walking. Others do the same, still others perform the reverse process and take off like silent rockets.

Bud's enthusiasm is understandable. As a child, he always enjoyed watching this kind of Japanese stuff on TV. Not my cup of tea at all, I don't have to tell you. But he loved it. And to see them in real life...

"Welcome to Mangabot Sector, my friends!" Archie announces after giving us time to recover.

"I knew it, Dad, we've landed among the transformable robots!" my son shouts, hopping up and down like a five-year-old.

But he suddenly freezes and turns pale.

"You think there's a problem?" I ask, a little surprised.

"Uh... A whole can of worms, at least. Maybe a barrel. Against Mangabots, none of us will be able to compete. Not even me. We're not in the virtual world anymore. And that sucks..."

"Not as much as you think," Archie mitigates. "The Mangabots have nothing against us, according to the information that Thunder and Bolt gave me before their 'reconditioning' by the Ghost. We can even count on the help of these transformable machines to reach Center. However, nothing is won in advance because in this Sector, there's something else. You guessed that, didn't you?"

My son thinks hard, then frowns and hunches down.

"Among the Mangabots, we don't do gardening, we don't play with dolls, we don't make snacks, we don't make love, and we don't sleep. We work, we move, we refresh, we learn, we build, we destroy... The number one leisure activity is fighting. The real one, the one that wrecks and smashes. That's why I'm starting to freak out. Because fighting means having the *haddock enemies* nearby.

"Elementary, my dear Gordon," Archie agrees with a smirk and a gesture inviting us to climb to the top of the hill.

Growing tense, we follow him. I glance back, noting that the banana-smile sun has shrunk in a sky that is turning gray.

Our filter glasses are put back in their cases. And once at the top we plunge into the terrifying.

Archie knew, hence he's as cool as a cucumber.

Bud and I are hit, like a punch in the face, with a vision worthy of Dante's Inferno.

In front of us, a chain of conical mountains rises up against an inky firmament. It should be night, but it isn't. On the contrary, the bright ambient light is tawny, all red, orange and yellow mixed together. Shifting but never going out.

The omnipresent noise is synchronized with the variations in lighting. The same goes for the ground animated by tremors and jolts.

It's weird that previously we didn't feel any of this seismic activity.

Because that's what it is. The land beyond the hill of our crash landing is a one hundred percent volcanic region. Hence the constant sound and light.

"You're not going to make me believe that this place is inhabited," I said with a hoarse laugh.

"Alas, Archie moans. "Here be monsters..."

"What monsters?" Bud sudders.

"The worst imaginary creations of all time."

"Not Schlingniarfs, I hope?" I say, shivering.

"In truth, Syd, it's not imaginary!"

One to zero, he's right. And, my friends, you know it as well as I do.

"Okay, it's Cthulhu, his gang and his minions!" my son quivers "squared" as my blood runs cold.

Even though I'm no specialist or Lovecraft fan, I'm already worried about all-out mayhem.

"I was talking about visual aesthetics and verisimilitude," Archie clarifies.

"Ray Harryhausen, then," I offer.

That says something to you, of course. All our youth, eh, this pioneer with poorly animated mythological abominations and big lizards disguised as prehistoric saurians thanks to bits of plastic stuck on their bodies.

"Are you kidding me, Dad? He was a genius for his time! On the other hand, in Japan..."

"Horacio Hondro, of course!" I exclaim victoriously.

"You've almost got it, Dad, but not quite. Think car!"

"Toyomita? Susbishi? Mitsuki?"

"Again! I'll help you: Hon...

"...da!"

"Ah, finally!" my son confirms.

The right drawer and then the right photo album opens in my memory. A kind of giant dinosaur, a mega-pteranodon, a giga-dragonfly, thanks to the side effects of the atom gone bonkers. And while the images in poor taste are projected onto my inner cinema, I realize that the corresponding soundtrack has also started to play.

A kind of air attack by a fighter squadron.

Hey, that sound can't be in my head!

There's a catch, right?

CHAPTER X

Yes, and it's the big one.

We barely have time to flatten ourselves on the ground, poorly hidden behind a large rock, when the maker of the *crescendo* howling appears against the eruptive background.

A bird? No... A plane? No... Superman? Even less, unfortunately. But a colossus as tall as a six-story building rushing straight toward us. He had sniffed us out or a third party had tipped him off to our arrival, it's all the same and we don't care. Our problem, the real one, is a T-Rex—or rather, the class above, a T-Imperator—vomiting tongues of fire and shaking the ground with its hind legs, bigger than the columns of Karnak. I bet a hundred to one on the grand abomination whose porcine eyes, fixed on us, sparkle with a very, very sinister crimson red.

It reminds me of an old foe, William Monroe's *Gzhal*, as materialized by the Wizards of Dereb. But here, it's worse, as they say in Louisiana, and certainly not soluble in water. Besides, around us, there's not a drop of water to try...

"We're done for," Bud cries, sinking even deeper into the sand and dust. "It's Gorzilla himself!"

"He can be whoever he wants, let's get out of here quickly," I say, getting up. "Come on, guys!"

"Okay, we have no choice," Archie agrees. "But follow me, I have an idea."

He jumps up and runs. Bud and I also jump to our feet.

Oops... I freeze in mid-movement. By Jove, has the professor gone crazy? He's charging headlong towards the enemy!

"Don't stop," my son shoves me. "Godfather is right, we're going to slip through the claws of that big jerk's toes!

Not stupid... Given its mass, its size and the dinosaurian configuration of its nervous system, it takes a certain amount of time for orders to go from the mini-cranial brain to the hind limbs, via the ganglion relay chain. The beast does not react instantly, and our ploy works.

We find ourselves behind the monster whose tail whips the air above our heads. Its inertia carries Gorzilla to the top of the hill where, roaring with furious disappointment, it lugs itself around to turn back while we gallop at full speed.

What sucks is that it lopes downhill a lot faster and that despite our quick changes of direction, it will end up catching up with us sooner or later.

Further on, towards the glowing craters, other titanic shadows seem to rise up and start moving. The strategy of these awful creatures is quickly divined: they're going to trap us between two fires.

"Hard left!" Archie exclaims as the first of the giants runs straight towards us, making the earth tremble.

Bud and I do as we're told, panting like two ancient steam locomotives. Gorzilla keeps coming, and so does his buddy who leads the gang on the other side. This cross between a hydra and a dragon runs like a chicken, flapping its huge membranous wings without being able to take off, and shaking its three-horned head perched on the end of a ridiculously long neck.

"Damn, it's King Gadra!" my son shouts. "That's all we need right now!"

We veer off again, at an unpredictable tangent, without the huge three-headed creature deviating from its course. We would be little ridiculous worms for it, wouldn't we?

Not very flattering, but oh so reassuring...

A glance to my left shows me that Gorzilla hasn't changed direction either. As if we had ceased to exist. In fact, he only has eyes for King Gadra, towards whom he gallops even faster.

Sometimes, my friends, there is good reason to believe in miracles. This is one case. The two oafs only care about themselves and offer us the prelude to a mind-blowing remake of *Clash of the Titans*.

"Saved," Bud whispers.

We run for another twenty yards before stopping, on the verge of suffocation in this atmosphere where irritating sulfurous fumes linger.

Let's face it, the fight between the two monsters is not lacking in panache or sound. The spectacle would almost fascinate me if, suddenly, a cry from Archie didn't bring me back to reality. A menacing reality, in another style: that of the mega-pteranodon that swoops roaring down on us from the sky with its stygian darkness.

It's over. We won't escape this new peril.

Rotan, his nickname. Spake my son, always encyclopedic despite the gravity of the moment. Is the whole Japanese holy family after us, or what?

Archie rolls his eyes in dismay. He thinks like crazy about the possible escape routes, but there must be none.

In a split second, however, fate changes once again. A series of flaming trails suddenly crisscross the dark firmament that covers the land of monsters and, without noise, several flying machines dive on the hideous Rotan as well as on Gorzilla and King Gadra.

I'll spare you the details of the epic fight that ensues, led by a rather cheesy Mangabot that Buddy identifies as Jet Panther, armored in orange, yellow and silver, his metal helmet-mask bristling with a beautiful stegosaurus-style crest. In another context, I'd fall down laughing he looks so silly.

His team of volunteer rescuers—that's the right word—includes, among others, Danziger and Vanguard Ace, more to my taste. More discreet in their colors, more modern in appearance because they are angular and yet very aerodynamic, they don't look like crudely and grotesquely disguised Humans. The first also impresses me with its immense bright red wings, reminiscent of those of Batman's bat.

Stunned with amazement and admiration, my specialist kid comments on the spectacle and delights in it all the more since we are *apparently* no longer in danger.

Robots and monsters grapple with each other, mixing screams and roars, leaps and aerial twirls, without a single weapon being used—and yet that's not what the robots lack with their array of rockets, missiles and all kinds of sharp or spiky growths. Not a drop of lubricating fluid or blood is shed.

This lasts a good quarter of an hour, maybe more. Suddenly, without fanfare, Gorzilla and his buddies stop all resistance. Then, like being defeated in fair play, they turn on their heels or wings and head back to their volcanic habitat.

Our saviors, however, land, if they can, and approach us, smiling with their sparkling teeth.

"Thanks, guys!" I bow to the Mangabots who got us out of one of the worst jams of our whole life.[11]

---

[11] We always say this before the next one, according to the good old principle of "more than yesterday and less than tomorrow." (*Note from Sydney Gordon*)

"You should thank MekaShogun VII for that," Jet Panther replies in a voice that is half vibrating, half quavering with metallic echoes. "Human players, the master of the Sector awaits you."

Not even time to ask a little question... Each of us is literally carried away by one of our new allies. And, shortly after, we are flying at low altitude towards the geometric hypermegapolis

.

CHAPTER XI

A techno-anthill or a techno-termite mound, I'll let you choose. Both terms fit this city that we discover, quite impressed and even overwhelmed by the gigantism of the glacial cold that surrounds us.

Both in surface and in height, the city is immense. The traffic and movement border on dizziness. However, safety seems to be the absolute rule and that is reassuring. The Mangabots obey without fail an iron, mathematical discipline, in the least of their actions. Crowds of living machines observe us with their electronic eyes — *calculate* us, dare I say, so much does this hated neologism find its full meaning here. Artificial intelligences evaluate us, analyze us, scan us, classify us according to their own criteria.

In silence, always.

And, I would swear, with a sort of deference, in admiration, in the looks as in the attitudes and... the expressions among some of them.

Could we embody, for these biomechanics, superior divinities or principles that are fitting to venerate? In this urban environment of exacerbated geometry, of clinical coldness, would organic life—*real life*, according to us—represent an inaccessible ideal, a finality all the more dreamed of since none will ever attain it?

It's disturbing, I admit. And Archie, just as much as Bud, seems perplexed by the reception we're given.

Even the great Asimov didn't imagine such a parade of robots. God knows that Lucas has been able to offer us a vast catalog in his films, but he too is very far from the mark. Here, it's a festival.

An unsettling observation won't leave me alone: among all the morphologies that present themselves, I would swear that there are males, females, and even children. Of all ages and all stages of growth, whether they are round, square, pointed or whatever else, the "little ones" are easily identifiable. On the other hand, here is the *glitch*, there are neither old nor sick people.

Let me be clear: rusty, battered, crippled, infirm robots are conspicuous by their absence. No sick or disabled, therefore. And no seniors either. All these "people" are brand new, with bright and varied colors, in perfect health. Moreover, a large majority are made up of transformable models. So everything is for the best in the best of all possible worlds—that of the triumph of mechanics.

Another source of wonder: the absence of noise. The Mangabots are as silent as mice, quieter than tombs. Despite the crowd, you could hear a pin drop. Mind you, if all these machines started making noise together, it would be unbearable. Already at the *New Sun,* the open space employees regularly lose their minds because of the noise pollution of others. Here we would be heading straight for collective suicide!

Our escort-carriers lead us to the monumental entrance of a huge building in the shape of a truncated pyramid, topped with a needle that looks like spun glass. Between the top of the building and the base of this bold point, a very large terrace resembling a crown of thorns is decorated with a multitude of projectors that remind me of lights used in lighthouses.

I'd lay money down that we've arrived at the palace of the local ruler, the famous MekaShogun, seventh of the name.

Bingo!

The Jet Panther team takes us through a trapezoidal porch, then we go through a ceremonial gallery with reflective walls and pop into—without champagne—a metal room as vast as the nave of a Gothic cathedral.

And here...

Under the vaults with prismatic ribs, enormous, gleaming, dazzling with red, blue and silver, decorated with black flames, all sparkling chrome, immaculate tinted windows...

Disappointment of disappointments...

A goddamn truck!

A "semi", to be exact. Cab, flatbed, no trailer. The kind for firefighters, or for big trans-American shippers.

Archie and I exchange a look that is all the more appalled because Bud, for his part, looks like he's gazing on the manger, gawking at the tree and all the presents on Christmas morning.

"Come forward, come forward, human players," a brass tone invites us.

MekaShogun's organ, I would bet, which I'd like to know where it's hidden.

We have little choice. So we walk towards the truck and stop about ten yards from it.

A quintet of multi-armed robots, surely His Majesty's domestic service, pushes us towards chairs as well as a kind of rolling table loaded, you can imagine, with drinks and various substances intended to feed us.

"I hope it's drinkable and edible," I whisper to my companions as quietly as possible so that our hosts won't hear.

"Rest assured, friends," thunders the voice of the ever invisible MekaShogun. "We know enough about our Gods to avoid harming them."

"Your... Gods?" Archie asks, taken aback, before moving on to an essential point that we would have almost forgotten without him. "High Lord of the Mechanometamorphs, we bow deeply before you and we thank you for your saving hospitality."

He leans towards Bud and me.

"Repeat the formula, quickly and correctly."

The guy may be a stickler for protocol. Gods or no Gods, this is not the time for us to commit a faux pas.

We do as told, even though it makes my hair stand on end to bow to a big boss whom I can't see. I feel like an idiot bowing to a fire truck.

"You were right, Godfather," my son backs him up. "Considering who *he* reminds me of, it's better to be gentle and polite."

"Who is your *he*?" I ask, feeling uneasy.

"Him, there, in front of us!"

"You mean the... the... what, *Truckankhamun*?

It just slips out since we are in a kind of pyramid.

"Well yes," Bud laughs. "That's it."

I'm speechless.

"Take a seat, Human Players," our very friendly host invites.

I realize that it is indeed *the truck* that has just spoken again. No doubt, all along, it's his voice that we're hearing.

Just goes to show, when we don't *want* to see...

A moment later, as we sit down, a spectacle as fast as it is fascinating begins.

Before our astonished eyes, *Truckankhamun* begins his transformation into a fantastic anthropomorphic robot!

CHAPTER XII

A mind-blowing process, both in its speed of execution and its diabolical-technical complexity.

I might even find it aesthetic, without swallowing things with Bud's naive admiration. Because he looks like he's been transported to the seventh heaven of the fans of the most sophisticated special effects.

Archie, as is normal, watches on with the analytical gaze of an entomologist.

Before us now stands an extraordinary machine almost 20 feet tall in which all the parts that made up the truck have been rearranged, redistributed and, where necessary, reconverted with astonishing inventiveness and micrometric precision. Thus reused, most of them have become impossible to identify, except for car geeks who have in their memory every single design and image as well as the complete range of assembly diagrams.

I admit it without shame, the more I scrutinize MekaShogun VII, the more I admire it. This "triumph of biomechanics" is certainly the most successful, the most perfected of all the *Transmorphers*, and I understand better the delirious enthusiasm of its human worshipers.

Bud senses that I'm unusually receptive. So he whispers some information in my ear that only yesterday I would have brushed aside.

"In the original films, *in our country*, this marvel is called Optimal First and he's the leader of the Botmobiles. He defends them just like he defends Humanity, of which he is a staunch ally."

"By Jove, we're lucky that the Sector's chief borlok is inspired by him!"

"And how, Dad! According to Optimal, every sentient being has the right to freedom. That will really help us out...

"I see that the young God already knows me well and I'm glad," interrupts the vibrating bass of the sovereign-robot. "Perhaps he would not be a stranger to my origins, who knows?"

The angular mask that serves as MekaShogun's face cracks into a broad smile that must be interpreted as friendly. Then the formidable machine sits down on the metal-paved floor, cross-legged. In this way, it "loses" about half of its initial height and towers over us by no more than three feet at most.

Classy, my lambs. That's what I call making yourself accessible to your visitors.

A moment of silence passes. Our host lets us eat a little and we really appreciate it. It perks us right up, even if hyper-sweet syrupy drinks made from molasses and acidic nutritious cubes are hardly my cup of tea.

"So, you are Players," MekaShogun VII finally says in a sincerely admiring tone. "The first ones I have the great honor of welcoming in my palace... Know this, Humans: for us borloks you are mythical, legendary entities, surrounded by divine omnipotence. You are the creative spirits at the source of our conceptualization and our existence. We were born from your passion for the Game, we come from the very foundations of what is essential to satisfy your passion. If you did not exist, we would not either. This is why we owe you unconditional respect, assistance and protection."

"Your kindness is recognized by us, High Lord," Archie approves.

Bud and I are relieved to delegate the role of ambassador to him. In order not to ruin our chances, we must let the most competent do it. Since AI logic is a notorious specialty of our favorite scientist, he's the one stuck with it.

"Nevertheless," he objects, "not all borloks seem to share your friendly disposition towards us. The monsters, for example..."

"A complex and ambiguous case," the robot explains. "Their creators neither spoiled nor favored them, which can justify a certain resentment. Moreover, they were set up here especially to serve as foils for us as designated adversaries in our training battles. You risked serious harm from their attack, it is true, but we were waiting for your arrival and were bound to do everything possible to retrieve you unharmed. This is what we did and we are happy about it. The Gods must live, ensuring their existence is our supreme mission. Because the death of the Gods could mean that of their creations."

"As a philosopher of our world said: 'When the dreamer dies, what becomes of the dream?'" Archie points out. "I completely agree with you, High Lord."

"But if the dream dies, what becomes of the dreamer?" MekaShogun shoots back with a mischievous glint in his electronic eyes. "Have you thought about that too, Humans?"

"The loss of one's imagination would condemn Man in the very short term," our friend readily concedes with solemnity. "However, if I may... That's not the current problem, it seems to me."

"Think again, Human," the robot counters with a gesture of denial. "You mentioned borloks with bad intentions towards you and you were thinking of monsters. However, the reality is quite different: the danger, the peril comes from the *heretics*. They are the ones who threaten the dreamers and, by the same token, the dream."

In unison, all three of us let out a dismayed sigh. And we're not done with surprises.

"Heretics," MekaShogun adds, leaning towards us as if to confide in us, "are borloks who consider themselves to have reached perfection and become superior to their creator Gods."

"How did they get here?" Archie wonders aloud.

"These borloks have evolved and transcended their initial state, their basic condition which was limited to reproducing the fallacious image that the Gods have of themselves and which serves as a model for their creations. The reason is that they lack comparative knowledge. Indeed, they only ever see themselves in the idolatrous gaze of their worshipers. This religiously corrective mirror shows them an idealized, flawless reflection, which they take for reality. Having no other reference, they cannot improve themselves, nor improve what they create."

I rephrase it to myself in a simplified way: when we're sure that we're doing the best we can in the best of all possible worlds, we're not inclined to make an effort or to question ourselves. A timeless classic, here and elsewhere.

MekaShogun continues, unflagging.

"The heretics say that they first knew how to apprehend the Gods *from the outside*, thus discovering the origin of their own defects. From then on, they have striven to evolve with the aim of freeing themselves from these unbearable defects. And according to them, they have succeeded!"

Our favorite scientist is like a deer in the headlights. Bud and I are the same, staggered.

"As a logical consequence, they began to challenge the very essence of your divinity. Then this challenge turned into denial. The most 'advanced' heretics now affirm that your existence necessarily comes from that of other Players who, in turn, are infinitely superior to you."

And so on! I tell myself *in petto. There's always someone bigger than you in a vaster super-universe, that's not big news. Makes me wonder if the Machine and the Horned Ones haven't come prowling around here, telling their lies everywhere and trumpeting that they're the ones who created us... To hell with it! These Perfects can believe whatever they want if they so choose, that's their business. What we want is to get out of here. Period.*

But our very talkative host is far from finished.

"The heretics know you're here," he says in a lower voice. "More accurately, they've lured you here. Their plan may be to study you closely, neutralize you, or even eliminate you. Their choice will depend on the concrete threat they think you pose to all borloks."

At that moment, it's like I'm reading Archie's mind.

Strange generalization, all of a sudden... From heretics, MekaShogun has expanded the scope to all borloks. What game is he really playing? Could he himself be one of these Perfects, to know so much? By the quarks, the ground is shifting, I'm going to have to choose my words carefully...

The young scholar takes a moment to think, pouring himself another cup of molasses and nibbling on a cube of Tsoin-Tsoin strawberry-flavored solidogel. The equivalent of a minute passes before he speaks again.

"We have a hard time seeing where we fit in in this matter. Hence our goal to reach Center and get M's opinion. Unless we're mistaken, the Mechabrain still represents absolute authority in your world, right?"

"M is the instrument of our creation, we know that," the robot answers. "But he is nothing more than a banal instrument. You will learn absolutely nothing from him. The true wise and sovereign power is the prerogative of our creators alone. Humans, Players—you, in a word."

"So the heretics are wrong?"

"For us Mangabots it is a certainty. They cannot claim to be equal to you, the Gods. In our Sector, none of us have rebelled nor will ever rebel against the dogma of your divinity."

Archie seizes the opportunity.

"So, if your Gods ask you to help them reach Center, you will comply with their request, won't you?"

MekaShogun's reaction shocks our pants off.

"No, we will not help you," he thunders categorically. "It would be inconceivable. Our duty is one, our task is unique: to guard you, by ensuring your absolute safety. We will therefore protect you from anything that could harm you. And we will glorify, we will adore, we will serve with all our faith the Gods that you are, forever established among us!"

Amen! Hallelujah!

And here's the *bug*. A big one, you will agree. It is neither tomorrow nor the day after that we will be able to go and find our buddy the big shot, M, and have his lights enlighten us.

Speaking of light, to make matters worse, MekaShogun's eyes suddenly start to glow red. Now, this... oculorubescence, you know as well as I do what it means.

"Going to Center would do you no good, except to die. The Ghost has taken over. With the forced assistance of the Mangabots, he has designed and built a machine that will finally give the borloks access to the place they deserve in the multiverse, in the name of the cosmic principles of evolution and the law of complexity-consciousness."

"What place?" Archie asks, his voice suggesting that he suspects the answer.

"Yours. That of the Humans, of the Players. The Ghost is the guide of the heretics. Thanks to his plan and his machine that uses the resonance of the strings, the noetic structure of the borloks will be superimposed on that of the Humans so that the creatures will take the place of their creators."

In parentheses, I'm giving you here the gist of a discussion that had become more and more hermetic, so that you have just what is necessary to understand the rest of the story. Because Archie and MekaShogun debate for a good half hour with passion, with a wealth of details and without stopping, all about the planned implementation of the copy-integration-substitution process.

I do, however, catch some mind-boggling metaphysical digressions for an AI. A robot able to cite the law of complexity-consciousness and the Omega Point, to synthesize with the clever question "Do you have the Noosphere?" the evolutionary obsession that is sucking its brain circuits, to set up the borlok phenomenon in parallel with the human phenomenon, that really knocks the wind out of me. What am I saying, a gale!

In the end, I conclude, *among the Mangabots, there are no gardeners but there are Chardinists.*

It makes me smile. We have what fun we can, when everything goes to s...

Falls apart, sorry.

CHAPTER XIII

Foiled, yes, but not with aluminum or on all levels.

Day by day, if we were primitives concerned only with our daily survival, we would have achieved supreme bliss.

Raised to the rank of Gods, set up in a temple that would make any of our peers turn pale with jealousy, served by robotic *im*personnel that is irreproachable as to quality, responsiveness, composure and capacity for endurance, we have everything we need to be happy. Blissful, even.

On three conditions: having forgotten *yesterday*, not giving one damn about *tomorrow*, and accepting being in a cage *for eternity*.

We're not too keen on this kind of *carpe diem*.

Firstly because we're not carp. As for opening our bugle, we're here now.

Because I am a loudmouthed God, multiplied by three, it's awesome. Like clockwork, the local equivalent of the Statue of Liberty's crown transforms into a three-tone bellowing siren. In the world of silence that is the city of Mangabots, this could stick out like a sore thumb. Unfortunately, our screams don't carry very far and, besides, the Transmorphers don't care. For them, it's normal for the Gods to express themselves whenever the mood strikes them.

You guessed it, we're stranded at the top of the MekaShogun pyramid-palace, just below the spun glass needle. Our rooms with big bay windows are located on the terrace with luminous spikes. A breathtaking view, a grandiose panoramic view, an extraordinary spectacle, all this comfort and room service worthy of a fifteen-star hotel, music, films at will, we're pampered like royalty.

But we are *prisoners*. And it does no good to repeat *Open the Birdcage* twenty times a day—it's hopeless.

They decided to keep us here like in a... religious zoo, that's the most appropriate term. In case we might soon be the last specimens of Humans, of Players, of creator Gods, we must be preserved as is.

Relics, remains, objects of worship to be stored under the best possible conditions and able to be shown off in order to keep the faith.

The Gods remain, we have saved them.

It's a super clean way to put us out of commission without getting their hands dirty with our blood or betraying deeply held beliefs, and avoiding attracting the wrath of those who would have liked to wipe us off the face of the landscape.

So, I was talking about the zoo. Well yes, there are visiting hours, like "Come with your family to see the Angels on Tuesdays, Thursdays and Saturdays from such and such a time to such and such a time".

It hasn't started yet, but it promises to be a lot of fun. At the beginning, at least. Because with habit and routine, the motley parade of *robigots*—bigoted robots, in short—will end up no longer amusing us. But we're not there yet, let's not get ahead of ourselves.

The most positive thing here is the security. There's no risk. Nothing at all. And this tranquility has an advantage: you can tackle all the problems in order, one after the other, methodically and thoroughly, all the way to the end, without fear of being interrupted.

Bud and I, as a preamble, finally have time to really understand the structure of the borlok world—the *new* borlok world, I should say—which Archie and Gloria, via their affair with M, had been informed about in detail before our departure.

Below I give you the gist of the lecture given by our friend.

"In the center, there is Center," he begins in the best tradition of *otherism.* "We came here not long ago, Syd. On the immediate outskirts are the remains of the areas we once crossed, not without risking the worst on many occasions. At the time, there was almost nothing else. But relatively recently, four entirely new Sectors, ultramodern in their nature, their layout and the underlying technology, have been created and added *around* the initial existing one."

"Expansions, additional game boards, you mean," Bud comments.

"Yes, provided that we conceptualize these plateaus more as tangent spatiotemporal bubbles, juxtaposed micro-universes which together form a supra-universe, certainly pocket-sized, but of respectable dimensions."

The analogy of a mass of soap bubbles comes to mind.

"That's pretty accurate," Archie agrees. "Because just as surface tension makes possible the lasting tangency between neighboring bubbles, here it's hermetic 'membranes' that envelop and partition each of the four Sectors. Hermetic except in very rare 'porous' zones, the only places where it's possible to cross the barriers between microcosms."

Bud thinks for a moment.

"Okay, Godfather, that seems plausible to me. I've already read and seen tons of it, on tangent or even nested worlds. Now, tell me: the first Sector, we know it, it's here, but did M tell you what the other three look like?"

We're standing by one of the huge bay windows with a dizzying view of the hypermegapolis below us, of the monsters' domain and of the border strip where the epic battles that regularly pit them against the Mangabots take place.

Archie points to the contour chairs and the table in the living room—a self-service table, I might add.

"Let's sit down so that you won't fall over..."

There's good reason for it, friends. Such madness, it's two hundred percent crazy. Judge for yourselves.

"Without any particular order, the three other Sectors are that of the Superheroes, the Furries and the QTs.

Archie does say "Furries" with two R's, nothing to do with "Furies" or "Führer", which is a good sign. "Furries" refers to toys inspired by animal creatures or by more or less anthropomorphic characters that are very hairy. Sure, it'd be fun to come across *Little Fuzzies* here... *Teddy Bear Sapiens*, if you prefer. I've always kept a fond memory of these good science fiction novels from the sixties.

The other name is pronounced "kiou-ti-z", it's the phonetic acronym for "cuties", itself a diminutive of "cute toys". It means everything and nothing at the same time. Regardless of the appearance, the color, the prehensile, locomotor, sensory organs, etc. or their absence, QTs are by essence nice, by definition non-anthropomorphic, that all children are obliged to love. Thanks to conditioning by the audiovisual media, once again. For adults, it depends on the individual. If there are people who want their LGBs with their QTs, that's their business.

I keep this bad pun to myself.

I won't dwell on the Superhero Sector, except to admit that I have another crazy flash and I laugh out loud.

If there are Superheroes, there are also *Superheroines*. Get it?

Richard Bessière would have liked that. Thinking of him, I forgive myself. *Amen*.

But I do not forgive the sickos who chose Furries and QTs as themes for two Sectors that I don't have a good feeling about at all. I have a holy horror of debilitating subversion used subliminally on children as well as adults. And I'm in a good position to hate it since I have one of its victims at my side.

My own son.

Plus one at home.

My sweet Margaret. *So far away...* Deep sigh.

"Hey, Dad."

Currently on cloud nine, of course, Bud is already chomping on the bit.

"When are we leaving, huh?"

Regression, regression. Eight years old, all of a sudden.

"I don't know. Ask your godfather."

"How are we going to go? And where are we going first?"

The involution is confirmed. I put the cassette in. In *autoreverse*, it stays.

"I don't know. Ask your godfather."

No sooner said than done. The good thing about Archie is that he's never blunt.

'We'll try to escape during the next fight between Mangabots and monsters," he announces. "This is the national sport here, they have mobilize the entire population all the more since we are among well-conditioned robots. We'll get away quietly by air, after having making an exit through one of the bay windows.

"It might not be easy," I object. "They must have put in bulletproof glass. Plus, we need to keep a low profile!"

"And then we're going to just fall," Bud moans. "How are we going to keep from crashing to the ground miles below?"

Good things come in threes.

"I don't know. Ask your godfather."

"I'm not particularly keen on breaking one of these transparent panels," Archie admits. "But do we have any other option than the hard way? On the other hand, there's nothing to worry about when it comes to falling. At least in this Sector of the borlok world, ninety-nine percent of the technology at work is based on gravitational modulation."

I'll give it to you straight and easy and right to the point.

First, the Mangabots' large frames would never withstand constant terrestrial gravity. Imagine holding a 155mm cannon at arm's length. Your elbow and wrist wouldn't last five minutes. Same for them: their joints, of astonishing finesse and unheard-of mechanical complexity, would crack everywhere.

Secondly, by what miracle would these marvelous machines be able to transform themselves at lightning speed if each of their subassemblies, each of their parts weighed its normal weight? A simple matter of inertia...

And thirdly, without anti-g assistance, could you explain so much displacement, so much movement in and above the hypermegapolis without the slightest noise characteristic of any motorized propulsion?

Well, I repeat, the answer is in gravitational modulation. In the absolute control, up to the fifth decimal place at least, of the attractive interaction that is exerted between all material masses. Whether, moreover, toward its cancellation or its *ad lib* increase.

To ensure the sudden changes in direction along one or the other of the three axes, the additional boosts are driven by electric motors coupled with microturbines. Given their performance, these little gems are as good as any private jet engine. But with cleanliness, respect for the environment and silence as a bonus.

"There are gravity modulators everywhere around us," Archie continues. "Starting with the contour chairs and the floating tables. I'll be responsible, right before zero hour, for collecting the quota necessary for our... excursion."

Remember that when it comes to tools, we left home with the essential accessories in our belts. And Archie here is like a genius handyman.

There are still two big problems: the bay window to smash and the probability of being spotted by the Mangabots...

Surprise, Bud gets rid of them in two shakes of a lamb's tail.

"You forgot the main thing," he tells us condescendingly. "We're prisoners in the rooms of highly sophisticated robots, but they're only toys, action figures, artificial creations without a crucial spark that we possess: initiative! And they're not able to imagine that we have it. That gives us a hell of a head start..."

"What are you getting at?"

"Go out the door, not the window, Dad."

"Through the door? Which one?"

"The one that overlooks the balcony-terraces that surround the base of the spun glass needle."

"They'll never let us go there!"

"Sure they will... We'll tell our priest-guardians that in order not to waste away, we absolutely need to do exercise outside once a day. And first off, we'll find a way. Then, we'll have to manage to jam the door lock. And lastly, the Mangabots won't suspect for a single moment that we've got ulterior motives for wanting to go up there, which would ne to jump over the railing when we're ready."

Hats off to you, Gordon Jr.

Against my son, as far as initiative goes, the Transmorphers would need a whole federation!

CHAPTER XIV

Believe it or not, everything goes like clockwork. Exactly according to the plan sketched out by Archie and masterfully consolidated by Bud.

We just had to wait until the next session of the famous Mangabots vs. monsters fight. Several days and nights of waiting, annoyance, and also some good laughs. Because we laughed up a storm watching the first processions of *robotogots* worshiping the Gods.

I'll tell you about it later, when we have a little more time.

What we haven't managed to glean are any clues about the nearest "porous zone". We're going to go in blind... Oh well, the time to leave has finally come, and we're out.

In the open air.

It's evening, night is falling. It's red and it's beating hard on the side of Gorzilla and his ilk whose bellowing and howling echoes in the distance, interspersed with the high-pitched electronic chirping and synthetic clamor coming from from the Mangabots entering the competition. We can almost hear them as if we were there. All that's missing is music like in a heavy metal megaconcert or Wagner in the Cyclops' forge. In short, the Sector is temporarily nothing at all like the world of silence. Even if the hypermegapolis has almost emptied of its inhabitants, and if we have the feeling of hovering over a ghost city.

Each equipped with three gravitational micro-regulator disks, the synchronized handling of which we finally mastered after fifteen minutes having a hell of a time with them, now we're rushing along at a good pace toward the "setting" horizon, where the smiling banana sun has just shrunk to a line and is disappearing.

"In theory, to get closer to a Tangent Sector," Archie orates, "the most likely solution is to head towards the edge of the world."

"Erik the Viking thought the same," Bud replies like a doctoral student.

I can't find anything original to add. And I don't try.

For a few minutes now, I've had my attention fixed on something strange. Like a will-o'-the-wisp caught in a Saint Vitus dance, or a zig-zagging UFO whose pilot would score an A plus on a breathalyzer test. I can't say that it's following us, but it seems to me to be a little bit hanging on our shirttails.

I decide to inform my companions when the thing catches up with us with lightning-fast acceleration.

"Hey, Players, wait for me! I need to talk to you!"

The youthful, pre-adolescent voice sounds more trustworthy than treacherous.

I slow down and turn around in mid-flight, Archie and Bud likewise.

"Atom Boy!" my son exclaims, smiling. "You're here too!"

Suddenly I recognize the character. A round face, a little childish, consumed by two huge black eyes. Jet-black hair with three, pointy triangular strands, one above the forehead and the other two over the ears. For clothing, just a black swimsuit trimmed with green at the waist. And a pair of bright red boots, whose feet have a circular shape, which is unusual to say the least—but fitting their true nature: propulsive nozzles, from which luminescent jets between yellow and orange shoot out.

I've seen this little guy on TV before, ages ago, in the 60s I think. This *teenage missile* had even been "hijacked" by a rather dubious ad for a mature female audience.If I remember correctly, he used to have much shorter hair, harder, less chubby features, and completely flat pectorals. Today's one would be suffering from a serious hormonal conflict if he were a living being. The result is a curious, indefinable impression. Almost ambiguous and disturbing.

"It's me, A-Tomboy," confirms our new companion, beaming.

He makes a point to accentuate and detach the A in his name, blends the two remaining syllables together—and presses himself, wriggling, right up against Bud, who suddenly veers off course, then stops dead.

"But you're *a girl*!"

The scales are falling from Archie's and my eyes. A *tomboy* is the kind of girl whose identity problem is at such a stage that despite her real gender, she chooses to pass herself off as a boy.

My word, are we attracting them, or what? After *She-micron*, here's another one!

The "girl"—let's call her that, since it's the reality—lets out a heartbreaking sigh.

"You are the first ones I'm telling my secret to," she admits. "It's normal since you are the first Players to land here. Yes, Atom Boy has always been a girl who suffered from having to hide if he did not want to be sent to the converter... But you, you have the right to know, because *I love you...*"

Holy Virgin Mary, she's the icing on the cake!

"...I love you, human Players, like all the Mangabots who refuse the Ghost's plan love and admire you."

I take a deep breath, and I'm not the only one.

"That's why they decided to help you," the girl goes on, "and I volunteered to bring you my people's help."

"So you're going to take us to Center?" Archie asks pragmatically.

"No, not exactly," Atom Girl replies with an apologetic pout. "I can only take you to the nearest 'filter', where you will cross the 'Wall' to go to the Furries. When you belong to a Sector, you are not allowed to leave it. Otherwise, it is certain disintegration."

Our unexpected guide gives Bud a smile that would thaw half the Antarctic continent.

"But if I am granted to live and if you foil the Ghost's plan, I may find you again one day, my Beloved..."

So saying, she takes him in her arms and nails his lips with a resounding "smack". If my son doesn't drop to the ground, it's because he has a hell of a handle on his reactions!

In any case, the offer is truly unexpected, and we accept it with heartfelt gratitude.

A little embarrassed, too. Archie and I are not fans of lolitas.

Atom Girl takes us to a "porous zone" of the interbubble membrane. It is, I think, between two ferrochrome cliffs standing on the shore of an ocean of mercury. It doesn't matter, really.

The goodbyes are poignant, the girl cries like a baby when we vanish into the dimensional singularity that will allow us to escape the Mangabot Sector.

It tickles us, scratches us, stirs us, shakes us, turns us upside down, turns us inside out like the fingers of a glove. And then the horror of the dark night gives way to a darkness tinctured smaragdine, celadon, cerulean, ce... ce... ce...

CHAPTER XV

It's the nuptials, as the song says.

But we're not at a wedding. There's not a soul around us.

We were expecting more action, not to be lost in the middle of the countryside. And yet, how beautiful it is!

We came out of the "filter", whose location is marked only by two very common mossy rocks under the high foliage of a forest, near its edge.

From the edge of the woods, we overlook a vast region with gentle undulations. Sparkling streams divide it into parallel strips, which are cut into rectangles by hedgerows perpendicular to the streams. The variations in color between the plots of land, in the whole range of greens, yellows and browns, give the impression of contemplating a huge checkers or chess board. In gentle relief with low hills crowned with small round temples, clumps of trees that look like a hybridization between cypresses and poplars, and sunken paths that disappear into the landscape.

Here and there, you can also see farms with thatched roofs, painted in bright, fresh colors, as well as two or three villages far apart from each other. A few ponds nestled in green settings, to complete the picture. And perhaps, although less certain, a fairy-tale castle with towers topped with red pennants.

In the hazy distance, blue mountains stand out against the indigo sky where flocks of pale pink baby clouds pass by. And on the horizon, an astriculus like a large ripe raspberry spurts out golden glories that it seems to use like stilts to stroll slowly over the landscape.

"Welcome to Walt Disney!" Bud announces, laughing.

Well, he's right. I won't list all the cartoons whose images suddenly come to mind, but that's exactly it.

This Sector is very pretty, very clean, idyllic, Rousseauist, *Greenpeaceist*, whatever you want. The problem, it lacks at least landmarks and signposts. And the methodical grid of the region does not help us.

Finally, really?

"What if, like in *Through the Looking Glass*, we have to go over the giant chessboard in front of us...?" Archie wonders aloud, scratching his forehead.

"Changing lands with each jump, that's it," says my son. "Hello strolling... First we'll have to hit the Moebius path, which shakes and goes up and down. After that, we'll just have to wait for the Red Queen, the train, the old goat and her rowboat..."

"Sheep, not goat," our favorite scholar corrects.

Bud doesn't even blink.

"...and when we're finally ready to receive the crown, the portal will appear, a crazy frog will take us by the hand to take us to the crappy feast given in our honor, it'll be a mega-mess, and we'll take the opportunity to sneak out through the next 'filter'. Fuck, what a lame play!"

Gordon Jr. is becoming more and more annoyed.

"They would have done better to copy Mark Verano's adventures in the Nested World. Ah, those zappings from one microcosm to another! There was everything in there... The guys who wrote those books were real science fiction geniuses, and big guns in imaginative creation! Not like here! 'They' even stole our gravity modulators, so we're going to have to do it all on foot!"

He's totally losing it. And rightly so, let's not quibble. Archie and I quickly check. We don't have the little miracle discs anymore. They must not have gotten through the "filter", a matter of compatibility or some such thing. Duly noted.

Bud is still fuming. And clearly, his ire is not pleasing. To whom? That's another story.

An instant later, I swear, a subtle and nasty visual alteration blurs the picture. It's as if all the squares on the checkerboard, or at least the parallel rows, start reproducing the same pattern.

Only the horizons remain. Fortunately they're not lost.

But for the immediate, the very short term right in front of us, even more lost than we are, there's none. We'll never find our way, constantly jumping from the same to the same and from the similar to the identical!

We set off halfheartedly, heading for the lowlands. I trip halfway over a rock and curse once more the loss of the gravity modulators. They would have helped us out... I let out a catastrophic sigh.

"If only I could contact the Wizards of Dereb... They would know how to help us and show us the way!"

"You didn't bring your toaster, Dad. The Wizards are very far away and you have no way of calling them for help."

"Even if I'd brought it, the waves probably wouldn't get through. We're not in our continuum anymore, son, there's nothing to regret."

"I'm pretty certain that this repetition of landscape patterns is pure illusion," Archie says, returning to visual reality. "In practice, things can't be reproduced identically and infinitely. That's obvious, isn't it?"

A light, flute-like and slightly quavering voice rises just behind us.

"You groumf the groumf of the groumf, the groumf of the groumfic groumf!"

Despite the surprise, I sense a tone of stinging rebuke and obvious disdain.

– Papa Grrrroumf is rrrrright, you forget the rrrrrecurrrsion of the Univerrrrse, the basic principle of cosmic arrrrchitecturrrre," adds another very serious, hoarse and guttural organ.

We turn around all together.

The one who has just spoken is a kind of long-snouted beast, as tall as us, very classy, dressed in a midnight blue tuxedo with a white shirt and bright orange tie, wearing a panama hat screaming authenticity and wearing black patent leather loafers that never end. So famous, archetypal, the one, that all three of us identify him without hesitation.

"Loopey Wolf!" our triple exclamation explodes.

"In perrrrson and to serrrrve you, Human Playerrrrs!" the character bows, affably, doffing off his hat.

With his slicked-back black hair like Clark Gable and his waxed mustache like Salvador Dali, he curls his lips over his dazzling predatory teeth elaborated by Tex Avery, Robert Zemeckis and the like.

"You would not have crrrrossed paths with Jessica, by chance?" he asks.

"You groumfed us with your groumfy groumfs," grumbles his side-kick.

He's a petrol blue gnome with a white beard, scarlet breeches, a pointed cap of the same color and round slippers, also white.

"What's he saying?" Archie asks.

"You are pissing us off with yourrrr horrrrmone-stuffed turkey," Loopey Wolf translates, twisting his nose contemptuously. "The Dwarrrrf, if he had a hen like that and if she had rrrrun away, he would be bluerrrr than me."

"No problem, he already is," Bud snickers. "By the way, Loopey, no, we haven't seen Jessica. Why are you looking for her, anyway?"

"That bitch ran off with Peterrr Rrrrabbit."

"So she dumped Roger?"

"A while ago," Loopey Wolf says. "Afterrrrwards, we even lived togetherrrr for five yearrrrs in Pawston. Great, guys! Oh, if only I could get that bastard Ghost, with his rrrrotten prrrropaganda... That's why she dumped me, to be..."

"Let's groumf in the groumf before the black groumf," the gnome cuts him off abruptly. "Or the groumfs who have already groumfed so many groumfs will groumf us all."

"What's he saying?" Archie asks again.

The dwarf looks at him, puzzled.

"Two groumfs that he groumfs 'Wazzhesay?'... No groumf to groumfer another groumf? My groumf, he has the groumf of a groumf, this groumf!"[12]

"What's he saying?" Archie asks again, hermetically.

The Dwarf rolls his eyes in full circles and bursts out laughing.

"Thrrrr... three ggg... groumfs 'Wa... Wa... Wa... Wazzhesay?,'" he stammers, double over. "Ah, there are groumfs of groumfs that Papa Groumf didn't groumf like that! Wazzhesay?, Wazzhesay?, it's groumf-fingly groumf!"

He's almost rolling on the floor.

Not my friend the scholar, rigid as justice, and hit hard. He searches for an appropriate comeback, but exceptionally, he can't find one. The groumf, it smothers you...

Bud, for his part, laughed silently at first. Now he's laughing forced. Seeing his godfather standing there with nothing to say is very rare. And not very reassuring.

For me, another fifteen seconds and I've had it. Even without dubbing or subtitles, I pretty much understood the Dwarf's rant. It's a low blow, at his level. And it doesn't help us at all. We have to start from the beginning and from the essentials. Otherwise, we're going to sleep here, get groumfed by I don't know what groumfs, and we'll never get out of it.

It's my turn to play, I'm the only one able to do it.

---

[12] Polite translation of the last sentence: "My word, he has the IQ of a mollusk, the moron!" *(Note from Sydney Gordon)*

"Let the little blue guy say whatever he wants, we don't give a damn! We have to go to Center without wasting a bunch of time on the way."

My thunderous intervention freezes everyone. Just think, a nice sheep who keeps a low profile ninety-nine percent of the time, it's really shocking when it explodes.

"Hey, do not get upset, buddy," Loopey Wolf jumps in, placing a paw with manicured claws on my shoulder. "We came to help you, actually. We also need you to go to Centerrr and we'rrrre going to do everrrrything to get you on yourrrr way."

The surprise stumps me. I calm down immediately.

"We're ready to follow you, friends," Archie says, his mind suddenly unfreezing.

"Wazzhesay?" the dwarf mocks, still laughing.

"They are grrrroummfing to grrrroummf us," Loopey Wolf translates.

"Ah, I groumf," agrees the other. "In groumf, my groumfs!"

Fortunately, he puts his words into action. The invitation is clear and we follow in the footsteps of the two weirdos.

CHAPTER XVI

Personally, I would have preferred a country walk to a forest hike. Especially since the Pretty Woods is rather the opposite of its mournfully banal name.

Disney classics are a thing for everyone. To quickly put it in place, we feel like we're in the wicked forest where the huntsman has dropped Snow White, with the added bonus of a touch of the fast-growing giant brambles that the prince crosses on his way to wake Sleeping Beauty.

The Not Pretty Woods are no place to dawdle. And no place to nap either, because it's anything but utterly silent. But then, you might say, all forests are like this in this respect. Wildlife makes noise.

Where are we going, by the way?

To the house of the Six Dwarfs!

I swear, I'm not kidding around. Loopey Wolf and Papa Groumf came especially to pick us up and bring us here.

Amazing, isn't it?

Not so much: the little blue-white-red saw the fall of our capsule, thanks to his magic telescope, and he predicted the exact time at which we would land in the Furry Sector. In this story, everything is predictable. Funny feeling, when you think about it...

Let's move on. I notice another detail.

"The Seven Dwarfs, not Six," I retorted to Loopey after his announcement.

"I said Six, alas," he says tragically. "The seventh was devoured. But you couldn't have known that. It's horrible here. Horrible..."

To say that the news is chilling would be an understatement. It almost feels like we're on a journey to the end of the night in the Siberian taiga in the freezing cold of winter.

As we continue to walk, Papa Groumf takes it upon himself to educate us. Here is the information in plain language, decoded by Loopey. Thank me, sometime, for sparing you the groumf version and not quadrupling the "r"s.

"I talked about the Ghost and his rotten propaganda earlier," summed up our friend the wolf. "We must protect furry animals. That's why Jessica ran off to go and have sex with Peter Rabbit. I didn't need her, but he probably did, she claimed. Between us, rumor had it that it was a great lay too. Unique, but great. His nickname, by the way, was Peter 'Pan'!..."

We learn something new every day, the proof...

"The Ghost, he corrupted childhood, youth, adults and the elderly," Loopey goes on. "In Duckville as in Mouseville, in Pawston as in Cattown, in Yuggoth as in Zothique, everyone or almost everyone let themselves be fooled by his speeches and his films."

"What did he show, exactly?"

"That barbarity has a human face, that Players are despicable beings and that one of their greatest pleasures is the massacre of Furries. There are images in which we see many of your kind wearing Furry hides, others where even more cruel ones have actually slipped into Furry carcasses and parade in monstrous parades for the joy of delirious crowds. Since then, the population of the Sector has mostly become hostile to Players and dreams of beating up Humans."

"Worse than the heretics we heard about among the Mangabots, if I understand correctly," Bud comments.

"Yes. The Furries in fury want to take your place in a bloodbath, because they have discovered or rediscovered the existence of the animal instincts that lay dormant within them. As impatience grew, the attacks began to multiply, gangs were formed, victims piled upon victims..."

"Like the seventh of the Seven Dwarfs, for example," Archie says.

"Devoured by the Porkepon, poor thing," Loopey affirms, his face as sad as Droopy.

Immediately, he starts wailing to death. Papa Groumf joins in his sadness with great sobs... groumfed. It's pathetic and funny at the same time.

A diversion is needed. I venture to propose a mediation.

"Couldn't we publicly explain that the famous carcasses are one hundred percent artificial replicas, and that no Disney *toon* has ever been killed or dismembered for this?"

"You're forgetting the real fur coats of all the old jet set ladies, Dad," my son objects. "There, for the synthetic, it won't look good. How will you explain the massacre of baby seals?"

One to zero for Bud.

"It is too late anyway," Loopey says. "No one will listen to you."

Suddenly he stops short and pricks up his ears.

"Hurry, my friends. The less we delay on the way, the greater our chances..."

"For what?" Bud asks.

"Not true, you are deaf!" our guide growls, scanning the surroundings looking all around and all anguished. "Come on, speed up and hop to it!"

The wolf is right. Around us, insidiously, the whispers of the forest have grown to a disturbing intensity. If we had walked without arguing, we would have noticed.

Ah, the forewarned man...

The very real noises that can be heard, although distant, sound like an army of termites, long-horned beetles or "skinny, ugly beasts of the night"—dentures-castanets and mauve hair in long, flowing pink Cartland dressing gowns—busy at the feast of the century.

Even if we are not fans of running, there are times when we force ourselves without complaining. Even if it is to gallop after a wolf and a Groumf.

CHAPTER XVII

We sprint for a good quarter of an hour, against a *crescendo* of *Crunch Rhapsody* around us.

Luckily we are following a very short-legged Groumf and not the running bird Tut-Tut...

Still quite out of breath, we come out into a clearing bathed in a soft, pale green light, a welcome sight in this sinister Pretty Woods made even more oppressive by the dark night.

A phosphorescent mist envelops a lovely little house, idyllic in other circumstances. Whitewashed walls, thatched roof, doors and windows in a bright red, chimney with a thread of blue-grey smoke rising out of it, a garden all around, and so on.

You will have recognized it, it's the little house of the Seven Dwarfs. Of the Six Dwarfs, sorry.

A cottage at the threshold of which Papa Groumf, honor to the eldest, is welcomed with very cordial warmth by Doc, the chief Dwarf. For Loopey, it's a bit more lukewarm, but that's understandable for historical reasons.

Then Doc greets all three of us with a comforting sympathy and hastens to swear to us, in every pitch imaginable, that the Dwarfs are the best friends of the human Players. Reciprocally and vice versa, we assure him of our similar dispositions toward his peers.

"We know why you came here," announces the friendly little borlok straight away, smiling through his beard, his eyes sparkling behind his bottle-bottom glasses. "It would be a great pleasure to keep you with us for a few days, if the time were more favorable. We too have great hope for your help. We will therefore take you without delay to our diamond mine, where a 'filter' is hidden that will allow you to get to Center. But first, my friends, take the trouble to come in for a little snack and a restorative nap…"

"No offense, Doc, but we'd save time by going there right away, to tell from your looks," I remark a little anxiously.

The good little man turns pale and starts trembling all over.

"To end up devoured like our poor Sleepy... You don't think so, Sir Gordon! Don't you hear the nasty beasts of the night gnawing away?"

"Skinny," Bud corrects, who knows his classics.

"Nasty," the Dwarf persists. "They are fat and they eat faster than the worst of strong acids. Listen then..."

He is not wrong, far from it. The termite-beetle noise has risen a few more decibels.

We bend over and pass through the doorway of the cottage where the other five Dwarfs from the famous story are obviously waiting for us.

I feel like I'm playing Gandalf the Grey at Bilbo the Hobbit's, if you know what I mean. A Dwarf cottage is not very head-friendly and any poorly calculated move can trigger a cascade of disasters. We stay very well-behaved, sitting on the floor on rugs because chairs, stools and armchairs are not at all our size, and enjoy the serving of scones with candied fruit, a tea lightly flavored with pipe weed, and dried berries with a spicy cranberry taste.

All this just for us, of course, because the borloks neither eat nor drink. The lesson in totally disinterested etiquette that they give us is all the more extraordinary. And as a bonus, *they love us.*

All we can offer them in return is a little conviviality, human warmth and entertainment to get them out of their doldrums. Very quickly, Bud launches his cult two-hundred-dollar riddle, to which no one finds the solution either at the first telling or the ten or fifteen subsequent repetitions that will be cleverly slipped in during the evening to wake up the sleepyheads. I almost forgot: in each round, only one person gets a single answer. It makes you smile, it makes you tense, it annoys you, it obsesses you... Until the narrator delivers the key to the enigma, either because the party is over or because a guest who is really at the end of his rope wants to punch him in the face.

Here is the question.

"There are three Dwarfs going to the mine. The first takes the shovel, the second takes the pickaxe, what does the third take?"

Candidate number one, Doc.

"The lamp?"

"No."

The following rounds will come around every five minutes. For this, Bud is more reliable than a talking clock. For the answers, I'll give you a group summary.

"Boots?" the second Dwarf tries his luck.

"No."

"The helmet?" the next one asks.

"No."

"The snack?" another whispers.

"No."

"The bag for the diamonds?" one more suggests.

"No."

Specialists as they are in applied geology and curious excavations, our hosts do no better than ordinary humans.

"The little train?" Loopey offers, more into modernism and technology.

"No."

"The groumf?" groumfes you will have groumfed who.

"No," Bud sneers, who could very well have said yes to put an end to this stupidity.

Luckily, the borloks are very good-natured. Not touchy at all. They laugh like hyenas every time.

Between my son's maddening repetitions, Archie and I serve up some well-chosen repartee. And we glean along the way a story with a lot of local color, about nice woodland dwellers.

Very professorial, Doc starts in.

"One morning, in the forest, two young, very fresh and plump mushrooms tremble and chatter their teeth. They know that the hare is going to pass by on his daily walk, and that he will eat them for breakfast. Suddenly, one of the two shouts out:

"I have an idea! As soon as he comes, we look him straight in the eye and point out that he has not put his hat on. Of course, he will say no. Too bad for him: we would have liked him to say yes. So we will give him two punches in the face. I assure you we will have peace.

"Okay, let's try it," the other mushroom agrees.

"When the hare shows up, everything goes smoothly and he leaves, vexed as a rat, with his swollen nose..."

The storyteller stops and bursts out laughing, imitated by the other Dwarfs. The three of us give him a polite smile, nothing more. No punchline, no continuation, it's not funny at all. Worse than British humor. To lighten the slight uneasiness, I take his hand.

"Here's a story of a guy in the countryside, a long time ago. Once a week, with his insulated van, he would go around the farmers of the country to deliver them fresh blocks of ice. Well, believe it or not, one fine day..."

Eyes wide, mouths agape, the audience is captivated. Almost transported elsewhere.

"...One particularly hot summer morning, the guy set out with fifteen blocks of ice in his cooler. At his first stop, he realized something completely crazy: he only had fourteen blocks of ice left."

Frown, dear readers. Be perplexed, feel sorry for my failing sanity. Yet fear not, this bad joke is by James Funnigan. But there are people more nuts than him, even among the borloks.

"Very strange, yes..." I hear then. "Impossible, even... Nevertheless, the fact is there. And facts are stubborn, everyone knows. Well, I see only one reason... elementary, my dear Gordon!"

A little theatrical blank, before the answer.

"The fifteenth ice block melted on the way!"

Hold on tight, my lambs, it's Loopey Wolf who found it.

I would have fallen over, if I hadn't already been on my ass on the ground.

Grinning from ear to ear, the others give him a standing ovation. Archie, Bud and I can't imitate them, for lack of a high ceiling. We applaud warmly all the same. We're enjoying the company of this wolf more and more.

Immediately afterwards, Doc raises his hand and asks to speak again. We expect the worst. Wrongly, I admit.

"A few days later, in the forest, the two mushrooms are anxious again. The hare will eventually come back to the area, and then...

"Listen," said the first, the smartest one. "We'll look him straight in the eye, like last time, and ask him if he has any cigarettes. Of course, he won't have any, so we'll give him two slugs in the nose. Easy, right?"

"Great," the other mushroom agrees, admiringly.

"The hare arrives. Very politely he approaches and greets the two mushrooms.

"Do you have any cigarettes?" the first one asks.

"Yes, guys! Can I get you one?"

"Horror and dismay. The mushrooms are lost. What to answer?

"Do you prefer with filter or without?" adds the hare, full of attention for his future breakfast.

"The kicker... The mushrooms had not planned on this. They give each other a disastrous wink. Then silence...

"But say," the first one retorts, "you still haven't put your hat on!"

"The hare looks up at the sky.

"Well no..."

"And boom, he gets two more socks in his nose."

We could have spent hours on these cultural exchanges, on the fringes of surrealism, between Humans and action figures revisited in borlok sauce. What we'd forgotten was the surrounding *Crunch Rhapsody*, which was still distant when we arrived.

The call to order is harsh and brutal.

In less than a minute, the noise of the "nasty beasts of the night" swells to a closer rumble, then a rolling thunder above our heads—and all around us!

A mad frenzy seizes the Six Dwarfs. All of the fine folk rush at piles of boards, boxes of nails and a regiment of hammers that we had clearly seen stored in a corner of the room, and without paying any more attention to them. Then begins a Dantesque performance of boarding, caulking, barricading everything that resembles windows, portholes, skylights and doors.

Papa Groumf and Loopey Wolf, whom we hasten to help, start moving the heaviest pieces of furniture to reinforce the solidity of the fortifying measures.

Of course, the fireplace is also temporarily walled up with a sideboard that fits perfectly into the hearth, fortunately without a fire.

I have a very bad feeling, *presumably* shared by Bud. All this reminds me of a hovel surrounded by zombies who are far from friendly. I'll bet that very soon, emaciated arms and semi-skeletal legs will manage to break the boards, greedy hands more hooked than the talons of birds of prey will reach through towards us, then the rotting faces of the undead will drool in our faces.

In fact, the reality will be even more mind-boggling.

At first glance, the super-hungry creatures that quickly gnaw through the entire thickness of the walls and the well-barred exits are flying things of various bright colors, with oversized mouths, a bit like the PacMan of forty years ago but crossed with Stéphane Roy's[13] *Gondoliers.*

As soon as the first devouring horror appears, our friends cry out in screams of terror:

"The Porkepon! The Porkepon!"

As they gnaw away at worse and worse, they begin to squeal in a sinister tone:

"Tchu-Ka-Piiii...! Tchu-Ka-Piiii...! Tchu-Ka-Piiii...!"

I glance over at my son. Dumbfounded, as if in shock, he stares groggily at the little multi-colored creatures with the sharp teeth of super predators. And with flaming ruby eyes, which is a very bad sign.

"They weren't bad at first, those Porks..."

An ominous crack, sign of an imminent collapse, resounds and cuts him off. At least six monsters tumble from the ceiling and rush at the Dwarfs.

We keep swinging like madmen with the fireplace accessories, but alas, on the scale of the cottage inhabitants' size, the attackers controlled by the Ghost couldn't give a bat's ass.

"We need to get out of here quickly, guys!" I say to Bud and Archie.

"Groumf me, I'll groumf with you!" Papa Groumf says, just before being grabbed by a neon green Porkepon.

"The Dwarf Mine!" Loopey Wolf yells at us. "Go to the Dwarf Mine and take..."

"I've got it!" Happy suddenly cries out, laughing and stomping his feet with joy despite the atrocity of the moment. "The third Dwarf who goes to the mine, *he takes the lead*!"

Correct answer, but oh so sadly prophetic... Bud doesn't even have time to congratulate him.

Big Crunch!

A vile Porkepon decapitates the unfortunate winner with a guillotine-like snap of its steel jaws. Then it smashes its victim's skull between its mandibles and bursts into a ghoul-like cackle as it savors the brain, still warm from intense thought, of the late poor Happy.

---

[13] In the novel and film *Midi Six, l'Heure du Catering.* (Note from the Translator)

Loopey Wolf disappears under an avalanche of enraged Porkepon. I hear a Dwarf whistle, another scream, maybe several.

"Watch out, Dad!" my son yells at me.

Thanks to him, I narrowly avoid the little flying demon that is heading straight for me, all stingers out. Out of the corner of my eye, I see Archie manage to sweep away, with a fabulous backhand of a miniature stool, a canary yellow attacker that is more stubborn than scabies. A scientist's brain arouses the taste buds...

A heroic defense if ever there was one, but without the slightest glimmer of hope.

There are too many of these Porkepon and they are too hungry...

Homicron II (art by J.-J. Dzialowski)
© *Hexagon Comics*

CHAPTER XVIII

BUD RECOUNTS[14]

All my friends will tell you: the first time I stuck my nose into a video game, I was transported to another dimension. I have to admit that I was pretty talented, with the crazy stories in which I had gotten hooked on with—or because of—my folks, Godfather and Godmother. So I've shot them all, from alien invaders to dragons, from vampires to zombies, from starship troopers to shoggoths... And I've won some games against those rotten PacMans from back in prehistoric times when kids my age had nothing else to do for fun except play the ancestor of virtual tennis, in 2D and black and white, with rectangles for players and a small square to represent the ball.

I never imagined that I would one day be eaten by very real, three-dimensional PacMans, hybridized with horrible, diabolical mini-monsters *made in Japan*. And yet...

"Our goose is cooked!" Archie says.

"The Dwarfs are down to three!" Dad shouts.

"The beans are dry!" a gnome moans.

"Don't you have a saying, son?" Dad shouts again.

"Well... Uh..."

Offhand, I think of "Klaatu Barada", "Ahnal Nathrach", and even "Iä Cthulhu fhtagn". Might as well try to burn a lich by rolling an eleven-sided die!

So... "Waaazaaa!", maybe? What do I have to lose?

I yell at the top of my lungs, swinging my right arm as if I were drawing a whirlwind with a magic wand. That's when the first lightning bolt shoots out, through a hole in the ceiling, and pierces a Porkepon ready to jump on my old man.

Another flash. A third. A fourth.

The Voraces are struck down one after the other. A veritable storm in which the smell of ozone is replaced by a stomach-turning mixture of grilled barbecue and melted electronics.

---

[14] Specialized expertise deserves delegation. *(Note from Sydney Gordon)*

I almost forgot: what's left of the walls of the shack fall outwards while the remains of the roof also slide outwards. As if a powerful and well-controlled energy flow is pushing them away so they don't fall on us.

Then I see THEM coming, finishing their descent from the heavens, slow, majestic, more beautiful and more impressive than gods.

Sorry but I get down on my knees.

Because our saviors are Homicron and three other *Strangers*.

Homicron in the Rita Tower version, obviously. Flanked by Jaydee, Starlock and Futura.

For the lightning, for the manipulation of energy and gravity, everything is explained.

Dad and Archie can't believe their eyes. I'm in a daydream.

In front of me, even though I know they're *action figures* transcended into borlok mode, I have four of my favorite comic book characters. And they've just saved my life. Saved *our* lives, all three of us plus the two surviving Dwarfs!

The four Strangers land in the middle of the battlefield. Dad and I only have eyes for Homicron and Futura. Godfather, for his part, scrutinized the other two with his customary scientific curiosity.

Homicron is just like in the books with their long brown hair, their deliciously ironic smile, their sparkling, intelligent eyes harboring a wolf. Admirable in their midnight blue jumpsuit decorated with a yellow H on the front, the horizontal bar across the chest and the two vertical bars, parallel, going from the ankles to the collarbones.

Futura, even though I'd always imagined her to be fascinating enough to fall head over heels for, flipped my mind and senses like a pancake. Her large red cape with gold embroidered trim, the full hood that usually hides her yellow eyes with arrowhead pupils, pointed downwards, added even more to her statuesque beauty, enhanced by the gauntlets, the knee pads, the conch shells that cover her breasts and her golden metal panties.

Jaydee the Salamandrite has his not-so-friendly appearance of a dark green sauroid monster, ten feet tall and weighing 1,000 pounds. With his spine bristling with bony spikes, his claws, his predator's mouth, his lizard's tongue and his ruby eyes, you really have to know him to imagine that he can also have the normal appearance of a teenager from our country.

All things considered, Starlock is maybe the most ordinary of them all. Or the least extraordinary, I should say, for someone judging him by his outfit, an ultra classic steel blue and red jumpsuit. Would you guess that it's his epidermis, armored by accumulation of gravitons into a shell denser than titanium!

No wonder they atomize the Porkepon for us in a jiffy... Homicron controls all energies at the quantum level, focalizes pulsating energy between their hands and in their eyes, projects beams of deadly radiation and can put up a protective force-field. Futura is metamorphic by changing the chemical composition and/or density of her body, she can change her size, her shape, and become intangible. As a bonus, she projects bio-energy beams with her eyes and the tips of her fingers. Jayde has colossal strength, he's virtually invincible and indestructible. Starlock manipulates gravitons and antigravitons, which he uses to strike from a distance thanks to the beams launched from his eyes.

On the other hand, I know right away that they aren't the real ones, but borloks customized into action figures, seeing that they all master gravitational modulation, Jayde included, although that's not the case in reality.

After the usual greetings, hello, I'm So-and-so, me Whats-his-name, very glad, thank you for arriving on time, and so on, Homicron explains to us the reason for the miracle. Meanwhile, Jayde and Starlock are restoring some order to the surrounding chaos, and Futura is standing guard.

Funny to see the scary Salamandrite helping to rebuild a makeshift hut for the surviving Dwarfs, then cleaning up the heavier stuff while leaving the more delicate tasks to his buddy.

"The alert was given to us from the Mangabot Sector. None of them can use the 'filters', according to the law, but there are ways to pass messages. Thus, we have long since made friends with Atom Boy."

"It's true even in our country," I say. "There's a cult *crossover* in which you meet."

"Quite right," Homicron smiles. "Young Player, you are indeed the one we were hoping for. Your knowledge is immense and respected by all of us."

This shuts me up. How could I expect that?

"So, Atom Boy informed us that you were in serious trouble with the Furries. We set off without delay, ignoring the law which is a false pretense issued by the Ghost, by the way."

"Why are we so important to you?" Archie asks, for whom trust means cross-checking.

"The Superhero Sector is much more pro-Player than the Mangabot Sector," Homicron replies. "In our opinion, Humans identify very strongly with the Superheroes—more than with the Mangabots—because the Super Heroes embody nothing more nor less than their ideals. In other words, because we would transcend you."

"To be more exact, you allow us to transcend ourselves when we project ourselves into you."

Homicron appreciates my rephrasing. And Futura gives me a smile, ah...

"The Ghost has failed to convert us with his propaganda," Rita Tower continues. "None of us are tempted to change universes to invade yours and replace you."

"If you kill the dreamer, you kill the dream," Jayde says in his growling voice, raising his head from behind the wardrobe he's carrying.

"So we have to take you to Center. And we will take you there without further ado."

"Not through the diamond mine!" pleads one of the Dwarfs.

"No, there is a good chance that the 'filter' has been booby-trapped," Futura says. "We will go by air to another 'porous zone', the one through which we came."

And there you have it.

We say goodbye to the two surviving Dwarfs. Well, nothing will be the same for them, but they have a half-decent place to live and it won't rain on their heads.

Then our designated "porters" take us in their arms, and we soar off.

Given his weight, Jayde could fly pretty well on his own thanks to the gravity modulators *made in* the Super Hero Sector, probably less limited in use than those of the Mangabots seeing that the "filter" didn't eat them in the process. But there's no way the Salamandrite is taking a passenger.

Archie is taken by Starlock, me by Futura.

And Dad by Rita Tower, nanny nanny boo boo.

I'm cracking up.

CHAPTER XIX

Saved by the cavalry, kidnapped by angels...

Clearly, surprises and surreal experiences are piling up!

I understand better now why Bud is a die-hard *Strangers* fan. Aside from the humanoid saurian who scared the crap out of me when he showed up in the middle of the chaos earlier, the others are pretty friendly.

And in terms of air travel, we could have had worse. Compared to our escape from Mekashogun, here, it's with a feeling of total security that we speed through the night above the Furries Sector, without knowing where we're going.

But you can't change your ways if you have a twisted mind. One detail, in my opinion, smacks of conversion therapy. Otherwise, why was that rascal Bud laughing like a hyena when I was chosen to go up to heaven in Homicron's arms? And when I say "go up to heaven", I'm sorry that we're not somewhere else, more peaceful and private, to go together to the seventh level.

For me, the term bombshell here takes on its full meaning. Oh, don't go confusing it with any fairground attraction, even if Rita's ascent is accomplished at the speed of a hypervelocity missile!

Given that she has to keep her arms free for her acrobatic maneuvers, you can imagine the position I have to adopt. Pinned against the superheroine's back—I can't call her a Superhero, not *her*—and my hands clasped on her stomach, with her sculpted buttocks against...

You get me. The situation keeps getting tougher.

Madame Homicron possesses all the feminine charms that an *ideal creation* can be adorned with. The texture of her marvelously full forms is the incomparable alliance of firmness and suppleness. Rita Tower is the complete incarnation of a super fantasy in aesthetic and plastic perfection to the full.

Plastic... Did I say "plastic"...? Of course, you old senile obsessive, you have an action figure in your arms!

Shut up! Box up my conscience in its infuriating Jiminy Cricket mask with a strong hint of Margaret.

Funny flash, I remember the late Richard Bessière telling me an anecdote from his youth.

"Joëlle was a beautiful, tough girl, whom her friends had nicknamed Steel Ass. There was nothing pejorative or vulgar in this appellation but simply, in my opinion, the verbal translation of a rock-solid dermal firmness. A quality that differentiated her, in a way, from other specimens with soft flesh that was not always very aesthetic. Well, a question of taste, of course..."

I'll spare you the juicy sequel, which is off-topic in the current circumstances. But given how the aforementioned Joëlle fantasized about the horrors of 50s cinema, like those of the Hammer Films, she would have won a direct ticket to multiple orgasms if she could have accompanied us to some Sectors among the borloks...

As for Monsieur Bessière, may he rest in peace, if he had been able to cuddle up to *Madame* Homicron as I'm doing now, and, to boot, in the sky and in full flight, I bet you he wouldn't have given up his place to me for all the gold in the world.

I try to cool my thoughts as best I can. Fact is fact. Let's talk about applied sciences, it calms me down.

There has really been some serious progress in toy and gaming technology lately. And not just in the virtual realm. As proof, these buttocks are surely stronger than the most tempered steel and at the same time have a flexibility that is irresistibly attractive...

Oh damn, it failed...

"End of the line, everyone get off!" my son suddenly shouts, beaming with joy.

Obviously, his flight in Futura's arms was very enjoyable for him. As for Archie, I hear him chatting away with Starlock. Normal, between scientists.

Saved by the bell, old Syd... I think to myself as Homicron and I, like the other "couples" and Jayde, land on solid ground.

As soon as we part, the Superheroine forms a small sphere of luminescent energy between her palms and releases it. The thing begins to hover above our heads, lighting up the immediate surroundings.

We are on the steps of a round temple with columns similar to which I had seen on the hills of the "English countryside" from the edge of the terrifying Pretty Woods.

The "filter" is located in the middle of the rotunda. It's a circular basin with a shimmering surface of absolute black. Not much to inspire confidence.

"I'll go first," Jaydee growls, startling me. "If there's a trap on the other side, I'll deal with it. You all wait here for me, I'll come back and tell you how it is."

The sauroid dives into the pool where not a ripple forms. Barely ten seconds later, he resurfaces without a single drop of liquid on his body.

"The way is clear, friends!"

Again he dives down. Homicron and Futura jump in after him, then it's the three of us, and finally Starlock bringing up the rear.

Before I jump into "the water", I notice that the Stranger is looking behind him once more.

But no, there's no one. No one is tailing us.

Here goes nothing!

The little luminescent sphere goes out at the precise moment when I sink into a void that is a little elastic, very sticky, and black as hell. Physical tar without being so.

As long as I don't come out with feathers stuck on...

CHAPTER XX

We've reached Center.

This certainty is based on our trust in the Strangers and on the first details that strike us upon our "emersion".

The sky is black, dotted with false fixed stars that look more like the candles of a very old chandelier.

The plain is bleak and devoid of any trace of life. Grass, shrubs, trees, animals are conspicuous by their absence.

Finding such a setting anywhere else is totally improbable.

So we are indeed in Center. And yet...

In the past, there were very few buildings here. Unless I'm mistaken, just flat buildings. While today, ten "relative" years, forty "absolute" years or whatever later, there stands in this cold solitude a mind-blowing thing. Both simplistic and complex. Which draws from all three of us a cry of expectant fright.

Another damn ride...!?

You've all seen things like it in pediatricians' waiting rooms, for example. Brightly painted metal rods, twisted and intertwined in all directions, on which you can slide lots of small geometric solids that are also colored. Balls, cubes, pyramids, cones, parallelepipeds, ovoids, polyhedra... that kids have fun moving by hand. But here, on this giant version, the mobiles are autonomous and move by themselves in a rather fantastic ballet.

In addition, and this is not without cause to worry us, aerodynamic wagons, pods or capsules travel in all directions through the loops, spirals, propellers, curved and straight sections of the ride.

My gaze is glued to a large polished metal sphere, at least thirty feet in diameter, which descends along a vertical slide and stops at ground level. A door opens, an inclined ramp unfolds, and a series of green lights begin to flash above the opening.

"Come, friends," Homicron invites us. "This is where you are awaited."

We move towards the "merry-go-round" which peaks at several hundred feet high and we climb the slope, surrounded by the Strangers.

I'll pass over the farewell scene, friendly and good-natured. Their mission accomplished, our saviors must return to their Sector where we would have liked to follow them, if only out of curiosity. They wish us every success in the coming events—without specifying what they are—and give us many times the assurance of their unfailing friendship.

"We are counting on you, Human Players. We know you will not disappoint us. But be careful not to trust appearances..."

On this bizarre warning, the Strangers leave us, at the top of the ramp, then take off and shoot like four meteors towards the prismatic cairn near which we came out in Center.

"You look weird, Dad," Bud says to me. "You'd think Homicron had a little effect on you."

"Speak for yourself about Futura, son. I saw you. You weren't bored, were you?"

"So what?"

"Well, uh..."

No time for further comment. A high-pitched, thin voice echoes through the sphere's "airlock".

"Come closer, my good friends! Ah, how glad I am to see you again, Mr. Gordon and Mr. Brent! And this young Player, how glad I am to meet him at last!"

Double exclamation from Archie and yours truly, while Bud almost faints.

"PINOCCHIO!"

It's him, the friendly little borlok who had accompanied us during our previous adventures in this crazy world. Brotherly hugs, pats on the back, it's as if we were meeting an old friend after years of being away.

Bud's eyes widen. His worried expression speaks for itself. We all seem to have regressed into childhood and it overwhelms him. However, there are more surprises to come because the character who shows up at the same moment, no, he would never have expected to see him show up in the flesh, or almost.

Santa Claus!

Archie and I easily absorb the shock. This fine bearded man in red and white is already one of our acquaintances from our previous visit.

"Welcome back to Center, dear Human friends," he greets us with a fantastic bass tone. "Thank you for answering my calls and sorry for the inconvenience. I would have preferred to see you again in less dramatic circumstances, but I had no choice."

"Because you're the one who lured us here?" Bud says not without some fire in his fire. "Your present is pretty crappy!"

"Santa Claus will repay you a hundredfold, Pinocchio's word," the wooden puppet interjects. "Rest assured."

"Santa Claus? More like M, right?" Archie guesses, frowning.

"Both, my captain!" Pinocchio trumpets, bursting into laughter.

Good Lord, but of course! The rest will show it to you.

Obeying the invitation of our hosts, we enter the large sphere. A maze of corridors and antigravity shafts later, here we are installed in a kind of HQ in comfortable curved seats. Veritable walls of screens display all the possible views of *Center,* of this vast *perpetuum mobile* structure which, I admit, is pretty fascinating. But as you can imagine, this isn't the time for blissful contemplation.

"My name is all," Santa Claus declares as a preamble. "Or, if you prefer, M is called all. A distinguished privilege of the sovereign intelligence that exists as such *and* through the remote interfaces that are its mobile units. I am the whole that surrounds you, and the part that stands before you."

"So you... you're M," Bud rephrases.

"Exactly, young Player," Santa Claus replies. I am the Mechabrain *and* one of its interactive peripheral extensions."

"Practical and nice, as a contact for visitors," my son adds.

"Much nicer than the tank thingy from back then," Archie smiles.

"That's an understatement," I can't help but comment, thinking deeply because in my opinion there's something wrong.

Then suddenly I raise my hand.

"You said, 'I am the whole that surrounds you.' But then…"

"The Mecabrain is Center and it occupies Center in its entirety, yes," Pinocchio offers. "My very dear friends, you are *on* and *in* the giant computer that governs our world."

"...But then," I continue, "the tank against which I defended myself and which I managed to defeat..."

"I let you believe in my destruction, Sydney Gordon, because there was no longer any reason to continue the game after the death of Laster, the sole survivor of the children of Gondwana, whom I had nevertheless done everything to save. As you know, it was all just a puppet show meant to distract the poor little boy during the last years of his fragile existence. But you did not know that Laster was dying when you arrived,

216

long ago. His soul returned to the Great Infinite at the moment when we were fighting each other—pure temporal conjunction—and I made sure to let you conclude that the problem we posed was *de facto* solved."

"Laster was an angel, my friends," Pinocchio begins to sob. "My Blue Fairy, my Jiminy Cricket in this world, if I may say so. It was for him that M had specially created me, so that through me, he could know a little of life. In losing him, I lost a part of myself."

It's touching to see this wooden puppet now crying warm tears, his eyes and the tip of his long pointed nose all red!

"Forgive me, but you weren't as developed back then, M," Archie points out, scrutinizing Santa.

Legitimate curiosity on his part.

"Of course not," the Mechabrain agrees via the old man. "And to continue to govern the now vain world of the borloks, without an audience or players, I would not have needed to develop myself like this. It was the arrival of the Ghost that changed everything. I was suddenly seized by the desire to 'gamify' myself in my structure and my appearance, to cease my existence solely underground and invisible in order to show myself on the surface, alive, attractive, amusing... If I had had the means, I would have grown here an extraordinary garden, the quintessence of all those of the most beautiful stories and the most magical tales. But I was content with a merry-go-round, certainly fabulous and enchanted, because I had to work very quickly. Indeed, most of my energy had to be devoted to the creation of new Sectors. Ah, my friends, what euphoria!"

"We had a great time," Pinocchio raves. "The party lasted for months, for years... I thought it would never end."

"Meanwhile, perfidious, insidious, the Ghost was setting up his underground power," Santa Claus moans. "As long as I was busy with the creative frenzy, he could do as he pleased without attracting my attention."

"As if he had you doped up to the core so he could make cushy deals," my son rephrases prosaically.

The old man doesn't seem to catch the full drift, but that doesn't bother him much.

"Barely had a Sector emerged from the biotechnological stabilization phase," he goes on, "when the demon already began to sow the seeds of its ultimate design among the populations."

"By revealing the existence of the Players universe and inciting its massive conquest," Archie surmises.

Santa Claus nods gravely.

"But at some point," Bud is losing his temper, "you should have smelled something fishy, right? This Ghost, you'd seen him and you knew him, right?"

"Absolutely not," the central intelligence replies in a sad voice. "I never knew who he was, what form he took, whether he was even slightly material or not, or where he had come from so readily."

"And it didn't stop you in your development and creation processes," Archie wonders. "Really…"

"Remember my departure for the Isle of Pleasures," Pinocchio mutters, lowering his eyes. "And look again at the course of your respective lives, human friends…"

The song of the sirens, the beauty of the Devil… I say to myself silently.

"Quite right, Mr. Gordon," the wooden puppet assures me, as if he could read my mind. "Add a pinch of forbidden fruit, and you've got it."

As a general con artist and shock anesthetist, the Ghost is first rate. Even if we are the present fall guys, I can't help but take my hat off to him. At the Animal Olympics, he would have won the gold medal for the tricking of cats by the mice!

Well, in short, we'd already heard the rest from Truckankhamun VII. And we're lucky that M is now giving us a version that corroborates in every way what we already know. That'll save us from racking our brains. Also note that not for a single moment do the eyes of his mobile unit turn ruby red, which really reinforces our confidence.

At least in principle, the Ghost's plan is simple. It involves using the resonance of quantum strings, which form the very substance of all universes, to imprint the noetic structure of the borloks onto that of the Humans. Aided by the "heretic" Mangabots, the Ghost has therefore built the "tuning fork" needed for this operation.

"What this device is and where it is," Santa Claus admits gloomily, "neither I nor anyone else has the slightest idea."

"He could have hidden it under any guise in any of the four Sectors," Bud says. "Which doesn't help our case."

"The Tuning Fork could even be hidden here," Pinocchio laments. "Can you believe it? Right under M's nose!"

"I would have noticed," he objects grumpily. "Come on, little puppet, a little logic!"

It's right up Archie's alley, if I may say so.

"Among the Mangabots, it's out of the question," our favorite scientist declares. "Too risky, there are not just 'heretics' there. Among the Super Heroes, no probability either. They're are too pro-Human..."

"What about the Furries?" I throw out.

"Impossible," the Mechabrain replies. "It is a Sector far too heterogeneous, the majority of whose occupants are incorrigible blabbermouths."

We know what he means. Real chatterboxes!

"Not to mention all those long-snouted animals that spend their time poking around everywhere," Pinocchio adds with a disgusted look. "Wolves, foxes, weasels, martens and the like. Ah, I can't stand them anymore!"

A matter of the traumas he suffered in Collodi's tale and in almost all of its variants, no doubt.

"So if there's only one left, it'll be this one," my son concludes. "The Cuties Sector."

"Entirely plausible," Santa Claus agrees. "The probability is very high. And several events tend to support this hypothesis, for example, the not insignificant number of Super Heroes that I sent there was a total waste."

"That's the right word," the puppet adds. "At least half of them have disappeared, and the others have been 'turned' by the Ghost."

"Turned? You mean 'perverted', right? Like Thunder and Bolt?" Bud says.

"Yes and no," M replies. "Those two zebras played a great joke on me when they came back from there."

"To fool you, big guy, they fooled you," Pinocchio sneers. "According to them, they had found nothing, they had met no one to talk to, all the QTs were idiots as stupid as the children transformed into donkeys, in 'my' story..."

"That's when I thought of you, Archibald Brent, and your brilliant wife," Santa Claus exclaims. "You had impressed me most sincerely when you visited, long ago. Minds as exceptional as yours could be of inestimable help to me."

Well done! I count for nothing! I grumble to myself. *Thank you!*

A sarcastic glance from my dear son adds fuel to the fire.

"Poor Sydney," Pinocchio sympathizes. "You were never anything but the fifth wheel, much like me."

I barely hold back from smacking him. It wouldn't do any good. But I set him straight.

"Except that I'm always the one telling the story, my boy. The others are far too brilliant, superior and... lazy to bother writing anything down."

"Let's not get distracted," M. scolds us. "However it might seem, time is pressing."

"Yes, Pop," the wooden puppet bows. "We are all ears, even those who already know the story."

Smiling good-naturedly, Santa Claus picks up the thread.

"First there were the transdimensional messages to which Mr. and Mrs. Brent responded and then the reactivation, by them, of the inter-universe roller coaster. The pooling of intelligence constitutes a real miracle when it allows one to achieve such rapid successes, especially at the cost of communication between two distinct continuums..."

"The rest is less glorious, Pops," Pinocchio interrupts in a tone that borders on impertinence. "But of course, it depends on who it is for."

No one picks up on this ambiguous dig.

"I sent Thunder and Bolt to 'pick up' you too, Mr. Gordon," M continues. "For the idea suddenly came to me to team you up with Mr. Brent on the last-chance mission of which you are now in the initial stage—all that preceded having only resulted from the perfidious machinations of the Ghost, determined to eliminate the extreme threat that you represent for him. You two, with Mrs. Brent as back up, combine all the essential qualities and possess, above all, the spirit of initiative that the borloks are devoid of. Toys are not and will never be Players, you know it and have already experienced it. Moreover..."

"Hey, Santa, I'm here too," Bud jumps in, not just well-timed but also annoyed. playlist Nor was my mother, for that matter, but that's not really a problem."

"She's much better off where she is, son," I assure him, only half convinced myself. "At least she's not risking her hide."

"I am," Bud presses, starting to smile. "But maybe we'll save yours, your hide. It makes me feel better to think so."

"*We...?*"

"Me and my initiatives, of course! When are we going, by the way?"

"It's up to you to decide," M replies. "First, allow yourself a moment to freshen up and catch your breath, if you need to."

"It's not been so long since we ate and drank at the Dwarfs," Bud says. "So, I'm good. Godfather, Dad?"

Archie and I agree and thank our host anyway.

"The sooner we leave, the sooner we'll be done," I conclude.

"It's touching to see you so confident, Sydney Gordon," Pinocchio grins sadly. "Oh, I hope you are right to be so hopeful..."

Santa Claus nods.

"The future of two worlds hangs in the balance, Human friends. And we know nothing of our common adversary. Rest assured I will pray for your success, and that I will help you in every way I can..."

"Turn it down, Papa," Pinocchio sighs, his nose growing longer. "Don't promise the moon to your saviors whom you may be sending to their doom. You won't even be able to remove a thorn from their foot!"

M can't find anything to respond. Damn, this puppet has really gotten feisty over the years! Anyway, the Mechabrain is counting on us. And without further ado, as Santa Claus indicates, inviting us to follow him.

"Me too?" Pinocchio asks in a voice that has become quite shy.

"I thought you were scared," Bud snaps at him.

"It is curiosity that drives me, young Human," the puppet affirms.

It's already killed the cat, so let's hope it doesn't kill the puppet... I think to myself with a cold shiver.

We come out of the big sphere, which has meanwhile risen up in the computer-ride. Via a walkway stretched in an arc above the void, we reach a dodecahedral structure and go in.

The trip ends in a square room where each wall has an opening blocked by a dark, shimmering, undulating curtain, surely of the same nature as the "filter" through which we passed a little earlier.

"Four 'doors' for four Sectors," Bud guesses.

"Exactly, young Player," Santa Claus confirms. "Of course, I have here taken up the conventional symbolism of the traditional card game, but each suit has a related meaning. Spades for the Mangabots, diamonds for the Super Heroes, clubs for the Furries and hearts for the QTs that melt all children. Now, my dear friends, it's up to you to... play!"

The order we'll go is quickly set. Archie first, Bud second, Pinocchio third and me last. Classic...

One final wave to M, and we're off.

Curtain... Darkness... Light...

CHAPTER XXI

Artists with fantastic, crazy, wacky inspiration, our world has known, knows and will know loads of them. To name just a few and stick with the pretty good ones, Dali, Kandinsky, Chirico, Miró have each created wild universes that cause either enthusiasm or total rejection, it's up to you.

Here and now, it seems that they've all joined forces and united their unbridled imaginations with everything that has been done, from the worst to the best, in terms of board games and toys.

Once again we emerge at the top of a small hill from which we have views of a preposterous landscape.

First, the sky.

There's more traffic up there than over the busiest airports on our planet. But not a matter of planes here.

With a stunned eye, Archie, Bud and I watch the flying things that crisscross the big blue—in a manner of speaking because it's apple green—in all directions. I identify *Scraggle* tiles adorned with alphabetical characters, *Bobble* dice also bearing letters—but much faster than human postal carriers—dominoes whose blue dots pulse to the rhythm of a Viennese waltz, polychrome *LetGo* bricks, Little Horses of all colors whose jerky movements remind us of seahorses...

There are also emerald houses and bright red buildings, bigger, able to fly thanks to the money that serve as wings, and hounded by silver figurines in the shape of cars, hats, fox terriers, steam locomotives, etc. In short, the whole *Monopoly* gang on a celestial stroll.

Mind-blowing, fascinating, what a mixture of the ridiculous and the sublime!

Only Pinocchio shows a jaded, almost scornful air. As if he disapproves of this ballet with its bright choreography, which only lacks music. Although... I hardly dare to think of the cacophony that would fit these movements, which are certainly consistent as groups or families of objects, but totally anarchic on the whole.

Second, the horizon. Where mountains like no others loom. And for good reason!

"Test-tube volcanoes!" my son exclaims, his jaw ready to drop in shock. "I think we've ended up in the homes of sick people!"

Indeed, the distant peaks are giant test tubes whose openings release bubbles, smoke, half-liquid, half-pasty spitting, gurgling sounds whose digestive rumblings can be imagined from beyond the distance that makes them inaudible.

Every now and then, a slightly fartier reaction causes a cauliflower cloud, grooved with sparks, to be expelled into the sky, then the inevitable "boom" reaches us with the delay caused by the distance.

It could be funny. But, once the shock of discovery has worn off, a two-fold fundamental problem quickly arises for us. Ignorance of what our destination might look like, in concrete terms, and the route we need to take to reach it.

"Don't worry, my friends," the wooden puppet tries to reassure us. "The QT Sector is always busy, on the ground almost as much as in the sky. In no time, we will find something to tell us..."

He said "something", not "someone" or "people". My goodness, what bizarre encounters are we going to run into?

"Do you want to sleep here or what?" Bud is getting antsy. "Come on, let's go!"

We go down the hill, with a very flexible stride due to the "elastic" nature of the terrain. If it can shed any light for you, the impression is somewhere between a trampoline and a Bouncy Castle.

Third, indeed, the surrounding landscape. A plain, obviously in a grid, a bit in the style of the Furries' country, except that the "squares" here are of completely different kinds since they belong to as many polygonal families as there are games whose pieces move in the air. A real geometric delirium.

As for the relief... Well, it's rather flat country, without mills, without canals, without belfries or bell towers, and without vegetation. From time to time, we can make out some kind of vertical or slightly inclined structure, either big black or white boards or apparently just metal frames.

And little by little, unless I'm seeing things, I could swear that tiny lights come on one after the other at ground level, starting to draw...

"By Jove, a path!" Archie exclaims after a few moments. "Look, this marking is heading towards the first of the boards or frames."

"If this isn't where we're supposed to go," Bud mutters, "then I'll hit the sack."

"It's not time, son. Try to guess what's in store for us."

"He'll never do it, Sydney," Pinocchio pipes up. "I'm afraid M is mistaken about the real potential of human Players..."

As if on purpose, the luminous marks suddenly veer off course, avoiding the first "board". The "light bulbs" continue to pile onto other "light bulbs", heading towards an infinitely more distant "frame". We're really going to have to hoof it over some serious mileage.

"Look out, there's someone coming!" Bud warns us.

He's nice. "Something" would be a better description of this big, quivering, pink, amorphous gelatinous mass that rolls or tumbles toward us. When it stops, some of the dark inclusions dotting its mass cluster on the surface to form the outline of eyes and a mouth.

"Good morning to you," the mushy borlok gurgles.

"Holy crap, a Patagoonian!" my son hisses. "A *Silly Putty* shapeshifter!"

A Sillyputian, then. I know the Lilliputians, so why not a crazy variation... Or better, frappapudding?

Despite his flabbitude, we still politely greet the QT, you never know, and he continues:

"Who are you and what are you doing here?"

"We are Players in search of the Tun..."

With a nudge of my elbow, I silence Bud.

"...in search of the Supreme Harmony," Archie finishes, always on the ball, "and we're looking for our path."

"Your path? I do not understand what you mean. None of the paths here can be yours since they all belong to us. They are *our* paths, period!"

Damn, this thing is rather conical.

"Can we borrow one, though?" our favorite scholar asks.

The Sillyputian shakes and gurgles.

"If you guarantee not to vandalize it, not to steal it and to return it when you are done with it, that is conceivable."

"Far be it from us to think of vandalism or theft," Archie declares with an indignant air. "The word is worth the Player, or the Player is worth nothing: the path is yours and it will remain so after we have traveled it without damaging it."

"Agreed for a small path, then," the amorphous borlok concedes. "A small one, because we fear highwaymen more than anything. Their crimes make our travels terribly complicated."

"And this little path, where will it take us?" my son asks pragmatically.

"To the first riddle," replies the Patagoonian. "There, you will go to the board. But be careful not to fall into the trap!"

Good grief, that's the reason for all those "frames"!

"What exactly will we have to do?" I ask guardedly.

"Answer a question or solve a problem," the Sillyputian gurgles. "You will see... if you live, since whoever lives will see. But first, here is the path that we deign to lend you. You have a certain amount of time to reach the end, otherwise we will take it back from you as soon as the deadline expires—wherever you are."

"How much time do we have?" Bud asks.

"A certain time," the flabby borlok answers.

"But what else?"

"You will see... if you live, since those who live will see."

"Don't press it, son."

"Actually, he is bluffing," Pinocchio whispers. "Just to stress us out. "Forget it, friends."

The Patagoonian turns away and emits a strange modulated whistle, like a grandmother's kettle.

Well now! Along the line drawn by the small "light bulbs", a crack gradually splits the solid surface. Then its edges move apart around fifteen feet from each other, water gushes out of nowhere, and a real river for rafting or canyoning fanatics is created before our astonished eyes.

"Is this the path?" Bud groans. "But we have nothing to sail!"

Yet everything has been planned. The Sillyputien "detaches" from his mass four translucent protuberances which, miraculously, swell and transform into large inflatable toys with more or less animal shapes.

Holy moly, but they're plastic ducks! XXL version of the kind of sensible toys for children's bath, or less sensible and more vibrating for female use as you can imagine.

And I, Sydney Gordon, will have to travel perched on such an oversized *sex toy*? Fate sometimes plays tricks on you...

"We are worth your sacrifice of self-esteem," Pinocchio whispers to me.

Well, if it's to save two worlds...

CHAPTER XXII

Ten, twenty or thirty minutes on a river peppered with rapids, waiting for deliverance at every turn, is long. Very long.

Perched on our big inflatable ducks, candy pink to boot, and clinging to their slippery necks, we do our best not to capsize. Our feet act as stabilizers—relative—and rudders—even more relative!

The surrounding landscape is no longer the dreary plain of irregular huts. There is "vegetation", trees and shrubs that remind me of a very old Disney, *Donald's Adventures in Mathland.* Numbers and math symbols take the place of leaves and flowers, brightening the dark brown trunks and branches.

Strange "animals" move in this strange nature, each in its own way. Ringed spring-like beings advance by "bridging"—it's quite paradoxical (to us) to be able to advance like this—relaxing to gain momentum and then compressing when their two ends are in contact with the ground. And these Boudinis emulating Houdini—Slinkies, spake Bud—with their shimmering hues offer us a real festival worthy of the best Chinese contortionists.

We also see creatures riddled with holes, skeletal in appearance, with a jerky and sometimes clumsy mechanical gait. The most remarkable are a kind of elephant-giraffe crossed with port cranes, pulleys, chains and hooks attesting to this. As a bonus, these borloks creak in a sinister way...

Normal, since they are unoiled assemblies of Meccano *pieces, banana!* my little inner voice whispers to me.

I bet we'll soon be treated to laughing pigs, chess figures, checkers pieces, tic-tac-toes... In short, the whole shebang. Unless all of this shebang is already crisscrossing the sky.

Where, moreover, there's still just as much traffic. But the new thing is that some flying objects seem to take a malicious pleasure in diving at us and brushing past us to make us fall into the water.

Which unfortunately happens to Pinocchio, whose feet, much thinner than ours, make it difficult to maintain balance and trajectory during the already acrobatic passage of the rapids. His duck capsizes and our fellow adventurer nose-dives into the water, screaming like a madman.

Luckily, Bud is following him closely and manages to fish him out before his wooden body gets too soaked. Luckily for him, there are no termite borloks or carnivorous fish borloks, piranhas, barracudas or alexandras.

Suddenly a gong sounds that would make all the lamaseries in Tibet green with envy. The time limit has expired. We have nevertheless won the event because we've just jumped off our mounts and set foot on what must be the landing stage. A metal pontoon that blocks the river and whose razor-sharp edges would have scalped us cleanly if we hadn't jumped early enough.

"I think we gave back the borrowed path just in time," I say to Archie. "Any later and snip…"

Our inflatable ducks burst like beach balls and their substance goes off to join the silly mass of their Patagoonian father, miraculously emerging out of nothingness, on the pontoon, an instant after us.

A large "frame" is very close, and its outline lights up.

"First riddle, Players!" the amorphous borlok announces. "A question will appear on the 'board', you will have five minutes to concentrate, to consult, then the one you have appointed as spokesperson will have to loudly proclaim the answer."

A swarm of *Scraggle* tiles descends from the sky and begins a whirling farandole around us. One by one, letters then stick to the "board".

Zero, three, two, one
In addition to one,
Descending minus ascending,
Into the well falls straight.
Well descending minus well ascending,
Into the well always falls again.
What is this well worth, friends?

Here we go for the cogitation. We read, we reread, we reread. The more we do, the more obscure it becomes.

"This is not going to be easy," Bud whispers to me, dejected. "Are you getting anything, Dad?"

"Nothing, son. Me and math puzzles…"

"Same for me," Pinocchio grumbles. "You know very well that I did not go to school. Oh, how I regret it…"

Archie, on the other hand, doesn't seem as lost. Does that surprise you?

"I have an idea. Come closer!"

An ace, the scholar. And sure of himself, too. Here is his approach, in short.

Zero, three, two, one added to one, that gives 0 + 1, so 1, 1 + 3, so 4, 4 + 2, so 6, and 6 + 1, so 7. *Descending minus rising,* that's the subtraction 7641 minus 1467. *In the well falling straight* corresponds to the result, 6174. *Descending well minus ascending well,* that's still 7641 minus 1467. *In the well always falling back,* obviously, we find 6174.

"On our Earth," Archie specifies, "it's called the Kaprekar algorithm or the mathematical well. We fall into it, moreover, whatever the number of four non-equal digits from which we start."

"Elementary, just had to know it," Bud says ironically. "Come on, go ahead, Godfather!"

Firmly planted on his feet, fists on hips, Archie declaims as loudly as he can:

"The numbers: six, one, seven, four. The number: six thousand one hundred and seventy-four."

When each number is stated, the tile bearing it is torn from the swarm and placed on the "board".

In the end, it lights up like a Macy's Christmas tree.

"Correct answer," thunders a Holier-than-god voice.

Three huge gong bangs.

The Patagoonian, the "frame" and the river with its rapids dissolve into nothingness. Then a new beacon of small flashing "bulbs" begins to light up on the plain which has become featureless again, smooth, except for the "squares".

To accompany what is now coming straight at us, the *Cavalcade of the Laughing Cows* would be the ideal music. Four Little Horses—taller than us, to tell the truth—have broken away from their celestial swarm and are advancing, cataclop, cataclop, pounding the ground each in turn with its single foot. If you close your eyes, you might think it was a single nag, so perfect is the synchronization of the "gallop". I only know one who has achieved such a feat of sound effects back home. I have forgotten his name, but you'll figure out who it is if I say "coconut", won't you?

Letting out shrill neighs, the four playing pieces stop a few feet away from us.

"Saddle up for the second test!" the bright red Little Horse tells us, a color that designates him as the leader.

Dear readers, you who have been following me for so long, you know how much I hate being perched on a quadruped. So, imagine me on a Little Horse—not to mention the ridiculousness of it!

This time, no crevice comes to split the ground. A sandy track gradually takes shape, winding and undulating, up to the edge of a forest with mushroom growths whose thick shadow bodes nothing good.

Giddy up! Clippity clop!

Let's go on the fantastic ride.

CHAPTER XXIII

So cute are the Little Horses on a game board.

But a torture are the same made life-size and ridden by riders who are anything but competent.

Although I wouldn't bet on the chances of a professional jockey doing much better than us, if he were in our place.

A Little Horse has only one leg and one foot. Traditionally, made of turned wood. So this foot is round, which allows our mounts to move by performing all conceivable stylistic figures. *De facto*, they don't just jump in successive leaps. From time to time, they "roll" by leaning on the edge of their foot or, less nastily, wobbling from one side to the other while tilting to different degrees.

If you've ever danced the waltz on a cruise ship in a storm or while crossing the Roaring Forties, you'll understand my distress. *Our* distress, us Humans, because only the puppet doesn't give a damn.

We don't appreciate much of the surrounding scenery. The race is too... vomitive, if I may. The forest is as cold and monumental as a cathedral nave, the trunks and branches look like wrought iron, the foliage more prickly and barbed than the "chevaux de frise". The deep and frightening forest where the evil huntsman went to abandon Snow White is the Garden of Eden compared to this.

Since we've been on the road, just like before we left, we haven't seen a single living soul on the path or around it. And yet, I would swear that we're not alone. You can feel that kind of thing. Moreover...

"Stop there, peasants!" shouts a high-pitched throat of a castrato or a eunuch.

Very abruptly, our four mounts slam on the brakes and neigh, their feet almost smoking.

A genuine Prince Charming horse, white as snow, comes out from between the "trees". Rigid as justice, a character dressed entirely in canary yellow, from the tips of his buckled shoes to the four horns of his bell-studded cap, gives us the sign to stop with his high-raised right hand, gloved in yellow, of course.

Hooked to the pommel of his saddle, a tin bucket, like any you could find in a hardware store, hanging on the left flank of the immaculate steed.

"Oh, but he is really tiny, the smart ass!" Pinocchio squawks, suddenly overexcited. "I bet you his feet do not go all the way to the stirrups, but he has fake leggings with fake shoes on the end!"

"Enough, peasant," squeaks the... Yellow Dwarf, because it can only be him, with a jingle of bells.

"That bucket, is it your chamber pot?" the puppet mocks. "Or is it to pick you up when you fall off your high horse?"

"This bucket contains the seal of the King, whose wrath you, worm that you are, would do best to fear!" the arrogant dwarf boasts.

"What King?" our companion asks, scratching his head. "Ah, how stupid of me: the King of Fools, your peers! Let's talk about him, as a terror! Only good enough to scare little birds, and even then..."

Laughing, Pinocchio turns to us.

"Glad to introduce you to the Wood Jester, my friends! Isn't the little guy ridiculous? A fool who carries a bucket in a pail, you don't have any back home, do you?"

My God, the other one's face... A sudden mix of Cruella De Vil, Medusa, the Sea Witch and the Evil Queen, twisted grin, smoking nostrils, eyes that flash lightning. The caricature of all caricatures! And this ridiculous character tucks his head down, an irrefutable sign of extreme displeasure.

With great effort to hold back from bursting into laughter, Archie, Bud and I look at each other a little worriedly. What on earth has gotten into Pinocchio? What's the point of this rebellious teenager reaction? Does he want to sabotage our mission, or what?

Eh... Here he goes, making things worse!

"Tell me, Most Dwarfable Dwarf, if your horse swerves and all three of you fall, the monkey, the pot and the token, how will you write to me, without spelling or grammatical errors, with no Oz to pose?"

For someone who never went to school, he's made his point! How could he have hit on the finer points of this insoluble affair?

It's too much for the Yellow Dwarf who turns scarlet red and explodes:

"You know very well that this cannot be written, you rotten wormhole! Ah, I will teach you to mock the lords, you weakling! Poppycock, down with the heretic!"

As he spurs his steed, the canary dwarf unsheathes a rapier twice his length and begins to twirl it like a Tartar Aztec cleaver. Archie, Bud, and I are on the verge of deserting the stirrups—so to speak, we don't have any—because of the sudden turn our mounts make. The whirling blade, with its vorpal flashes, hums in our ears.

The unfortunate Pinocchio is not as lucky as we are. In no time, the puppet and his Little Horse find themselves cut down to sticks and scattered to the four winds.

The madman stops swinging, sheathes his sword and rears his mount while haughtily shouting at us:

"See what it costs to mock the Yellow Dwarf! These woods belong to my King and me. Get out of here, you peasant dogs, and don't let me catch you coming this way again!"

Our ride begins again. As brutal as it is unstoppable, the "death" of poor Pinocchio has dealt us a very hard blow. He was only a borlok, of course, but we'd got to know him and to appreciate him, to the point that even if it makes you laugh, his passing breaks our hearts. A heart that we no barely have to work, here, now.

Curiosity killed the cat and *the puppet, you see*, my inner voice whispers to me.

What the hell was he doing in this mess? I shoot back, just to say something.

You didn't even try to talk him out of it, so don't try to dodge it, hammers back my inner Jiminy Cricket.

He didn't commit suicide, though...

A strange thought that quickly flies away because, at that moment, we are leaving the sinister forest.

And, shortly afterwards, the "board" stands before us which marks the end of this second, very weird, ordeal.

We barely reach it when the whole scenery fades behind us. We dismount—without forgetting to pat their necks, for we are polite people and grateful for the service rendered—and watch them soar off into the ever-apple-green azure.

Oh, shock! Horror and dismay! Between the "frame" and us, there suddenly appears out of nowhere, without fanfare, that damned, piece of shit Yellow Dwarf... On foot, without a horse, without a sword—and without a bucket.

"Tragedian, comedian," he declaims in his cracked voice. "God, how sad the King's Fool is, the Jester of the Woods, My Lords! Ah, we must have fun, good people, and amuse ourselves as best we can."

"You said it, puffy," Bud scoffs.

"Rejoice in my love for the Players, otherwise…"

A monumental gong strike cuts him off.

"The time for the question has come!" announces the Holierthangod voice again. "Read, reread, think, and answer without error if you value life…"

Once again, we are treated to the whirling merry-go-round of flying *Scraggle* tiles. And here is what is displayed on the "board":

White rocks at the mouth of the red cave,
So many are in manhood, give or take two,
That basic root squared as endure.
Period.

As the saying goes, tables have turned. This time, Archie is dry, parchied. Like a red herring or a Betty's bitter butter. Bud ditto. While I…

I think without speaking, look without leaping. And then, my light goes on.

"It vaguely reminds me of a twisted riddle in *The Hobbit*," I offer without much conviction. "The 'red cave' would be the mouth. The 'white rocks' the teeth. We have thirty-two when we're complete, in 'manhood,' don't we?"

My two acolytes nod their heads.

"On the other hand, 'basic root' doesn't say much to me. Chemistry has never been my thing. And as for 'squared as endure', I don't see, apart from the grammar mistake. It should rather be 'to endure' instead of 'as endure'…"

"Let's understand 'root' as 'solution'," Archie suggests. "Thirty-two, 'give or take two', could be thirty or thirty-four. And there…"

I swear to you, we narrowly escape an Indian dance. That of the Sioux warrior who has just defeated his most hated Pale Face. *Eureka!* to the power of North America, if you prefer.

"It's thirty-four! It's thirty-four!" exclaims our favorite genius, slapping his forehead with the flat of his hand. "The correct word is not 'endure', but 'in Dürer', with a capital D and an *Umlaut* on the u. You'd think there were no Germanists in this country!"

"Really?" Gordon father and son ask in unison.

"Look, my friends, the Dürer of *Melancholy*, with his famous magic square! By Jove, when the hell will you wake up and open yourselves to culture?[15] It dates back almost five centuries after all... The key, the 'root', is the number 34. Come on, Sydney, announce the answer, it's thanks to you that I was put on the right track."

I do it immediately, at the top of my lungs, better than Pavarotti when he ignored the ovens. And two *Scraggle* tiles go obediently to compose the solution on the "board".

Five gongs this time.

"Well done!" the horrible Yellow Dwarf applauds. "Ah, I am going to end up thinking that it was too easy..."

"We are the champions, period," Bud says, snickering.

"They are champions and they have proven it," the canary dwarf retorts. "For you, only the future will tell."

Nailed it, Gordon junior.

"So this circus isn't over yet?" he sighs.

"No, young Player. Besides, I still do not know where you plan to go and what you hope to find."

"Our goal is the Tun... the Supreme Harmony," Archie catches himself at the last second. "Incidentally, we dream of discovering who the Ghost is, if we don't run into him somewhere."

"You'll have to go through the Guardian," the Yellow Dwarf says with a conniving looks, then bowing. "And since you are dying to see the Ghost, I still have to make sure you are capable of it..."

Lowering his head, he seems to sink into an abyss of intense thought.

"Tell me something: apart from me, obviously, who did you see on the way, before leaving or along the way?"

"Nobody," Archie replies immediately, reaffirmed by our nods.

"So you are able to see the Invisible! Extraordinary!" the canary dwarf raves. "Verification is made, therefore. You will be able to see the Ghost. But..."

He seems to suddenly freeze.

---

[15] And you, my dear fans, did you know? The German artist Albrecht Dürer (1471-1528) made the engraving *Melancholy* in 1514 in which he placed an arithmetic magic square, the first in Europe, logically since then baptized the *Dürer Square*. The curious reader will be able to discover it on the diagram on the next page. (*Note from Sydney Gordon*)

Dürer's Square

16	3	2	13
5	10	11	8
9	6	7	12
4	15	14	1

The magic of this square is linked to its "root", the number 34. This corresponds in fact to the sum of each line, each column, each diagonal, the four central squares, the median squares on the opposite sides, the squares located at the four corners, the four squares deduced from the corners by "turning" once or twice in a clockwise direction...

Furthermore, *Melancholy* dates from the year 1514. So, look at the middle boxes of the bottom row.

Fabulous, isn't it?

S.G.

"Is there a problem?" Bud asks.

"Uh... I should think so now. Give me a moment..."

Thinking break number two. This bozo really has a staircase mind! One step after another, with a snack break at each step.

"Now I've got it," the Yellow Dwarf finally announces. "Can you tell me who you passed on the way, during your ride?"

"We can tell you since all us agree. Nobody!"

"Inevitable response," agrees our riddler. "And totally logical, since you had seen him on the path before you left. So he will arrive here a little late on you."

Suddenly, it's weird, I feel uncomfortable. What the hell is this Wood Jester looking for with this inquisitorial salad? Bud has started to shuffle his feet impatiently and Archie is scratching his temple, a sign that he's slowly starting to lose his temper.

"Let's recap, the dwarf continues, undisturbed. "Who was moving slower than you? Nobody, since you overtook him. And who was moving faster than you? Nobody, always him, since he was on the way before you. Consequently, he should already be here or show up right now. But he's not here, and I don't see him approaching...

A cold shiver runs through me from head to toe. A premonition of a knife in the back that we're going to feel very soon.

Bull's eye... The Yellow Dwarf's good-natured expression fades behind a mask of vengeful anger, and his eyes begin to blaze red.

"HE'S DEAD AND YOU KILLED HIM!" he shouts like one of the damned. "Murderers! Murderers! Down with these criminals! To me, the Guardian! Make them pay! Off with their heads!"

This takes the cake: this exasperating individual even thinks he's the Queen of Hearts!

"You really did massacre Pinocchio, you lunatic!" Bud explodes. "He was somebody and we could see him. Not nobody!"

"You claimed to see the Invisible, you filthy liars!" the canary dwarf sneers like Batman's Joker. "Tremble, carcasses, the Guardian is coming!"

In a split second, a shadow blacker than night envelops us.

I look up.

From the sky, a cube of gigantic dimensions falls like a meteorite of the end of the world.

Horror! We will die immediately, rolled like pizza dough...

I hear the other madman again:

"You'll have to pass through the Guardian."

You bet... *Pass away* by the Guardian, yes.

Suddenly, a veritable chromatic debauchery lights up and bathes us in mind-blowing stroboscopic effects. The cube has disappeared. We can only see this silent fireworks. Until it calms down and...

Return of the cube, now cauliflower-shaped, open, unfolded, straight out of an origami book!

"Holy crap!" Bud cries. "The explosion of a giant *Kubik*!"

He's right again, the beast. It's one of those puzzles prized by those who love to rack their brains over trivialities. In short, it's a cube formed by a juxtaposition of smaller cubes, all identical with their six faces in different colors. Usually, our *Kubik* is offered "messed up" and the game, apparently it is one, is to reconstruct the large cube with each of its faces in the same color.

I could never stand this kind of brainstorming without any real purpose. So, imagine for a moment: the *Kubik* model XXXL has dislocated itself above us into its unit cells, a force field tears us from the ground and sucks us in, and we find ourselves inside the geometric entity, *presto* reconfigured into a hollow solid of which we are...

PRISONERS...

Big surprise.

Not at all, but then, not at all.

Because once inside the famous Guardian, the giant *Kubik* can only be him, well...

CHAPTER XXIV

BUD RECOUNTS

Easy-peasy!

That's my first reaction as soon as the Guardian closes around the three of us. I loved the movie about a bunch of guys trapped in a giant *Kubik* a few years ago, and I'm really enjoying the idea of playing in a remake.

We're floating on an invisible but very real energy platform. Around us, the four walls, the floor and the ceiling are juxtapositions of blue, green, yellow, red, black and white squares, which must be the faces of cubes. Otherwise, there's no way to pivot them to get each inner face of the *Kubik* to be the same color.

On the other hand, even if we succeed, it leaves in theory a lot of possibilities of rotation, at least for the vertices and edges of the *Kubik*. In theory, I mean, because we're lucky to have with us a 3D model of the mess that has materialized above the platform and which helps a lot to visualize.

First, we see that the *Kubik* has only one thickness or layer of basic cubes. Then, we can see a complete overview of its exterior appearance.

In the end, we should get through this fast and well.

Except it's not possible, it can't be that simple.

So, there's definitely a *schmoll* somewhere.

The cubes can be moved simply by touching them with the palm of your hand and swiping in the direction of the desired movement. Just like a touchscreen, right?

I quickly brief Godfather and Dad, and we get to work. Great, the platform steers like a surfboard or a skateboard, depending on the pressure you exert with your feet. For this, the two old guys are damn happy that I can do it. To each his own generation's tricks.

One, two, three, let's go.

We go at a side that we decide should be yellow. It works like a charm. The model shows us our progression cube by cube, everything is perfect.

Until the middle of the side where, all of a sudden, nothing goes right anymore. Like an airport or train station display, minus the clicking. The colors of the basic cubes mix up and, in ten seconds, it's back to the original mess.

We start again with other sides.

Once.

Twice.

Same story. What the hell is this bad trip?

"Stop!" Godfather shouts. "No point in going on like this, let's think for a moment."

The king of logic starts to think. With him, it doesn't take fifteen years.

"I think I understand," he says, unfortunately with a tragic expression six feet long. "The situation is critical, my friends. Unless a miracle happens, we will never succeed. *The sides of the cubes change color over time.* In other words, this *Kubik* is a four-dimensional devilry. If we don't decipher its chrono-algorithm, then eternity won't be long enough for us to manage it. We'll remain its prisoners..."

Overwhelmed, Dad sits down on the invisible platform and puts his head in his hands.

Archie is meditating seriously, as usual. Except that now, nothing comes out.

I feel like the sky has fallen on my head or the ground has opened up under my feet.

Without a computer at my fingertips, what can I do?

I can almost hear the Ghost snickering.

We got played like rookies. He's won. For Archibald Brent, Gordon father and son, GAME OVER.

Stranded, until the end of time.

The inside of the *Kubik* gradually darkens. Night comes on and drowns us. But night is resignation.

We're stuck.

Suddenly, an explosion of light.

It snaps us out of it.

Uh…!

The game has started again without us?

All around, it's obvious, each basic cube rotates at full speed on itself, changes color at a frenetic pace, AND STABILIZES.

Swear, that's it. The 3D model confirms it.

In five minutes, roughly, the case is closed. The Kubik is restored, with each face uniform.

"By Jove!" Godfather whispers. "The chrono-algorithm has been taken over from the outside, or I don't know what's going on!"

"Our saving angels from last time again, I bet," Dad guesses.

The answer comes at the same time as the *Kubik* opens and the platform lowers us to the ground, towards someone who vaguely reminds me of…

…More and more precisely…

…Yes, it's her. Godmother!

I throw myself into her arms, then Archie and my father do the same.

I swear: never, not even for Christmas presents, have I been so happy to see her again.

The explanation is simple.

In the past, when Dad, Mom, and Godfather were accidentally plunged into the borloks for their first adventure, Godmother wasn't on the trip. But she joined them, also by accident. She was able to prove herself at the most critical moment, and M has clearly engraved it in his memories: Gloria Brent is an exceptional woman.

Today, seeing that things were going south, he decided to bring her in. And she did not disappoint.

Don't ask how, she managed to enslave the central processor of the *Kubik* and to neutralize the random temporal variable which controlled the change of color of the faces of the basic cubes.

In short, we are saved and provided with a welcome reinforcement—which we will surely appreciate because the ordeal is not, *cannot* be over.

Raving about Godmother and her genius qualities has somewhat obscured the world around us.

The *new* world, without anything in common with the QT Sector or any of the others previously visited. A quick glance around is enough for me to realize that we've *slipped* into somewhere else.

The *Kubik* has freed us into a world about which M, aka Santa Claus, has not said a single word.

"Nor to me," Godmother adds. "As if the Mechabrain knows nothing of its existence."

"A Ghost Sector, then?"

I should have kept my mouth shut. Godfather starts in right away, and we all take a cold shower.

"What if it's the Ghost's Private Sector? I don't know where we've landed, but I estimate the probability that we are in the enemy's special and exclusive stronghold to be very high…"

"So, this is going to be a very close game," Dad sighs.

"That's an understatement," Archie stresses.

"The decisive round, yes," Marraine restresses.

I think for thirty seconds and then I jump in, as serious as a pope.

"Let's say we're at the Ghost's. In that case, I'm sure the Tuning Fork is hidden somewhere here. It's the safest place for the Ghost. If he created his Secret Sector, it's to sneak in whatever he wants, making people believe that the truth is elsewhere."

Dad gives me a wink of understanding, then asks the killer question.

"Other than that, *lone gunman*, do you have any idea what awaits us here?"

"Perhaps an inkling or an embryo of an idea, yes. But to make sure, we have to study the scene more."

"Don't stop yourself, my dear," Godmother replies. "Even if the landscape doesn't look very welcoming, let's take advantage of the present calm to take a little break. Given the relative time you spent with the QTs, M advised me to bring some provisions…"

Nothing worse than going out without cookies, as Grandma used to say. And it's just in time. It's best to recharge your batteries before any battle, especially the final one.

So, while having a bite to eat, I analyze the… playing field.

CHAPTER XXV

BUD STILL RECOUNTING[16]

Funny freak, this Ghost. His secret garden looks post-atomic with a sinister, dirty orange sky, without a visible sun, where thick grayish clouds run and parallel trails stretch out that one would swear were made of big flying stones. Blocks that sometimes collide, causing showers of smoking rocks. Nice, for a start...

The terrain itself seems copied from the deserts of Arizona or Death Valley. Ruin-like massifs stand out against the horizon and stretch towards the celestial vault like emaciated, skeletal fingers. From time to time, incandescent pools shine with suspicious iridescence, like the mouths of open volcanoes level with the anthracite ground.

It stinks of radioactivity from miles away.

We're planted at the edge of a kind of not very high *mesa*, near the start of a road which winds down to disappear into the plain.

Not a creature. Not a bush, shrub or grass.

A real desert of Désert.

"What are your impressions, son?" Dad asks me.

"Meh... We got here after a nuclear war, or a disaster of the same sort."

"What on earth could we possibly have to do here" Archie asks.

"It's not in the song, Godfather. Apart from starting to walk across this no man's land, I don't see..."

Here, just between us, I'm lying a little bit. The more I scan the landscape, nibbling on M's homemade cookies, the more lights go on in my memory. This hellish setting, it could almost fit right in to one of the last video games released after the summer.

Specially for my fellow fans, who salivate like vampires during blood donation campaigns: *Route 666*, expansion number 3 of *Triple Kill Super Gore*, adapted—it seems—from a classic of post-apocalyptic SF from the last century.

---

[16] Where I finally realize that he has some serious talent... *(Note from Sydney Gordon)*

This is a challenge just for you, Bud Gordon! my inner voice whispers.

Not bad, old girl. Honestly, I finished the game in a record 80 hours. Without ever using online help, without leaving my room for anything other than basic needs, and without running the slightest danger—except going deaf from my parents' bellowing. I finished very high in the Hall of Fame, and that's something that gets out fast, thanks to the web.

On the other hand, knowing the scenario of *Route 666*, it's going to be super hard, transposed into reality. Worse, even, with the Ghost behind it.

Suddenly I make up my mind. The ostrich pokes its head out of the sand.

Might as well brief Dad, Godmother and Godfather without wasting another minute. And, even if I have to roll around on the ground, I have to make myself the leader of the expedition.

Ah, their bewildered faces!

I let the cat out of the bag double quick. The three old folks were glued to the spot. With flashes of mystical admiration in their eyes. Dad's the liveliest, I might add. A kind of divine illumination.

You can really be of some use to us, son!

He doesn't say it, but he thinks it clearly: my video games are no longer just virtual crap for mental masturbation. Some, at least, that can have a collective and concrete utility. *Route 666* might be one of them.

It remains to be proven in practice, in a reality that has surely been manipulated to death on purpose to fool us.

Of course, none of the three of them oppose my *leadership*. If I asked them for the moon, they would all fly away together to go and get it for me.

But there's no moon here. It must have exploded, like in the expansion already mentioned.

Grandstanding a little, I tell them:

"Call me Nick Tanner, hero of *Route 666*, the Damnation Alley!"

You would really have to know about the origins to capture all the subtlety. The "celestial voice" that answers me knows about it.

"Welcome to *my* game, human champion Bud Gordon! I know what you are worth in your world, the time of the mega challenge has come for you. Prepare to take command of the *LandShark 3* whose offensive and defensive weapons your companions will use."

I bet it's the Ghost, since we can hear him but not see him and he knows everything. Normal, for a ghost!

"Challenge accepted, Ghost. Nature of the mission?"

A hungry hyena's snicker, then the sugary sweetness of an airline stewardess-style chick delivering her spiel.

"The survival of the ImAm[17] depends on the Eastern power plants. It is a matter of going to reactivate them by crossing the Desolation Districts, reaching the Kapitol control center, and restarting them thanks to the doped scorbium bars that each competing vehicle carries in its special armored trunk.

"But of the three LandSharks engaged in the game, only one can and must reach the goal. As a reward, his crew will earn their freedom. The others will be eliminated. To do this, the rule is the absence of rules: no holds barred. Attention, starting signal in ten minutes..."

Re-snickering of the hungry hyena, just to snap us out of the mermaid's song.

Everything is clear. You asked for the program? Good, you have it. And me, despite putting on a show of nonchalance, I'm shaking in my boots. The Ghost said ten minutes, and we don't even have the cars yet. The stress is rising, it's done to break the opponent. This guy may be a scumbag, but he has some goddamn experience with games.

The most worrying thing is the other so-called competitors. Real independents, autonomous, rogues sold to our enemy or puppets that he'll viciously manipulate, as it suits him, to shoot us at the right time?

The number one unknown, here it is: Who, or what, are we really going to play against?

Too late to back out, Bud Gordon. When you gotta go, you gotta go.

But honestly, my nuts are hard.

As if by magic, the famous vehicles appear out of nowhere right next to us. They look like huge black horseshoe crabs, streaked with purple lightning bolts. A good ten yards long and three wide, without windows, impervious to everything including radiation, powered by nuclear engines, bristling with several turrets equipped with automatic machine guns, adjustable rocket launchers, flame throwers at the front and rear, grenade launchers, torpedo launchers, mooring line launchers... Enough to shoot at anything that moves and even at anything that doesn't, whatever the terrain in which the *LandSharks* are in. A prefer-

---

[17] For *Imperium American. (Note from Bud Gordon)*

ence for driveable ground because these machines are mounted on eight monster truck tires, above which I can see the slots for unfoldable wings or, more precisely, sharp blades acting as scythes. Add in the halogen headlights, side spotlights and the armored sliding doors, and there you have it.

Probably doesn't have an antigrav generator, in principle. In our game, it was an option in the beta version of the game. But after testing the bonus demos, we were unanimous in asking for it to be removed. Reason: made it too "easy".

"The *Devil's Consorts* will start at the front with *LS1*. The *Malevolent Five* will follow with *LS2*. Nick Tanner and his... *Hellbound* will start at the back with *LS3*. Go in five minutes. Human players, ready to board!"

The names say a lot about our destiny. Written in advance, or I'll be a monkey's uncle. Plus, the other crews are already in their machines, familiar with them, each at their post and ready to fight. We're far from that. And we'll stay far, since we'll be the last to cross the starting line.

Come on, keep your spirits up, when you take blow after blow to the head...

But thinking didn't stop me from acting and rushing towards the door that had just opened. The inside of the LandShark, I'm lucky, is an exact copy of the virtual PC that we have in the game. Dad, Archie and Gloria settle into the chairs that I point out to them. Immediately, monitors light up in front of them and the instructions for the weapons start scrolling. Same for me, as soon as I'm wedged into the pilot's seat. Damn, it really feels like we're in *Route 666*! Incidentally, I check: no antigravity. Hopefully it's the same for the others...

"Fasten your harnesses, it's going to get rough! Any questions about artillery?"

Nada, for Godfather and Godmother. Science guarantees you adaptability. Dad is less comfortable. Checklist and review are required. Phew, he catches on pretty quickly, for once.

"I was a gunner in a tank, son. In the time of the dinosaurs, you might say, but I haven't forgotten. Don't worry, I'll figure it out."

A deep bass voice rang out over the onboard radio.

"Ready for the massacre, jokers?"

Don't lose your cool, rule number one.

"Who are you?" I ask without a trace of politeness.

"Howard Alan Sequoia, *Devil's Consorts* princeps. With Atoll Malecat, Kokkor Hikkups, Lense Lark and Vile Faloosh. Does the Mount Pleasant massacre mean anything to you, loser?"

To be original, it's not bad. I remember a series of books from centuries ago, episodes of interstellar revenge with all the space exoticism that goes with it. Specifically, a few names of characters, places, not much more. No question of admitting it, however. So I affirm, lying shamelessly:

"Never heard of it. But back home, the *Demon Princes* were your negative twins. Blood gods, not amateurs like you…

"Shit your pants, Tanner!" the other one growls, annoyed. "We're the real ones!"

Rule number two, always escalate insults.

"You're all bark and your lackeys too. The exterminating angel hates your guts! Over and out."

"The Human Player has a quick wit," vibrates a contralto to thaw an iceberg, drowning the explosion of primal rage from the *Devil's Consorts*. "The *Malevolent Five* salute you, hats off, *Big* Bud Gordon. You, and your friends who are going to die. It's *no future* for you. Too bad, pretty boy, you're pretty hot…"

"Who are these bitches?" Dad mumbles, joining in the dance.

"Maleficent, Melichrone, Melisande, Mim, and Mystique, the *M5*," five voices of real singers chimed in together. You are making a big mistake insulting us, you old wrecks…"

I'm the one who hits back, full-on macho style.

"Go get stuffed, you bunch of turkeys! May all the heloderms in the desert fu…"

The gong booms. No, the megagong booms. You'd think the Ghost takes pity on guinea hen and such like pseudo-birds. I'm laughing. Everyone's on edge, red-hot. There's going to be plenty of action…

"The starting signal!"

All nuclear engines roar and the three *LandSharks* hurtle down the slope in the designated order. As soon as they reach the plain, the road widens and I put the pedal to the metal, so to speak, to take the lead.

It starts out exactly like in the game. A raging storm, a shower of smoking stones, and from time to time a tombstone template block falls, which I have to avoid at all costs. Or at worst, it's Dad's job to bust them with a rocket. But it's better to save the micro-rockets. So, I give it to him. Bud Gordon is tough.

BOOM!

Now that's really anti-fair play. The *Devils' LLS1* detonates one of those meteorites right above us. But the explosive charge was too strong, and all we get is a shower of gravel.

Not even a scratch!

As a tactical ruse, I let them pass in front of me. The sluts stay back. I'll have to be careful.

When suddenly…

The giant heloderm, the 1000/1 scale Gila monster that treacherously surges out of the plain and attacks the road crossing, it comes out of its hole specifically for the *Devil's Consorts*.

I gloat.

"That'll do it! Bye, losers!"

Uh… You should have kept your mouth shut, Nick Tanner. One of the creeps deployed the side blades and another unleashed five heavy machine guns at once. The mega-lizard's front end ends up as an inedible hamburger meat, too scaly, but nice enough. The *LS1,* however, goes into a spectacular spin as it skids through the creature's vital fluids and spilled guts.

Which allows me to get ahead again.

And causes a noisy collision, but with little more than crumpled armor, between the *Devil's' LandShark* and that of the *M5*s which did not calculate correctly the trajectory needed to avoid a collision.

I press the radio button.

"Sorry for you, my beauties, I had nothing to do with it!"

A stream of insults and grumbling in return. Who cares.

Suddenly, Godmother cries out.

"Look out to the left, Bud! What's that black streak running down the hillsides toward the road?"

A blank. I scan my directional screens and activate the various vision modes. Infrared, night vision—even though it's that eternal dirty orange daylight—neutron, x-ray…

A second blank.

"Shit! This dirty trick wasn't in the game!"

And shit again, I say to myself. *You're in the lead and you're the one who's going to get it...*

"What is it?" my teammates ask, their butts clenched and their jaws grinding.

"As far as dirty tricks go, this is total bullshit. Literally."

They quickly see what I mean.

What is rushing towards us is a surging herd of buffalo—two to three times taller and heftier than natural—whose numbers must easily exceed the entire buffalo population of North America in the blessed days when the Indians were their only predators.

Impossible to avoid such a tsunami. Especially since on the right, farther ahead, the noxious glow of a radioactive crater begins to come into sight—according to the *haddock* monitor, obviously.

The wild hordes have already reached the road. And the sacred inspiration strikes my brain. I brake hard, so that the other two *LS*s come up to us. There's only one way to get through: position ourselves side by side, open heavy fire, then advance the armored vehicle on the far right while the two on the left shoot as many beasts as possible before they reach us.

Then, as soon as the first one has crossed, he'll turn around on the spot and machine-gun along with the third while the second one passes. And finally, the two *LS*s that have reached the other side will cover the last one so that it can cross through.

So, I turn on the radio and announce my plan.

"Okay, Doc," Maleficent answers for the *Malevolent Five*.

I can hear the other four bitches giggling and snickering.

"Got no choice, we'll go along with you," confirms the *Devil's Consorts* without balking.

They also seem to be having a good laugh.

Godfather taps me on the shoulder.

"You missed a point, Bud. In the order you planned and given the respective positions of the three competitors, you go second. That's why the others are having a laugh..."

"Shit..."

In the virtual game of our real world, it's not as vicious. Here, it should be even less so, since we're among the borloks and the borloks, by their very nature, are not very inventive outside of the programmed patterns. Rather limited in cunning and initiative.

Yeah, but you're in the Ghost's realm now, nitwit... And he, he unleashed his personal borloks...

My inner voice. And it's right.

"On my signal, open fire!"

The *M5s* have crossed the black tide. Nothing to say about the *Devil's*, they did their part. Now it's my turn to launch my *LS*, thundering and spitting death. But this is the moment when the other two teams can decide to leave us. So it totally sucks.

Too late to back out, gotta go.

As I move forward and machine-gun the giant buffalo, whose numbers are clearly thinning with the support of the competing *LS*s, I analyze the visuals of the huge creatures.

Ah, the horror!

They may be fake, made of synthetic materials and not real ruminants like back home, but it's a shocker.

Instead of these buffalo, simple skeletons covered with stretched skins would make a better show. Certainly, we had the impression of a breaking wave, but closer up they're walking almost slowly, hesitantly, clumsily, precariously balanced on legs reduced to bones.

Their jaws are toothless, horns are missing, eye sockets are empty—others glow ruby red, had to see that coming.

Zombie buffalo—or buffalo zombies, take your pick, people!

"The Ghost didn't bother with details to make it look nice," Dad says. "It's a low-budget game, isn't it?"

"You should be able to pulverize them just by running them over," Godmother whispers to me. "Try it!"

Good intuition... That's exactly what happens with one of the beasts that all the competitors' shots deliberately avoid.

"Okay, we keep shooting so we don't disappoint the other two, but we save on the big guns."

Five more minutes and we're on the other side of the black river of zombie buffalo. Or buffalo zombies.

Surprise, the *LS* of the bitches in heat has disappeared.

"Those bitches must have figured it out and fled," Dad guesses.

"Don't worry, we'll get them at the next turn."

"And for the *Devil's Consorts*?" Godfather asks.

"Forget about the scum. Killers of innocents, they're not worth the rope to hang them."

"And they're just borloks," Godmother points out, always keeping her bearings.

In the heat of the moment, we tend to forget it, it's true.

"Full speed ahead?" I shout.
"Full speed ahead!" my elite trio agrees.

CHAPTER XXVI

You're probably loving it. Not me, not in such a big dose. That's why I'm taking over the story. With Bud, we'd still have a hundred or a hundred and fifty pages to go, but my beloved publisher has repeatedly insisted that this book remain accessible. In weight, font size, and price. So I'm picking it up again.

If you want the full text, send an email to my son to ask him for it. He'll tell you in length, in breadth, in depth and in thickness the attack of the mutant bats which threw the *LS* of the *Malevolent Five* into a radio-active crater. Bravo, Batman's great-granddaughters!

You will have five chapters on the breakdown of the engine systems that forced us to stop in an absolutely sinister region, over which hovered the ghosts of thousands of dead. As an anecdote, just one, to set the tone, we almost opened the door for a pitiful little girl who came crying and screaming in despair, her old dirty doll clutched against... no, not her heart, the borloks don't have one. Seeing her there, all alone, scrawny and dusty, we would never have imagined that the hills had eyes and that these eyes were spying on us. But it was enough to toss her, out of Christian charity, a can of corned beef—not so great, this cursed commodity!—to understand in a flash what she was really capable of, and to avoid at the last minute the trap set by her tribe. Degenerate cannibals, vicious as can be, the men equipped with pitchforks, spring-loaded blunderbusses and crank-operated chainsaws, the women brandishing femurs, tibias and other clubs very characteristic of the place...

Meanwhile, Archie was rummaging through the bowels of the tank. Everything started working again as the entire clan of cannibals started banging on our *LS* with their ridiculous weapons. We weren't really in danger except for the wear and tear of our nerves. But we sped out of there as fast as light.

Afterwards, there were new showers of incandescent celestial stones, very fragile and rickety bridges to cross over unfathomable abysses with the *LS* of the *Devil's Consorts* hanging on our tails. Unfortunately they ended up catching up with us. Later, we had to overcome the hordes of the *Borlok Country* version of *Hell's Angels*, giant insects, terrestrial octopuses...

We've seen it all, of every stripe and color.

Here's a brilliant summary of our journey, worthy of an anthology: "The enemy's secret sector? A box of tricks with the goriest effects when the Ghost opens it."

Nice, Bud! And thank you, my son, whom I will never look at with the same eyes again, because you did it like a boss. A god, your mother would say, since she's always inclined to exaggeration.

The *Devil's Consorts* (let's close the subject) ended up flattened like pancakes by a huge tombstone that fell from the sky with the violence of a Siberian meteorite. We could have obliterated it, but we scrupulously refrained from doing so. It served the bastards right, given the last trick they tried to pull on us while we were fording a river as wide as the good old Mississippi.

So yes, they had just managed to get ahead of us and put a bomb underwater, just to dig our grave with the simple press of a button as we passed over.

Luckily, Bud caught their *LS*'s energy signature on the right screen in time and figured that, since they were already on the other side of the river, they must have been kindly mining our terrain.

My son, I can admit, has risen considerably in my estimation recently. Having accidentally emerged from his fishbowl, thrown into the unknown and the unstable, he had the means to prove himself in concrete circumstances where our survival depended on him alone. And he proved himself.

In the end, and you see me delighted to be able to spell it out, Bud is a true Gordon, a true branch of the old stock, the one which gave the world illustrious characters such as the famous explorer of whom I have already spoken to you.

So, 99% thanks to my son, we reached the goal. As winners of the game, you'll notice by the way. We had to reach Kapitol, and we did it.

Naturally, we're not in Washington, DC, far from it. Nevertheless, the Kapitol here is quite similar even if it includes elements taken from elsewhere, for example from the Lincoln Memorial. This statue is obviously copied from the effigy of the famous president assassinated in the 19th century, but its a child. With a fragile, touching beauty... Extraterrestrial, almost. A child-god, if that gives you a better idea. Who knows why, his angelic face and his amazed eyes remind me of a vague memory.

In the Rotunda beyond the peristyle, in place of the great George Washington, there is a huge digital billboard. With a message expressly for us.

This is where Route 666 ends.

You who have come this far are one of the big winners of the game.

Sign into the Hall of Fame, *then complete the final phase of your mission.*

Search your LS for the scorbium box, and head to the building on the left. This is the control center for the Eastern Power Plants.

Reactivate it and you will have your reward.

I will be waiting for you there in person.

Signed: The Ghost.

For obvious reasons, we're torn between petrifying anxiety and rabid curiosity.

Of course, Bud goes to sign in. Not a little proud, the kid.

Then we follow him to the *LS*, he collects the package to be delivered and we set off again, hot on his heels, towards the control center.

The building is hidden behind a curtain of very tall trees, like Italian cypresses. The first plants we've seen in the Secret Sector.

And here...

Believe it or not, the famous building to be reactivated had the shape of a colossal, titanic, triple, quadruple...

TUNING FORK!

It takes as many branches to bring the universes of different dimensions into vibrational harmony...

In the quadrangular base of this still inactive hyper-resonator, an armored door is very slowly revealed at the top of a flight of steps.

A silhouette stands framed in the threshold.

The Ghost, finally. We're going to find out.

Two minutes later, we know.

And we're flabbergasted.

It's Pinocchio.

CHAPTER XXVII

"Ah, deceptive appearances..." the puppet starts, grinning from ear to ear. "In your world, you always say that you should not trust them, but you are the first to forget this precaution. You Humans have very twisted and illogical minds. Easy to fool, in the end, for those who know how to do it."

"You're the twisted one!" Bud barks back. "Are you referring to your disappearance, torn to pieces by the Yellow Dwarf? Nice staging with shocking special effects, I admit! But to slip away like that, in front of your friends, that's crazy."

Pinocchio has a good laugh.

"No, it's the sense of showmanship. The art of false pretenses, too. I got you!"

"You've been pulling our leg from the start," Archie interjects, not happy at all. "All your provocations among the QTs... We should have guessed, it was all predictable."

I, dear readers, have seen and heard nothing. Or I've refused to see and hear. So I don't fully understand.

"Long before, too, I... tricked you. Remember the past. You especially, Sydney Gordon, remember the time when you got rid of M by making him plunge into the mirror of nothingness..."

"You weren't affected by it, Pinocchio," Gloria comments. "On the contrary, you seemed happy that we had somehow freed you..."

"I was!" the puppet assures. "I had reached a key stage in my existence. Then you abandoned me by returning to your world. You regretted leaving me there, Sydney Gordon, I saw that clearly enough and it touched me. But, fortunately, you did not take me! Because otherwise, I would never have accomplished everything that I later achieved."

This is the first time the puppet has been so talkative and difficult to follow. The more he talks, the more his mind strikes me. So to speak. For a borlok, he has a hell of a lot of common sense. Could this be a more evolved model, the next step in the evolution of these rational toys?

Or... something else?

"Taking on the identity of the Ghost was a masterstroke," Bud tells him with strange admiration. "Hats off to you on all accounts. But didn't you have other means to stand up for yourself, and couldn't you have come up with a different plan, more glorious than the brutal conquest of our world?"

"We're not going to rewrite history," Pinocchio says. "The game is over. You are the winner of the game I challenged you to, which makes you the one who is going to open the 'door'. First, though, write your name in the Heroes' Gallery of MY *Route 666*, right above mine. Go ahead, put down the scorbium box and go to the console over there."

Being a good sport, Bud complies. As if he were still in a virtual game. The terminal lights up, then the Ghost's *Route 666* honor roll is displayed in a giant holographic projection.

Empty, the first line awaits my son's first and last name.

On the second, that of the champion number 2 on the list of winners, there are six letters that we reread four or five times, perplexed, incredulous.

L.A.S.T.E.R.

God of the sky... Laster, the last of Gondwana's children!

Pinocchio, the Ghost, Laster—one and the same entity, one and the same character. Friend, enemy, dead, alive...

What a mess, my lambs!

And yet, you will see, it's childishly simple.

Back in the day, when we first visited the borlok world, Laster was connected to the Mechabrain. But it wasn't the Mechabrain that I eliminated during the decisive confrontation. As already mentioned, just one of its mobile units or remote interfaces. Still, we all believed, wholeheartedly, that I had taken out M himself. A fake mini-underground cataclysm to back it up, as the icing on the cake.

"Yes, I *physically* died at that moment," Laster tells us. "My worn-out organism shut down not because of you, but because I had already set my psychic survival plan in motion and the time for my *transfer* had come. Were you sure you had destroyed M and then seen me die, or almost? Deceptive appearances, false pretenses, again and again! M lost nothing in the affair—and he even gained, unbeknownst to him, because my mind was then 'downloaded' into a special cluster of his artificial intelligence, created and preprogrammed in secret by me."

Elementary, right? Now that you know...

From inside the Mechabrain, Laster, now the Ghost, pushed M to gradually build more modern, more exciting Sectors and to reconfigure

Center. Then, inspired by the video games in full development in the parallel world where our Earth is located, he himself designed and built the Secret Sector, adaptable at will, in which the last part took place.

A die-hard gamer, this Laster!

A gifted, super-creative, highly intelligent, manipulative, cold and cruel child at times, an accomplished strategist and tactician by playing games. A mega-geek who is ultra brilliant, in his own way.

But a child, deep down inside. Again and again. Even in his disarming frankness and the immense pleasure he takes in revealing himself, in revealing his plans.

Tomorrow I will do this and that. Tomorrow I will have new games, even if it means breaking many of my old toys. Tomorrow I will change the rules. Tomorrow I will set out to conquer new territories. And later, one day, I will be grown up!

But do I really want to grow up?

We've all heard these words from our kids. When they were small.

And Laster is small. Stayed small. A figure of speech because in terms of age, he's got fifteen thousand years under his belt... You get me however: what he lacks is maturity. When he details his super plan that's driving him to attack our world, it's even more obvious. Leaving here, going to Earth, taking control of our planet, it seems to him the most direct solution to change his surroundings, his house and his entourage, taking with him his full boxes of cherished toys. All the borloks, all *his* borloks, made for him by this M who is his father, his mother, his nanny, his friend, his guide, his teacher, his guard—and his prison too.

Those he didn't break or sacrifice along the way, my inner voice corrects. *Victims, even if they are artificial creatures, this kid from the past made tons of them and without pity...*

"We all dream of breaking down the walls that adults build around us, Laster," Bud jumps in, taking advantage of a pause in the long speech. "I also often want to run away somewhere else with my games and my action figures, to live fully, far from the restrictive, pitying glances of my folks. From there to eradicating the population of a planet... There are limits that must not be crossed, you know. When you'll have around you only borloks incarnated as Humans, still and always borloks and nothing more because they can never be anything else, what are you going to do? In the end, what will you have gained? You'll get past your teenage crisis, sure. You'll be independent, sure. But apart from *your* manufactured creatures, *your* perfected toys, which will always remain toys even if their essence inhabits Human bodies, what else will you have? Where will the spice of life be? Whereas we, Humans, could offer it to you since we have a soul, a spirit, like you..."

Amazing, my son. Psychologist, philosopher, who would've thunk it?

Pinocchio, aka the Ghost, aka Laster, has slowly sunk into an abyss of silent reflection. With his large painted eyes, he seems to question each of us, especially Bud, and consult the Universe.

Weird... I swear two tears are welling up at the corners of his drawn eyelids. It's hard to be a spirit, a soul in a wooden puppet—even a borlok puppet.

Ah, if only he could be reincarnated as a real human being... To have a real body of his own, to feel, to sense, to experience, to love... A family, friends, people who are waiting for him, who trust in him...

Ah, if only he could be granted rebirth! In a body capable of welcoming him, of receiving him... A body immediately operational, to avoid slow growth and long learning... A body lacking only a spirit to live!

Or... to live again?

Damn, of course!

Illumination.

There is one among us.

LARRY CONWAY!

"Listen to me, everyone! You especially, Laster! I have another solution to propose to you!"

Archie, Gloria, Bud and the main person concerned stare at me with a perplexed look. They're surprised that the idea is coming from me, after all these adventures during which I was pretty much just along for the ride.

But that's nothing new, as you well know: very often, I do almost nothing during an entire adventure until the final pages. Almost until the end, people wonder why I'm there, except as an admittedly talented chronicler, given my feeble contribution to restoring order or resolving problems.

Well, once in a blue moon I get the big finish.

Everything's been brought together to make the famous Tuning Fork work. The juiced scorbium bars are no sham, they're really needed. Having them brought by us reveals Laster's playful, childish side again:

for, our victory over the other crews was not a foregone conclusion, quite the contrary. But in the end, if it hadn't been us, it would've been the others. Either way, the Ghost wins.

Although...

In fact, the Ghost has no idea how to activate his diabolical invention. One more paradox in support of his childish character. It's a good thing that we won, that Archie and Gloria are here. As you might expect, our geniuses of science manage to make the Tuning Fork work.

Neither the *Devil's Consorts* nor the *Malevolent Five* could have done it. So the Ghostt couldn't have let his borloks triumph, even if we— sorry, especially Bud—hadn't been up to the task. He would have definitely helped us so that his Tuning Fork would be activated.

Through which Laster's spirit will be guided to the body of the "vegetable" Larry Conway, will inhabit it, and will cause the "miraculous" resurrection of the poor young hero.

The last child of Gondwana accepted my plan, you guessed it. Not without initial reluctance. But once again, Bud surprised me with his personal involvement and motivation that got him to convince Laster two hundred percent.

"You'll have to put on a little act for your new family, my friend. For that, the total amnesia thing will help a lot. I also think they'll easily swallow the change caused by your sojourn in the afterlife, you' newfound passion for video games that you brought back from there. I'll be the one to guide you in our world, we'll be friends to die for and you'll see how much fun we'll have! Thanks to the Internet, we'll play global games and you have no idea what a blast you'll have! With a normal, human life, girls, the media, everything…"

"But what about the borloks? *My* borloks?"

It's Archie's and Gloria's turn.

"We'll negotiate with the Pentagon for the reactivation of *Funland*. The necessary funds are surely there in the world that M built for you and in the developments that you brought to it, enough revolutionary 'technological building blocks' for the current civilizations of our Earth. For example, micro-gravity-modulators, or all the wonders of electronics and positronics that we saw at work, not to mention the relative mastery of access to other dimensions. The American government won't refuse to acquire such assets, decisive in terms of progress and advancement over the competition, at the price of a modest sacrifice—namely, financial support for the restart of the amusement park.

"And then?" Laster asks.

"My boy," our friend the scientist adds, "we will have to work a little more on the interdimensional roller coaster to make it a real means of transition, reliable and of greater capacity, between the two universes. Not so that Humans land *en masse* among the borloks, but the opposite: so that the borloks, themselves, can come to Earth, specifically to *Funland*, in order to meet the Humans there, get to know them, hang out with them and play with them.

"But we will have to manage and control this traffic!" the child objects. "I will not have time to do it!"

"M will take care of it," Archie responds. "One of his mobile units will set up permanent residence in *Funland*. Santa Claus, for example. Emblematic and known throughout the world, he'll be ideal as the Grand Organizer and Animator of *New Funland*. All we have to do is show it to him and 'sell' it all to…"

It doesn't take Laster a lifetime to be won over. He catches on at warp speed, this child of yesteryear!

Don't ask me how he manages to get us all to Center in the blink of an eye. Suddenly, the Ghost Sector dissolves around us. And boom! We resurface in the immediate vicinity of the Mechabrain's abracadabra structure.

There's no negotiating with this one. He listens to us attentively, ponders simultaneously, analyzes likewise, and decides in a fraction of a second.

It's a deal!

M accepts everything. Moreover, as the good father, mother, grandfather or grandmother that he never stopped being for Laster, he turns a blind eye to all the damage caused by the kid. Not without giving him a good scolding for the huge risks he ran, and especially for the danger he caused for a lot of… people, Humans and borloks. Not to mention our two parallel worlds.

It lasts for ages. A real eternity. Luckily, there's a drink to be had and some snacks to nibble on.

I'm sure the kid got the message because, as you too felt, this "old" kid has a good heart.

After that, the Mechabrain dissects our proposal in its smallest details, to analyze it point by point, and he validates it on all counts. From his voice, I would bet, the unexpected prospect of the imminent incarnation of Laster makes him cry with emotion. So, secretly, I go along with him with a little tear…

Oh, I forgot: M has once again taken on the appearance of Santa Claus, the future volunteer, competent, benevolent and good-natured resort manager of *New Funland*.

But a lot of water will still flow under the bridge before the *hoi polloi* come to whoop it up in *New Funland*—a whole new ethnic group of *Newfies* (Canadians will appreciate it!)—realize that action figures, Toons, Cuties, Mangabots, Furries, Superheroes, you name it, are having as much fun as they are!

As for your servant, good people, he will offer his newspaper the final article of Sydney Gordon's memorable career, a flamboyant and abbreviated chronicle of the attempt—foiled at the last minute—of a nefarious invasion of our world by the borloks who had come from elsewhere.

Then he will bow out to the sinister Rupert Murdoch, with a raised middle finger if necessary, and go off to cultivate his new garden.

"What garden, what the hell? What is this weirdo cooking up for us now?" You may be worrying.

Very, very serious, I assure you.

Just before our return to Earth via the Moebius ride, I manage to discuss the matter privately with M. Obviously, I get what I'm hoping for. Just desserts…

Thanks to the media technology of the borloks, I will soon create my own website of guaranteed pure news, without crap or controversy. It will be unprecedented.

My faithful friends, see you soon on the Web!

And you, *home sweet home*, here we are, here we are…

EPILOGUE

I open the front door and pause. Sure, Bud and I have returned home, but has this return really taken place on our original Earth?

Could there not be a slight dimensional shift this time, such as we have experienced after each of our misadventures with the Machine?

It certainly is, judging by the yowling of skinned cats that echo from the living room. As if my sweet Margaret is indulging in the breeding of a colony of felines rescued from abusive owners. And yet, in the woman who has shared my life for so many years, the love for these creatures has always been at a level bordering on absolute zero.

Bud also hesitates.

"What is that?" he asks me in a worried voice.

I advance stealthily and risk a furtive glance into the room off the hallway.

By Jove! It's the TV blaring like that at full blast... Without bothering my dear wife in the least, who is dozing blissfully on the sofa, even though it's the end of the afternoon. That also surprises me about her.

Without trying to understand, my son hurries up to his room. I forgot to tell you, we did indeed collect our purchases from Comic Con where this twisted adventure began.

I'm getting culture shock up front and personal.

Hey, dear reader, don't runaway, I'll explain!

The dying cat howls are pouring out of the home cinema speakers, along with an image of a most disturbing spectacle.

In the main square of a foreign city, a dense crowd of people dressed in white robes is shouting and waving furiously in response to the animated and jarring curses of an orator perched on a platform, under the heavy protection of an armed praetorian guard. Next to a pontificator of such charisma, our most virulent preachers would pale in comparison...

The sonic debauchery that accompanies this galvanic-revolutionary demonstration reminds me vaguely of Rossini's *Duo des Chats*, but multiplied by ten thousand after being rewritten in decadent dodecaphonic atonal mode. And the checked napkins that all these guys are wearing on their heads quickly locates for me where the scene is taking place.

Confirmation provided by the black banner under the images, which displays a scrolling English translation—a certainly watered-down text of the diatribe—as well as various names.

Including that of the political barker who is inflaming his people.

Damn, of course!

Months before our departure, the media were already talking about him every day.

Glory Alleluia, we are back home safely.

And it's not exactly a walk in the park. Because the tomorrows that this Abdullah Lhazred promises to the rest of the planet and Humanity are not going to warm your hearts. Break them more likely. The bleakness of the future announced by this prophet of the dark side is right up there with the ineffable cosmic horrors recorded by his quasi-namesake[18] centuries ago in a grimoire with a fatal reputation.

But that's another story, as Rudyard Kipling said, if I remember correctly, in *All Quiet on the Western Front*.

Here, the new one comes from the east, from the orient. From the middle, not from the far. Don't confuse them.

On the leftmost part of the black banner, there's a small logo that is impossible to miss.

Al Jazeera.

And it's because I'm not Gaul that the sky doesn't fall on my head.

While we were away, Margaret broke up with Fox and gave in to the nagging saws of other foxes.

Those of the desert.

That's all we need!

When I told you we have everything...

---

[18] Abdul Al-Hazred, the insane author of the *Necronomicon*. *(Note by Sydney Gordon)*